DARKSIDE

FINDERS KEEPERS

'Surprise, of course, is the most potent aspect of suspense.
And Belinda Bauer knows exactly how to manipulate that element,
right until the very end. What's more, she's shown, not just how
to keep surprise bubbling explosively away, but to do it with
extraordinary dexterity, maturity and feeling'
Daily Mirror

'Belinda Bauer's third book represents a remarkable achievement:
almost a return to the good old Victorian triple-decker novel of suspense,
but created with a deftness that allows each book to stand alone'
Independent

'Bauer is not occupied by writing a "crime story"
– although there is a crime at the heart of it –
she is more interested in writing a novel'
Karin Fossum

'*Finders Keepers* has an enjoyably creepy premise . . .
But it's the book's humour that really shines. Bauer reveals
her Gold Dagger-winning writing credentials in her neat
skewering of everyday pomposities and her wry asides'
Observer

'Belinda Bauer hit the big time with the excellent *Blacklands* and
continues to explore her theme of West Country cruelty and corruption,
balancing the procedural and psychological aspects of crime. Once again
she nails the petty grievances, prejudices and loyalties of village life, and
shows how some law enforcers operate at the outer edge of competence'
Financial Times

'Compelling...Bauer blends a psychological crime story with
a darkly humorous narrative . . . I can't wait for the next one!'
Bookseller (Booksellers' Choice)

'One of the leading names in crime fiction'
Stylist

On line Services

'... s great gift is her ability to surprise the reader: in the sense of making you jump out of your chair, certainly, but also in that she makes you think a bit differently about the world'
Daily Telegraph

'Contains one of the most startling plots in contemporary crime fiction'
Sunday Times Culture

'This could be the most astonishing whodunnit you are ever likely to read'
Red Magazine online

'As good as Mark Haddon's *The Curious Incident of the Dog in the Night-Time* . . . and with more twists and coils than a hangman's noose, it deserves to do equally well'
Sunday Express

'The exciting result reads like a collaboration between Mark Haddon and Barbara Vine'
Sunday Telegraph

'Breathtaking. I read this and wished I'd written it'
Val McDermid

'This excellent, thought-provoking novel will hold your attention from the very first page'
Bella

'Taking the psychological thriller into new territory'
Independent

'Bauer has once again succeeded in creating an innovative path into detection'
The Times

'*Rubbernecker* isn't your average crime novel:

THE FACTS OF LIFE AND DEATH

'Belinda Bauer is one of the best British
crime writers out there right now'
Simon Kernick

'Bauer at her best . . .
the true heir to the great Ruth Rendell'
Mail on Sunday

'Belinda Bauer's thrillers are always compelling,
always original, always brilliant. I will rush
to read anything she writes'
Mark Billingham

'Our most inventive crime writer'
Metro

'She writes so beautifully, plots so cleverly and exhibits
a razor-sharp understanding of people and places'
Literary Review

'This gripping, unsettling tale blends a murder
mystery with a blackly comic look at the
gradual erosion of "normal" family life.
You won't want to put it down'
Bella

'Gripping and original'
Sunday Times

'Lingers in the mind like an unwelcome guest,
albeit one with a dark sense of humour . . .
powerful, compelling reading'
Spectator

'Belinda Bauer is the most interesting crime
writer in England today'
Val McDermid

Belinda Bauer grew up in England and South Africa. She has worked as a journalist and screenwriter and her script, *The Locker Room*, earned her the Carl Foreman/Bafta Award for Young British Screenwriters.

With her first novel, *Blacklands*, Belinda won the CWA Gold Dagger for Crime Novel of the Year. In 2013 she won the CWA Dagger in the Library for her entire body of work. Her fourth novel, *Rubbernecker*, was shortlisted for the CWA Gold Dagger and won the Theakstons Old Peculier Crime Novel of the Year Award. Her latest novel is *The Facts of Life and Death*.

Belinda lives in Wales.

RUBBERNECKER

BELINDA BAUER

BLACK SWAN

TRANSWORLD PUBLISHERS
61–63 Uxbridge Road, London W5 5SA
A Random House Group Company
www.transworldbooks.co.uk

RUBBERNECKER
A BLACK SWAN BOOK: 9780552779494
9780552779692

First published in Great Britain
in 2013 by Bantam Press
an imprint of Transworld Publishers
Black Swan edition published 2014

A CIP catalogue record for this book
is available from the British Library.

Addresses for Random House Group Ltd companies outside the UK
can be found at: www.randomhouse.co.uk
The Random House Group Ltd Reg. No. 954009

Typeset in 11.5/15pt Caslon 540 by Falcon Oast Graphic Art Ltd.

The Ra   supports The Forest Stew   rdship
Council®   forest certification or   nisation.
Our boo   ed on FSC   ertifi   paper.
FSC is   pported by th   ading
                                                       including Greenpeace. O
      80 2164564 4   policy can be found at

To Simon, for all the early days.

PART ONE

PART ONE

1

Dying is not as easy as it looks in the movies.

In the movies, a car skids on ice. It slews across the road, teeters on the edge of the cliff.

It drops; it tumbles; the doors come off; it crumples and arcs, crumples and arcs – and finally stops against a tree, wheels up, like a smoking turtle. Other drivers squeal to a stop and leave their doors open as they rush to the precipice and stare in horror, while the car—

The car pauses for dramatic effect.

And then bursts into flames.

The people step back, they shield their faces, they turn away.

In the movies, they don't even have to say it.

In the movies, the driver is dead.

I don't remember much, but I do remember that the

Pina Colada song was on the radio. You know the one. Pina Colada and getting caught in the rain.

I hate that song; I always have.

I wonder whether I'll tell the police the truth about what happened. When I can. Will I have the guts to tell them I was trying to change channels when I hit the ice? Because of that song. Will they think it's funny? Or will they shake their heads and charge me with dangerous driving?

Either would be a relief, to be honest.

I was on my way to pick up Lexi from Cardiff. She'd been away somewhere; I can't remember where – maybe a school trip? – but I do remember how much I was looking forward to seeing her again. She often got the train home with her friends, but now the weather had turned and the trains weren't running. Ice on the line or something – you know how many excuses train companies have for their shoddy reliability. When I was Lexi's age you could set your watch by the trains; now you can hardly set your calendar with any confidence.

Where was I?

Oh, I was coming down the A470 with the old tips looming over me and the ground sloping sharp away into the valley below. It's all grass and trees now, of course, because of the old Coal Board planting, but tips is what a lot of them used to be, however much we all called them mountains. Mountains don't turn to black porridge and bury little children at their desks the way this very one did, all those years ago. I remember *that*, you see, and I remember the little Williams boy with the wonky eye, who came to rugby practice one week and not the next, and never again. But other memories are jumpy or not there at all.

I do remember thinking, *Whoops, you didn't see THAT coming, Sam!* And then hitting the barrier and wondering about the lie I'd have to tell to Alice to explain away the dent in the Focus. Only had it six months, and she's always telling me I drive too fast. But before I could even *think* of a good lie, the car sort of jumped in the air and then all of a sudden I was the *wrong* side of the barrier, with not much between me and the River Taff but a two-hundred-foot drop.

That drop came in four parts.

The car hit the ground nose-first and the windscreen shattered into lace with a sound like squashing a giant beetle.

Then came the silence while I flew like a happy lark.

Then it hit again – all crashing metal, and the grass an inch from my nose. I tried to jerk my head away but I had no control, and I saw the damp tufts and the crystals of leftover ice, as big and sparkly as dinner plates.

Then came more lovely silence, as I watched the dull snow-sky pass by in slow motion and wondered who would pick Lexi up now. We've only got the one car. Maybe she could stay the night with Debbie – she's a nice girl.

This time, when the car hit, I bit my cheek and tasted the iron of blood down my throat. The door came off and I watched my right arm flail close to the opening as we took off again – me and the car we bought together at Evans Halshaw in Merthyr. It was an ex-demonstrator so we got two grand off, but it still smelled new, and that's the main thing, Alice said.

She's going to be so cross with me.

I don't remember coming down the fourth time, but I'm assuming we must have, or I wouldn't be here – I'd be the first Ford Focus driver in space.

With my luck, I probably wouldn't even remember that.

The traffic had slowed to a crawl and eighteen-year-old Patrick Fort could see the blue flashing lights up ahead.

'Accident,' said his mother.

Patrick didn't answer pointless statements. They both had eyes, didn't they?

He sighed and wished he were on his bicycle. No bother with jams then. But his mother had insisted on driving – even though Patrick didn't like riding in cars – because he was in his good clothes for the interview. He was wearing the only shirt with a collar he owned, the grey flannel trousers that made his thighs itch, and the shoes that weren't trainers.

'I hope nobody's hurt,' she said. 'Probably hit ice on the bend.'

Patrick said nothing again. His mother often spoke like this – making redundant noise for her own edification, as if to prove to herself that she wasn't deaf.

They edged towards an impatient-looking policeman in DayGlo who was flapping an arm, ushering cars past in the open lane.

Now they could see where a car had gone over the side. The dull silver crash barrier was stretched into a deep loop, as though it had tried to hold on to the car for as long as possible, but had finally had to let it go with a bent sigh. A knot of firemen stood and looked over the edge of the precipice; Patrick supposed their training qualified them for that, at least.

'Oh dear,' murmured Sarah Fort. 'Poor people.'

The car ahead of them had stopped and Patrick could see all its occupants craning to the left.

Rubberneckers. Desperate for a glimpse of death.

The policeman shouted something at them and flapped his arm furiously to get them to drive on.

Before his mother's car could move again, Patrick opened his door and stepped out on to the tarmac.

'Patrick!'

He ignored her. The air outside the car was bracing, and the slope above him suddenly seemed more *real* – a looming hump of solid matter, covered with a yellow-red carpet of dead winter grass. He walked over to join the firemen.

'*Patrick!*'

Patrick leaned against what was left of the barrier and peered into the valley. A car lay, wheels turned up in death, wedged against a small stand of trees close to the riverbank. A trail of debris marked its path from the road – a door, a magazine, a length of twisted trim. The radio was still on in the stricken car, and Patrick could hear a song floating tinnily up the side of the valley. 'In Dreams' by Roy Orbison – 1963. Patrick didn't care for music, but he never forgot a release date.

'What happened?' he said.

The nearest fireman turned to him with a roll-up clamped in his lips. 'Who are you?'

'Is anyone in there?' said Patrick.

'Maybe. Get back in your car.'

'Are they dead?'

'What do *you* think?'

'I can't tell from here,' shrugged Patrick. 'Can you?'

'Look, smart-arse, get going. We're working.'

Patrick frowned at his hand. 'You're smoking and staring at a car.'

'Just bugger off home, will you!'

'No need to swear.'

'Piss off.'

'Patrick!' His mother appeared and took his elbow and said sorry to the fireman, even though she couldn't have known why.

Patrick took a last look. Nothing was moving down

there. He wondered what things were like inside that car – still and twisted and bloody, and awash with Roy Orbison getting higher and higher like the torture of angels.

He shook his mother's hand off his arm, and she said sorry to *him* then. She was sorry about everything, always.

They got back in the car and his mother continued driving – but much more slowly.

2

Tracy Evans had imagined that the Cardiff neurological unit would give her plenty of time to catch up on her reading. All that quiet; all that stillness; all those comatose patients not vomiting into paper dishes, not peeing into cardboard bottles, not ringing those buzzers that made her feel like an effing air hostess – without the perks, or the prospect of marrying a pilot.

She'd been looking forward to the lack of hassle, and to *Rose in Bloom*, the third in the Rose Mackenzie series. In the first, Rose Mackenzie had graduated from the orphanage, shy and beautiful and still a virgin, despite several titillating attempts on her virtue. In the second, she'd had her money and her heart stolen by the cad Dander Cole – only to be rescued from imminent ruin by Raft Ankers, her tall, dark and monosyllabically handsome guardian. Raft's secret (and therefore, no doubt, tragic) past kept him from paying any but the most formal attention to her, of course, but Tracy knew what Rose could not yet see – that embers glowed in the depths of his unfathomable eyes, waiting to burst into flames of passion.

The title alone of *Rose in Bloom* promised much in the way of conflagration, and twenty-four-year-old Tracy had filled the opening on Cardiff's neurological unit with that very vow in mind. She'd imagined rows of sleeping patients, serene among the machines, and herself moving silently between them – more a night-watchman than a nurse – or turning slow pages by the light of a single yellow lamp . . .

The reality, however, had turned out to be quite annoyingly different, in ways Tracy had barely imagined, let alone encountered. A few patients *were* deep in comas – ostensibly asleep, motionless – but others were in a range of vegetative states. Tracy undertook all the usual nursing tasks – changing drips and catheters, sponge baths, administering medication and nutrition, and noting alterations in respiration or motion. But here there was also cream to be massaged into skin to keep it supple, guards to be raised on the beds of those patients who thrashed and flailed, and bedsores to be prevented on those who did not. There were grunts and moans and blinks and incoherent shouts to be translated into sane requests for water or a switch of TV channel. There were nappies to be changed and arses to be wiped clean of soupy orange excrement. Physios wrestled noisily with stiffening limbs and clawed hands. There were splints to be strapped around legs, and dead-weight bodies to be hoisted into wheelchairs, or on to tilt tables, where patients hung as if crucified – all in an attempt to keep them from contracting into crooked foetal balls from which there might be no return.

Basically it was bedlam. Combined – for Tracy, at least – with a prickling fear that the dead-eyed patients were *watching* her, and biding their time . . .

To cap it all, there was the ward initiation – a painful C-diff infection that had Tracy doubled over in the toilet half a dozen times a day, and left her literally and figuratively drained. The other nurses called it 'the diff-shits' and told her it wouldn't be so bad the next time. Tracy vowed to learn by her mistake and to start applying now for other jobs, before the next time could ever become *this* time.

In the meantime she learned that there were good coma patients and there were bad coma patients. A more experienced colleague, Jean, told her this in a way that let her know that such things were understood, and that it was OK to understand them, but not to talk openly about them.

Good coma patients were quiet. They didn't make noise; they didn't lash out when you tried to help them. They didn't get pneumonia and require a lot of extra attention, or pull out their feeding tubes and drips. Good coma patients had families who were polite and didn't clutter the place up with bits from home, and who brought little gifts – bribes, really – for the nurses, in the hope that they would take good care of their loved ones in the long hours filled with their absence. There were always at least two boxes of chocolates open behind the nurses' station; Tracy liked the nuts, and would lift up the top layers before they were finished to get at the hard centres below, before anyone else had a chance.

It was also understood – by the nurses, at least – that good coma patients had been good people in their previous lives, too. They were here because of strokes brought on by overwork, car accidents that were not their fault, and falls from ladders while helping neighbours clear their guttering, or rescuing cats from trees. *Good* coma patients got their brows stroked and kind words in their ears, encouraging them to return to the world in one mental piece.

Bad coma patients cried all night long, or choked on even the thinnest porridge, or gripped their bed guards and rattled them like the bars of an old cage. They shouted out and flailed, and sometimes connected with a fist or a foot. They soiled themselves into freshly changed nappies – apparently just for the hell of it – and got constant infections that required extra nursing all night long. Bad patients were here because of drug overdoses and speeding and drunken brawls outside pubs. Their families were demanding and mistrustful. Bad patients got pursed lips and brisk handling, and their restraints tightened 'for their own good'.

Nothing of this distinction was written down or discussed with doctors or families, but all the nurses knew the difference. When Jean first showed Tracy around the ward, she walked from bed to bed, filling Tracy's head with biographies that were never to be rewritten or erased – or even verified as truthful.

'This poor lad was going to buy his girlfriend an engagement ring when he was hit by a taxi. Driver was on his phone, I'll bet,' said Jean. 'The girl comes in after work and just cries. Every day for seven months. Sweet little thing says she still wants to marry him. Breaks your heart.' She sighed and sounded sincere, so Tracy nodded in a way she hoped denoted that she, too, was a little bit heartbroken – even though she thought that if *her* (hypothetical) boyfriend were in a coma for more than a few weeks, she'd probably just cut her losses and move on, not stick around to watch him shit in his pants for the next fifty years.

Jean was on to the next bed. '*This* one,' she said with a brusque tug of the sheets over the chest of a middle-aged man, 'fell off that bridge at the end of Queen Street. Drunk, most likely. Or running from the police. Shouldn't have been on it in the first place; it's a rail bridge, you know, not pedestrian.'

Tracy did know. She herself had staggered under it many a Friday and Saturday night as she wove the mile from Evolution back to the house she shared with three other girls. People were always hanging over the parapet of the bridge with spray cans, or playing chicken with the trains as they left Queen Street station.

'A right pain, this one,' whispered Jean over another man. 'Bawling and shouting. Sometimes in a foreign language, makes me think he has something to hide.'

Tracy nodded, enthralled.

'He has us all running about like headless chickens. Gets violent too.'

'Really?'

'Well,' shrugged Jean, 'he doesn't *mean* to, I suppose, but he can knock things about. He's very strong. He broke Angie's finger.' She nodded at a pretty, dark-haired nurse with white tape on her left hand, then looked back at Tracy seriously.

'So you take care.'

'I will.'

'And the *families*,' said Jean, with a look that said that Tracy would soon find out for herself. 'You mustn't let them bully you. *You*'re the professional, not them. Remember that.'

'I *will*,' said Tracy firmly, and looked around the unit. Two wards, twelve beds – ten of them containing people who were neither dead nor alive; who had bought tickets to the afterlife and then had somehow had their journeys interrupted, and who were even now debating whether or not to go on, or to turn around and make their way back home.

3

He had seen a lot of doctors, but it wasn't until he'd started school at the age of five that Patrick realized there was something wrong with him. He hated the disorder of his classmates and the physicality of the playground – where nobody else was interested in clearing the quad of gravel, then grading it according to size.

In the classroom there was no task too complex for him to tackle, and few he could not complete. While the other kids rushed out to play, Patrick would wriggle and shriek if the teacher tried to encourage him away from his alphabet or his sums. He was a barnacle for learning.

He deconstructed his lunchbox and discarded anything red, and was obsessed with parroting any sentence spoken to him, emphasizing each word in turn to taste the changes.

PUT the chalk down.
Put the CHALK down.
Put the chalk DOWN.
And still he'd be holding the chalk.

Nobody rejects difference as quickly and brutally as children. Soon Patrick was not invited to houses and parties, and was excluded from groups and games. But he didn't want to go to parties, hated groups, and didn't understand the games, so it didn't bother him. After all, he was fascinated by the rhythm of ants, but it didn't mean he wanted to *be* one.

Until he was seven years old . . .

Children weren't allowed in the bookmaker's, so while his father watched the horses and dogs on the big screen, Patrick sat under the counter nearest the door, hemmed in by bikes and an old black Labrador, which was either always wet or just smelled that way. Sometimes men would stand in front of Patrick without even knowing he was there. They leaned their elbows on the counter to read the pages of runners and riders that were pinned to the walls, and he looked at their knees and their crotches, and the muddy prints their boots left on the lino. He could hear the scratch of the cheap little biros as they scribbled their selections over his head, and their muttering when they lost, which seemed to be all the time.

Occasionally they noticed him and bent down and said, 'Hello, down there' and 'All right, boyo?' But when that happened, Patrick always edged towards the dog for support, and said nothing back. Once a man held a Milky Way out to him and the Labrador snatched it and swallowed it in two gulps – wrapper and all.

'Don't say much, do he?' an old man once remarked to Patrick's father, and his father replied staunchly, 'He's thinking.'

His father always told the truth: Patrick *was* thinking – about the way air smelled like rubber when it hissed from bicycle tyre valves, about the odds that changed on the screens, making horses' names jump up and down the list like fleas, and about why dogs had pink gums but black lips.

Increasingly ignored, Patrick grew to enjoy his post by the door, where he could observe without being observed.

It was a hot summer day, and Patrick was tracing the Labrador's slumbering outline on to the lino in biro, when a shocked groan went up from the men in the bookies – followed by a terrible silence.

Patrick crawled from under the counter and crept forward past the shoes of the men, until he stood up just inches from the giant TV screen.

Pixellated by proximity, a purple jockey trudged up the emerald grass with a saddle on his arm that should have been on the back of a horse.

Patrick touched the grass and felt the green buzz warmly around his fingers.

'What's that kid doing in here?' somebody called out, and his father got up and held out his hand.

Patrick drew back. He hated to hold hands; it made his bones itch. But he was perplexed to see that his father had tears in his eyes. For some reason he didn't understand, it made Patrick take his hand without complaint. He even held it while they crossed the busy road, and then all the way to the lounge bar of the Rorke's Drift. There his father bought him a Coke in a bottle that looked as though it had been squeezed in the middle, and touched his own pint to it with a dull click.

'To Persian Punch,' he said huskily, and pinched his nose, which was like wiping it on his sleeve but not as common.

'To Persian Punch,' agreed Patrick, although it was only later that he would learn that Persian Punch was a horse.

Had been a horse.

He never forgot the feeling that it had given him. The curious sense that he was closer to his father at that moment than he'd ever come to anyone. That he could almost *share* what he was feeling. For the first time, Patrick had an inkling of what it was that the other children seemed to know instinctively – that they were part of something bigger, something mysterious.

Something he finally wanted, but still didn't know how to get.

* * *

Discovering that he was missing a critical link turned school into a daily misery for Patrick. Everybody else possessed the key to popularity and happiness, and his clumsy attempts to find his own key always ended with other children looking at him funny, or calling him names. Classmates hid his pencils just to watch him rage, and a group of boys wrapped his winter coat round a rock and threw it on to the roof of the bike shed. The frustration left him confused and angry, and obstinate at home, where he made his parents shout at each other behind closed doors. Patrick would press his cheek to the cool, painted wood and listen to his mother's voice cracking hysterically: '. . . can't go *on* like this! I wish we'd never *had* him!'

He liked it when she got like that, because then his father would take him on long walks across the Beacons – just the two of them – while she stayed home and drew the curtains so she could sleep. 'I need to recover,' she'd say wearily, and they'd return much later to have tea in a darkened house – silently, so as not to wake her – and his father would put the vodka away somewhere different each time.

Finally, when Patrick was eight years old, Mark Bennett – a monster of a farmboy – had shouted 'Twpsyn!' and punched him in the back as he swung on the monkey bars. Patrick dropped into the dirt and lay gasping at the sky until his breath came back to him. By the time he'd got slowly to his feet, the bigger boy was already high on the swings, laughing. Patrick had stood to one side and waited for the swing to swoop down and past him – then smashed Mark Bennett square in the face with a rounders bat. The combined speed of the swing and the bat knocked him out cold and off the swing, in an impressive somersault that a generation of Brecon children would claim to have seen with their very own eyes.

The school had called Patrick's mother, who'd burst into tears and hung up, so they'd called his father, who had left work in the middle of the day to fetch him.

And had died because of it.

4

I'm asleep and I cannot tell you how hard I try to wake up.

I dream of Jesus hanging on a cross in his pyjamas, his hands twisting in agony while Mary in a blue uniform tugs on his drubbing feet. Other times it's a birdman in a black cape and a gas mask, come to plunge its long beak into the jelly of my eyes and drag me off by the sockets – and I scream until my throat hurts, but nobody comes.

Because it's a dream – as if that makes it any better.

Sometimes I'm asleep but I'm *aware* that I am not awake. Then I swim for the surface in a bottomless well. The water is thick and dirty and I can't always see the disc of light. Only the fear of what lurks beneath me in the sinuous darkness keeps me fighting, keeps me swimming.

And yet, whenever I get close to the top, I turn away from the greater horror overhead.

Up there, beyond the water, somebody screams in pain or in anger – a tortured soul howls obscenities and roars its agony. A hell above me. A holocaust in a foreign tongue. Tears are shed; women and children heartbroken and scared. 'He'll be all right. He'll be all right.' But the sobbing doesn't stop – just moves further away.

Some unseen fish bites the back of my hand and my arm goes cold, and there's a tugging at my insides like a leech sucking my belly inside out. My shoulders ache, my legs cramp, my neck hurts. Hands run over me like I'm a cow at market and – like a cow – hot shit slides out of me, unhindered by decency.

There are voices far above me, as if people are passing by the well with buckets and other things mechanical. I hear them coming and I hear them going: a slow Doppler effect. I don't recognize them but they seem to know what they're doing; they're very busy, very *efficient*, even though I can't make out the words.

The voices drift in and out, and *I* drift in and out, too – in and out of life and dreams for days, for weeks, for years? But when I'm *in* I listen all the time for somebody I know. When I hear them, *that*'s when I'm going to break the surface and shout out, *that*'s when I'm going to make them know I'm here.

I'm going to call out: *Hey! Hello! I'm down here!* And

they will look down the well and see me at the bottom, and wave in surprise and go and get help and pull me up in a big wooden bucket, like a kitten that's been lost for ever.

Hey! Hello! I'm awake! I can hear you! I'm awake!

The words are always on the tip of my stagnant tongue. All it will take from me is the air to form them with, the effort of pushing them out, and I'll be away.

But for some reason, I'm frightened to try it.

If I can't force myself to wake from my own dreams, what if I also can't shout out when I need to? Or if I *can* shout out, but nobody hears me? What if they pass right by the lip of the deep, dark well, and never look down, however hard I'm screaming?

That would no longer be a dream.

That would be a nightmare.

Tracy Evans noticed that coma patients were not visited with Get Well cards and grapes; coma patients were attended by those who loved them, or by those who felt a sense of duty. It was easy to tell the difference. Those who loved stayed for hours, touching, washing, talking, playing favourite music through iPod earphones, bringing in childhood toys and adult knick-knacks, holding scented flowers under breathless noses, singing 'Happy Birthday' with tears in their eyes and croaks in their throats.

Those who loved hoped for recovery.

Those who came out of duty hoped only for an end, one way or the other. They sat and read or brought their laptops to catch up on their emails – and asked endlessly for the password for the free Wifi. They bit their nails and tapped their feet and read any old magazine they could find, even the gardening ones. They stared out of the window, down across the roof of the car park and the city beyond it – as if even that were preferable to looking at the person in the bed who wouldn't make up their mind whether to live or whether to die.

Tracy Evans liked those visitors better. They never asked for vases or for the blinds to be opened, or thought they'd seen a twitch or a blink, or a finger tapping out SOS in Morse on the lemon-coloured blankets.

The ones who were there for love were a bit of a pain. She'd only been here a few weeks but already she'd had a girlfriend leave a boyfriend a life-sized stuffed leopard, a woman bring in an electric frying pan to cook bacon by her husband's bedside, and four karate club members performing some kind of routine, complete with loud yells, in the hope that the sound would kickstart a brain that no longer worked. She couldn't even tell them off for waking the other patients, because waking the patients on the coma ward was sort of the whole *point*.

It was all mildly diverting, but in no way did it

replace or facilitate Tracy's obsession with the progress of Rose Mackenzie's life.

The one bright spot was Mr Deal.

Mr Deal came every night after work to see his wife, whose notes told Tracy that she had been here for nearly a year, after suffering a brain haemorrhage following a fall downstairs. Mrs Deal was forty, which meant Mr Deal was old enough to seem far more exotic to Tracy than the young men she routinely met in Evolution on a Friday night. Those young men hunted in packs and vomited in gutters; she couldn't imagine Mr Deal doing either of those things.

There was something authoritarian and brooding about him – something of the Raft Ankers, if Tracy were honest – and every time his visits coincided with her shifts, she got a little thrill.

He never came at weekends, and seemed just un-interested enough in his wife during week-night visits to make Tracy think that a bit of mild flirtation might not be such a sinful thing – or a wasted one. She hadn't done it yet – not properly – but she knew she would quite soon, unless Mrs Deal died or got better. Actually, only if she got better. If Mrs Deal died, Tracy thought she would still be in with a chance. Men hated living alone and were no good at it; Tracy knew this because her father had tried leaving her mother once, and had been so thoroughly hopeless that he'd returned home just two weeks later with his tail tucked between his legs, right where his balls should have been.

Mr Deal wasn't a pilot or a doctor, but he was obviously rich and important. Tracy guessed the former because he had a set of keys on a Mercedes fob, which he often twirled on his finger while he looked at the car park with his back to his wife. She guessed he was important because when he spoke on his BlackBerry about work, he sounded as if he were giving orders, not taking them, and frowned and sighed as if he were running the United Nations.

Rich and important, and just a little bit dangerous.

Tracy Evans pulled a fresh sheet tight over Mrs Deal's slowly curling body, tucked it in hard, and hoped she wouldn't get better too soon.

5

It was only the first week of August, but Patrick had already packed his bags for college.

Bag, singular.

Sarah Fort stared down into the battered old suitcase, open on his bed in the room under the eaves that looked out across the smooth green hills of the Brecon Beacons.

She had told him to take everything he'd need for the twelve-week term, so he'd packed his laptop, his textbooks and his hoodie with the word HOODIE on it.

Nothing else.

With a sigh, she opened Patrick's drawers and started to fill the suitcase with sensible things. Sweaters, shorts, socks. His washbag held only toothbrush and paste, cheap shampoo, and a razor with innumerable blades, each one supposedly more efficient than the last. Sarah smiled at the razor. Patrick got so angry about the lies advertisers told: the best ever, the longest lasting and eight out of ten cats outraged his logic. But he'd bought the razor anyway – prey to the power of advertising, just like any normal person.

Normal.

It was all she wanted for him – to be normal. Of course, she wanted him to have a job and a wife and a family, too – but she'd settle for normal. Normal would be a relief.

Down below, next to the ramshackle wooden shed, on the patch of weed-strewn gravel they called the driveway, Patrick was leaning over the engine of her little Fiesta. What could be more normal than a boy fixing a car on a sunny day? The scene gave Sarah hope. He'd got that from Matt – that obsession with mechanical things, even though Patrick had never learned to drive. The Fiesta was twenty years old now, and still ran like a dream, thanks to him.

She watched him tinker. From this distance she could see the boy *and* the man; the way he was changed but still changing. Big hands on the end of wiry arms, wide shoulders but narrow hips, and cropped hair that came to a childlike curl at his nape as he bent to read the oil level.

Sarah sighed. Patrick had been such a sweet baby; a boisterous toddler. But then – increasingly – a strange little boy. He'd started to stiffen when they tried to hug him, to look away when they spoke. His teachers said he was the cleverest in the class at sums, but then looked down at their hands while they mumbled about everything else: his fixation on detail and routine, his isolation and his lack of eye contact.

After Matt had . . . died, Patrick had got worse. He shrieked if Sarah reached out to him, and barely spoke – except to ask obsessively, 'What happened to Daddy?'

The doctor said it was understandable.

When it went on for a year, the doctor turned his palms up more cautiously, and said it was an understandable obsession.

Sarah hated the word 'obsession'. She preferred to call it a 'phase'.

But it had gone on so long . . .

Patrick had started to bring home dead animals. Birds, squirrels, rabbits. He sat and stared at them for hours, rolling them gently back and forth with a stick, or spreading a dead wing to watch the feathers move into place. After a while he'd begun to slice them open, peering into cavities and unravelling intestines. Making his bed one day, Sarah found a peeled shrew under the pillow. After that, dead things weren't allowed in the house. She had caught him testing the padlock on the shed door instead, and warmed his backside for him.

No means no, Patrick!

The dead-animal phase had lasted years, and then

Patrick had become more focused on mechanical things. When he wasn't fine-tuning his bicycle gears, he was peering at the engine of her car, or those of neighbours, coaxing dead and dirty metal back to life with a spanner he wielded like a wand. Now his hands often reminded her of Matt's, with the whorls on his fingers mapped in oily isobars.

Sarah frowned. This sudden desire to go to college – to learn anatomy – seemed like an unwelcome return to that earlier obse— that earlier *phase*. No good could come of it.

She watched her son tighten the spark plugs, then put each of the old ones back inside little cardboard tubes for disposal and line them up neatly on the ground, making sure each one was parallel with the last. She knew that when the time came to throw them away, he would take them out of the tubes one last time and check each one again before dropping it into the bin.

What went on inside his head?

Sarah had been asking herself the same question for eighteen years and knew she probably would for another fifty, if she lived that long. What was it that made Patrick panic if his T-shirt was too tight? What hitch in his brain made him arrange his books by publication date, and eat his food in alphabetical order?

Sarah never asked him. They talked – but never about the things that mattered. It was all *Bring down your laundry* and *Don't forget your coat*. Part of her yearned for more; another part shied away from anything deeper or more difficult. The truth was, she didn't want to know why he was the way he was, or whether there was anything she could have done about it.

Or *not* done . . .

She caught sight of her reflection in the window: tight-lipped, no make-up, mousey hair scraped into a utilitarian knot. The face of a woman who has no one to wake up with.

Through her own ghostly eyes she watched Patrick wheel Matthew's old bike across the gravel and disappear down the lane. She knew he'd be gone for hours, and felt the relief.

There were two dusty framed photos on Patrick's bedside table. The first was a picture of Matt on the Beacons, taken from a child's angle that only accentuated his stature.

He'd been such a handsome man, thought Sarah, and they'd shared such dreams. Not grand dreams, but humble ones – of a better couch, a holiday in Scotland, and of going together to watch their son on the rugby field or in the school play. They hadn't wanted much, but they'd been denied even that.

The other photo was of her and Patrick standing awkwardly together – not touching – next to the old blue Volkswagen she'd once loved but which she couldn't bear to look at after Matt's death. Patrick was only seven or eight in the photo – a thin child with dark-blue eyes and brown hair that was always clipped too short, to save time and money. She'd framed it because it was one of the few pictures she had of him where he was actually looking into the camera. No doubt because Matt was behind it, she thought with an unexpected flicker of the old resentment. Patrick had always been more Matt's son than hers. Matt would explain things to Patrick in a low, soothing voice, and never cared if Patrick said nothing in return, or got up and left in the middle of it.

Both of which drove her crazy.

The least you could do is nod your head, Patrick!

If you're not going to sit at the table like a big boy, you can bloody well go hungry.

It wasn't often Sarah was able to hold Patrick's gaze, and now she picked up the photo and thumbed a path through the dust so she could study his eyes. Even though they were ten years out of date, they were still the same – solemn and wary. He didn't trust her; she knew that. Even as a small boy he would turn and look to Matt for confirmation of anything she'd said – each glance a needle in her heart.

On a whim, Sarah slid the photo under the hoodie, where Patrick wouldn't notice it until it was too late. It knocked against something wrapped inside the thick material of the sweatshirt.

Sarah took out a black hardcover notebook with a red cloth spine, and opened it – expecting that Patrick had already begun making notes for his anatomy classes. He was the most conscientious of students.

Instead there was page after page of dense pencil lists in his firm block capitals.

. . . CHARGER, BELLADONNA, HOSTILITY . . .

She frowned at the long columns of random words.

. . . EXIT STRATEGY, SLEEPER, COMMON GOOD . . .

Sometimes there was a date, or an asterisk next to a word, or a symbol that meant nothing to her. *None* of it meant anything to her. She doubted it meant anything to anybody apart from Patrick. She flicked through dozens of almost identical pages, increasingly uneasy, yet not knowing why. Partly it was because she'd never seen the book before, which meant Patrick must have kept it hidden. That alone was disturbing. But mostly because its contents just seemed so *odd* – and she discouraged odd wherever possible. Odd had never done Patrick any favours, and never would.

As she was about to close the book, it fell open near the back where the pages were still clear, and suddenly she was looking at a black and white photograph of a little girl in a white dress.

Panic squeezed her throat, and gooseflesh rose down her forearms. What was *this*? Her mind – always primed to expect the worst – launched like a firework, spinning crazily through a ruined future where the police knocked on the door, where she had to find the money for solicitors, where people spat at them in the street and broke their windows, whether Patrick was found guilty or not.

Then she realized that the photo was not so much black and white as sepia.

And that the child was dead.

She gasped and bent her head over it more intently, with the little bedside alarm clock ticking suddenly loudly in her ears.

This was beyond odd.

The little girl in the picture was aged about five. Her face was pinched and workhouse poor, but her flaxen hair had been brushed and a dark ribbon tied into it over one bony temple. She wore a long, carefully arranged dress full of lace frills and impractical flounces. It was a dress worn only for such photos, Sarah guessed – likely to have been provided by the photographer, and probably the only decent dress the little girl would ever have worn.

The child in the picture was propped on a chair; Sarah could just see the tips of her shiny black shoes dangling below the pristine hem. The girl's eyes were closed, but that might just have been the taking of the photograph, Sarah knew. Those Victorians had to keep utterly still during long exposures, and children often couldn't make it. They blinked, they twitched, they yawned . . . they blurred. So the eyes might have been caught mid-blink.

No, it was the hands that gave it away.

A cheap doll had been placed on the girl's lap and

her arms arranged around it, as if she were holding a favourite toy. But this child's hands were beyond holding. The wrists were curled inwards, and the fingers were slack – and the photographer had failed to notice that the pinkie on the girl's left hand was bent backwards under the doll, in a way that no living child would have suffered.

This girl was dead.

Somewhere Sarah had heard of such photos, but she had never seen one. Pictures taken of the dead for their families to remember them by, in a time when few could afford to spend precious pennies on such fripperies for the living.

She felt overwhelming relief, then gave a short, nervous laugh at the thought that she could be relieved by finding a picture of a dead child among her son's possessions.

Her brief illusion of normality popped like a soap bubble and she looked out across the Beacons, where sunlight illuminated the very top of Penyfan, throwing its swooping drop into ominous shadow. She remembered the day Patrick had been suspended from school – how she'd swayed on that crest, staring into the abyss, while fingers of mist caressed her calves and encouraged her to take a closer look.

She hadn't been back since. This was close enough.

She heard again the smooth, cultured voice of Professor Madoc on the phone a few days after Patrick's interview – talking in careful circles, tying her up in condescending knots about empathic response and special requirements – and her registering none of it but the single word 'quota'. Patrick had got into college because of their disability quota. That was the bottom line. Not because he had smashed national academic records in A-level biology and zoology, but because of his Asperger's Syndrome.

Professor Madoc could patronize her till the cows came home, but she wasn't stupid; she'd had an education once; she'd had a life! And no amount of politically correct verbal acrobatics could hide the fact that, although they were letting him take anatomy, Professor Madoc thought there might be something badly amiss with Patrick.

At the time she'd felt killing tears scorch her eyes. Now – sitting on her son's bed, with his cryptic notebook in one hand and a photograph of a dead child in the other – she wasn't sure he was wrong.

6

Patrick lay on his back and watched the clouds obey the breeze. The sheep-shorn grass was warm under him, and the smell of hay drifted over him from the farm in the valley below. Good enough to eat.

On late-summer days like this, with his eyes starting to close, it was easy to imagine his father was still alive – lying beside him in a silence that had only ever been broken by a quiet word or a gentle snore.

But even in this warm cocoon, he could never remember his father without thinking of that day . . .

He'd followed him out of the school gates, staring at the back of his blue overalls, and at the Doc Martens with the steel toecaps that felt like lead when he stepped into them at home to play Deep Sea Diver.

His father rarely walked so fast, so Patrick guessed he had forgotten he was behind him. Every few

48

paces, Patrick had to break into a jog just to keep up.

He was glad to be out of school. Everybody looking at him, and all the loud words. Nobody had seen Mark Bennett punch him in the back. No adult, at least. But they had all come running to pick the bigger boy off the ground, and they had all seen the blood. Mr Jenkins had shouted and asked him if he understood how *wrong* he'd been, but Patrick didn't feel wrong, and couldn't lie about it, which made Mr Jenkins even louder. Then, when his father had arrived, Mr Jenkins had been loud with *him*, as if *he* were eight years old, too.

'Follow me,' his father had said as he left, without looking at him, and so that's what Patrick had done – followed him out of the school gates and down towards the town.

The garage was at the other end of Brecon. Patrick knew he would sit and wait in Mr Harris's broken chair in the grimy little office, which was always covered with pink invoices and black fingerprints, with Miss February forever on the calendar. Her name was Justine, she liked beach volleyball and kittens, and her nipples were dark brown.

Near the bookies, his father turned and took Patrick's hand and started to pull him across the quiet road. Patrick stiffened. His father *never* just grabbed his hand without warning! The feeling of it made him want to scream. He twisted free and stepped back towards the kerb. His father spun on his heel.

'Oh, for *fuck's sake*, Patrick! Take my hand!'

The car hit him so hard that it knocked him out of his shoes. One moment his father was coming towards him with his hand outstretched; the next there was a space, with only the Doc Marten boots to show where he'd been – one lying on its side, the other rolling awkwardly down the road, like a dumped dog trying to find its way home.

The car never stopped.

Patrick breathed hard into that space for a long, deafening moment, then slowly started to follow the second boot. Further up the road, people were running. Running from shops and cars, and out of the bookies. Running away from him.

Patrick reached the second boot, which now stood on the white line, upright and obedient, the way his father left it in the hallway every night.

All the running people had stopped in a bundle further up the road. Between their legs, Patrick could see something blue lying on the tarmac. Blue and jumbled, and with angles that made no sense.

'Don't let him come here!' shouted the Milky Way man. 'Keep him there!'

A young man in a striped shirt blocked his way, and Patrick stopped before he could be touched.

'What's his name?' said Stripey over his shoulder.

'Don't know,' said Milky Way. 'Just keep him there.'

'What's your name, boyo?' said Stripey.

Patrick ignored the question and craned around

him, desperate to see what everyone was looking at. Then someone moved and – just for a second – Patrick saw his father's eyes.

Looking nowhere.

Patrick waited at the police station until nearly midnight, when they finally contacted his mother. She couldn't come to fetch him and when they drove him home he understood why. She had been recovering and could barely stand. The older policeman had tried to explain things to her, but she kept losing focus on him. Eventually he had made them both hot, sweet tea, and then had cooked Patrick beans on toast, before driving away under the fullest of moons.

'What happened to Daddy?' Patrick asked his mother.

'Daddy's dead,' she said hoarsely.

'Why?'

'Because of you,' she said, and her voice broke in half. 'Because of *you*!'

Then Patrick watched her howl, and slap her own head, and crawl about the kitchen floor – and thought that she hadn't really answered his question.

For a long time after that day, Patrick had searched for his father. He roamed the Beacons, he peered through the doors of Harris's garage, he was chased out of the Rorke's Drift, and he crept into the bookies to huddle beside the Labrador, waiting for his father's blue legs to pass him. At night he lay awake, restless and alert, sure that he'd hear the key in the lock and catch his father creeping in by moonlight; in the mornings he stood breathless at the top of the stairs and looked down into the hallway, expecting to see the Doc Martens in their proper place.

His father had been there one moment and gone the next. It was like a magic trick that he might expose, if only he looked up the right sleeve.

In his dreams he always took his father's out-stretched hand, and they crossed the road together.

His mother didn't go to work in the card shop, and Patrick didn't go to school. His mother slept and slept and slept. He barely saw her, and found that calming. He made his own meals. Every day was sandwiches: breakfast, lunch and dinner. He stopped bothering to put the lid back on the jam.

Two weeks after the accident, a woman and a man came to the cottage and spoke to his mother with files on their laps, while Patrick watched through the crack in the door. They said the car had not been found, that the driver had not been traced. They said someone had seen a number plate but that someone had got it wrong. They said they would keep trying but that the trail was going cold. His mother sat on the couch as limp as a rag doll, and nodded her head now and then. When she looked up, her eyes were almost as empty as his father's had been.

A doctor came and gave her an injection. Patrick

slipped out the back way and ran across the Beacons, scattering sheep.

After that, he went back to school. For the first few days, he got a lift with Weird Nick and his mother. Then one day when he got home, they had the Fiesta instead of the blue Volkswagen and a new jar of jam, and life returned to some kind of normality – on the outside, at least.

The school counsellor asked him how he felt and he didn't understand the question, so she told him.

'You feel sad,' she said. 'That's normal. You've lost someone you loved very much and if you want to cry, that's not being a baby.'

Patrick didn't want to cry; he only wanted to find out what had happened to his father.

The counsellor sighed. 'You see, Patrick, when somebody dies, it's like going through a door. Once that door closes behind them, they can't come back.'

Patrick had never heard of a door you could only go through one way. He hadn't seen a door opening or closing – or even his father moving towards it. He'd simply been *there* and then *not there*. But the counsellor seemed very sure.

'Then I can just find the door and open it and find out what happened,' he told her.

'Oh, Patrick,' said the counsellor with tears in her eyes, and reached out to give him a big hug.

He'd had to hit her to keep her at bay.

7

I can smell bacon! Frying bacon. I can even hear it sizzle – and the waves of memory crash saltily into my mouth.

Sunny mornings outside the caravan down on the Gower.

Why don't we sell the house and live like this? That's what Alice and I always say to each other, sitting in our old stripy deckchairs, after the breakfast and before the washing up, while Lexi and Patch chase each other through the tufted dunes, squealing and yapping.

Flying the pink plastic box kite I bought Lexi in the little shop festooned with beach balls and buckets; feeling it dance and tug at the end of the line. And then suddenly we're holding nothing but falling string, as the kite breaks free and soars into the Wedgwood sky like something that knows where it's going, and can't wait to get there. As it disappears into a dot, Lexi slips her little hand into mine and says, 'Look at it *go*, Daddy!' – and my heart is overwhelmed with joy, because watching it go *is* better than holding it back, even if we'll never see it again.

I can feel her hand now, squeezing my fingers so hard that it hurts. But I don't pull away because holding her hand is so special; so precious . . .

All *that* from the smell of the bacon. All that wonder and joy . . .

Somebody tells me they love me. It's not Alice but it warms me anyway. Love is never bad, wherever you find it; Alice taught me that.

I wonder where they are, Alice and Lexi. Do they even know I'm here – waiting for them to come and find me while a stranger holds my hand? Until they're with me, what am I? Not a husband and not a father.

I'm lost without them.

The only noise is a soft *blip* . . . *blip* . . . and the sound of my own breathing. In and out . . . and in and out . . . and in and out . . . and in and out. My chest rises and falls to the maddening rhythm. It makes me think of Lexi learning to play the piano. 'Chopsticks' outrunning the metronome, and 'Twinkle, Twinkle, Little Star' lagging behind it. But she stuck at it, even though her fingers were never going to be long enough to be good. That's my fault; I brought the stubby hands to the marital table. Alice brought the even temper, the sense of fun, and all the looks.

And the sad eyes.

When did *that* happen? Is that *my* fault?

In the cot next to the bed, Lexi cries as if her heart is breaking.

So sad. *So sad!*

I want to roll over and comfort her, before she wakes Alice. In my head, I do.

'S OK, I whisper. *'S OK, sweetheart, go to sleep.*

But I'm the one who sleeps, down the dark years.

When I wake again, sliced white bread is laid out in neat squares for buttering. For a party, perhaps? A catered event, and here's all the bread, waiting for the tuna and the cheese and the coronation chicken. I'm not hungry, but a sandwich would be nice. A sandwich and maybe a sausage roll, and a pint of Brains bitter. My mouth is so dry.

I open my eyes anew and realize that it's not bread; it's ceiling tiles!

I'm happy because that is dull enough to be real. No writhing Jesus, no giant man-crows, just square tiles suspended in a metal frame like the view at the dentist's.

I think it means I'm definitely awake.

It must be night now. The tiles were off-white before, which is why they looked like bread, but now they're grey, and in one place there's a small black triangle where one has slipped or broken.

There's a miserable sound somewhere nearby. It's

the sad whine of a puppy left out in the rain. Shivery and cold.

My head's not working, so I slide my eyes to the very corners of their sockets, so that the ceiling disappears – at least, the bit over my head does – and I'm looking over there, to my left.

There's a water jug and beyond that a bed, so I assume I'm in a bed, too, because I'm lying here on *something*, which makes that *another* bed. And two beds in one room indicate a hospital. Or a dorm room. But I have a sense I've already graduated from Bristol, where I shared with Artie Rinker, who could whistle through his belly button.

So, a hospital then.

The snow-sky passes silently by, and my arm flaps at the window.

There's a man in the other bed. And there's a machine beside him with a soft grey-lit screen. That's where all the blips are coming from – they sound in time to a point of light jerking across the screen. There are tubes running to the man's arms and stomach, and somebody stands over him. This person's back is to me, but even in the dim glow of the screen, I can see he is wearing blue scrubs.

Two and two equals a doctor.

This is my moment.

I call out to let him know I'm awake. Or, at least, I thought I was going to call out, but I can't hear myself. I try to clear my throat, but my tongue is big and sticky and I can only really make a little *whirr*. I try again to speak, and realize that my lips are moving but nothing else is. No air is coming up from my lungs to shape itself into words in my mouth. I've forgotten what every newborn knows.

I try to sit up, but that doesn't work either.

I nearly panic, but all I can do is look at the ceiling, at the little black triangle, and tell myself to calm down. I have to get pretty stern with myself: calm down, Samuel Galen! This is *not* an emergency. I have time. I have lots of time. I have been here for a thousand years already; another minute won't hurt.

I concentrate on sensible things; on what I know. The man in the bed must be the one who swore and begged; whose wife and children wept when they visited. The mumbling and the crying wasn't Lexi at all, because Lexi's almost thirteen, not a baby in a cot. That bit must have been a dream, I think.

So much of life is.

Also, if this is a hospital then the man in the next bed must be a patient. Like me? I suppose so, if the crash I dreamed was real. And if we are patients, then the doctor will not ignore me, whether I can shout or not. If I am a patient, then I am here to be cared for, and that's what doctors do. So I don't *have* to shout. I don't *have* to wave my arms around to attract attention. All I have to do is calm down and wait until he's finished helping the patient in the next bed, and then he'll turn to me and see that I'm awake, and help me too.

Ding dong bell. Pussy in the well.
Simple.
Click.
The sound of a switch is soft but unmistakable, and is accompanied by the extinction of the grey light.

The blips have stopped, too.

I turn my eyes again. The doctor's hand is on the dark machine and the man in the bed is moving a little. Then a lot. Straining; feet kicking under the covers like he's having a fit; like he's gasping for air.

Like he's dying.

My God, he's *dying*!

Now I panic. It seizes me, but I can't shout or run or wave my arms about to share the feeling, so instead it splashes through my chest like electricity, then shoots down my arms and legs and up the back of my head until every part of me tingles with pointless shock.

In my mind I am already there beside him, clearing an airway, pinching his nose, breathing into his mouth, the way we all learned that time from the St John Ambulance. In fact, I can't move a muscle.

My head screams: *Help him! Help him!*

But the doctor doesn't help him.

Instead he just leans over the man and watches him suffer. It seems to take a forever of choking and rattling, and when it's all over, there's a vast silence filled only by my heart in my head. Then I hear the soft click of the switch again and the dim light returns, making me blink. I wait for the blips, but they don't come back.

They never come back.

Is this another dream? I hope so. I beg the grey tiles, *Please let it be a dream. Please don't let this be real.*

I hear quiet footsteps squeak towards me and quickly close my eyes. I don't want to see the doctor, and I don't want *him* to see *me*.

I no longer want him to know that I'm awake.

PART TWO

8

Patrick entered a large space filled with dead people and thought of an art gallery.

The Cardiff University dissection room was brighter, whiter, lighter than he had ever imagined; films like *Flatliners* and *Frankenstein* had apparently misled him. This was more a hangar than a lab, white and airy under a lofty ceiling filled with skylights, but with no windows in the walls. There were no views out on to the tree-lined bustle of Park Place, and definitely no views in.

It was only after his eyes had lingered on the pale-blue October sky that Patrick looked at the bodies.

Cadavers. He would have to get used to calling them that now.

They were the artworks in this exhibition. Thirty still-lifes – bloated by embalming fluids, and a curious shade of orange – lay on their tables waiting patiently to be deconstructed and analysed more thoroughly than any Mona Lisa, any Turin Shroud.

Each body lay in a cocoon of its own cotton swaddling, like a tender chrysalis. Each head was wound in lengths of unbleached cloth. To preserve moisture, Patrick knew from their anatomy prep sessions – to keep the face from desiccating, the eyes from wrinkling to raisins, and the students from being freaked out.

It was warm, and the smell was . . . strange. Patrick had been expecting formalin, but this was sweeter than that, although with an odd undernote that was not entirely pleasant.

'I'm going to be sick,' somebody whispered faintly from behind him.

'No you're not,' said another student encouragingly.

A dark-haired girl beside Patrick nudged his arm. 'You OK?' she said. 'You're very pale.'

He nodded and removed his arm from her orbit. He could have told her that pale came from excitement, not nausea. He could have told her that this dissecting room was where his quest would succeed or fail. A quest for answers he'd been seeking since he was eight years old, and which nobody had ever seemed willing or able to give him, so that eventually he'd simply stopped asking out loud.

Patrick didn't tell the girl that, because it wasn't in his nature to tell anybody anything.

They were each carrying *Essential Clinical Anatomy*

and wearing one of the twenty white paper lab coats they'd been issued in what looked like a gift bag – poor imitations of the thick white cotton coats doctors used to wear. Each had been given a four-figure code to allow them into the dissecting room via a key pad on the door. Patrick's was 4017 and he hated it on sight. There were no patterns, no progressions, and the number had no shape other than spiky. He wondered whether it was worth engaging with another student to see if he could swap.

Just inside the entrance were three large bins filled with bright blue latex gloves. Small, medium and large. There were a few nervous giggles as they struggled into them. Patrick took a large left and had to pick up six more before finding a large right. He toyed with calculating the odds, but the boxes held an unknown number of gloves.

The blue latex seemed irreverently jolly here in the dissecting room, like bunting at a funeral.

Next to the gloves were white plastic boxes full of the tools of their new trade. Saws, hooks, scalpels, forceps, scissors – even spoons – all tossed in together. They were tools a handyman might use; a common labourer with calluses on his palms and dirt under his nails. It was a stark reminder that these – their first patients – were already past saving.

Clutching their gift bags and textbooks, the students shuffled forward gingerly towards Professor Madoc. The 150 students barely looked at the cadavers as they filed past them – as if to do so before they were given the green light to start cutting might be rude. They kept their eyes averted and fixed on Professor Madoc as he started to speak.

He was a tall, elegant man in his sixties, with neat white hair and a sailor's tan. He welcomed them, giving them a brief overview of the anatomy syllabus and stressing the fundamental nature of the work they would learn in this room and how it would inform their studies and their rotations on the wards of the teaching hospital. He thanked the retired professors and junior doctors who had returned to guide the students through what he called the 'infinite intricacies of the human body'. He nodded at the assorted men and women in white coats at the back of the room.

Then he mentioned the Goldman Prize, given to the best anatomy student every year, causing looks and smiles to be exchanged in silent challenge. The professor ended by saying that he was sure he didn't have to tell them to respect those who had donated their bodies to medical science – and then told them anyway.

'Ladies and gentlemen, you may have heard stories of eyeballs in Martini glasses and skipping the Double Dutch with intestines, but those days are gone, thank God. The thirty cadavers you see before you now are the mortal remains of people who donated their bodies because they wanted to help you through your studies and into a noble and caring profession. They wanted to do that even though they didn't know you. And even though *you* didn't know *them*, and never will, please show your appreciation of their gift by according them the same respect that you will one day show to your living patients.'

Patrick heard little to nothing of the professor's speech. Alone among the students, he stared openly at the cadaver closest to him – an elderly woman with withered breasts, an apron of stomach fat and neatly manicured fingernails – still with a layer of chipped varnish on them. He was eighteen, but had never seen a live woman naked, and couldn't reconcile this one with the images he had browsed on the internet. They didn't even look like the same species.

He reached out and pressed a finger against the upper thigh. The consistency was that of a raw roast – cold and yielding, yet solid underneath. He thought of the way his mother stabbed the lamb on special occasions, and then pushed garlic and sprigs of rosemary into the gashed flesh.

He wasn't sure he wanted to look inside a woman.

The noise from Professor Madoc stopped, and the silence brought Patrick back to the here and now. Names were read out, and he was relieved to find himself soon standing at a table that held the body of what looked like a middle-aged man. It was hard to tell the age with the head wound in cotton strips, but even in death this body looked tighter than the old lady's had – more muscular, the skin less folded, and the abdomen swollen by embalming fluids rather than by fat.

Four other students joined him, including the dark-haired girl, who smiled at him as if they already shared common ground.

Their table mentor was a junior doctor – a young man only a few years older than they were, and in a *real* white coat – who introduced himself as David Spicer. He picked up the clipboard hanging at the dead man's feet in an incongruous echo of a patient's hospital notes.

'Right,' he said. 'Everybody, meet Number 19.'

'I don't want a man,' said a short Asian boy with thick glasses. 'I'm going to be an obstetrician. Can I swap with someone else?'

'No,' said Spicer.

'Why not?'

'Because I'm an uptight arsehole who wants you to fail.'

The Asian boy pursed his lips and looked sulky.

'You'll all get proper access to a female cadaver and the relevant prosections as the need arises during the course,' Spicer reassured him. 'Plus you will be doing various clinical rotations in a range of medical departments, so that you get plenty of exposure to a variety of real patients and conditions, OK?'

The boy nodded and Spicer went back to reading. 'Let's see . . . Number 19 here is a Caucasian male who died aged forty-seven.'

'Of what?' said Patrick.

'That would be spoiling the fun.' Spicer smiled. 'You should be able to diagnose cause of death during the dissection, but if you're really stumped and you don't mind being a *big fat failure*, you can go and ask Mick in the office.' He inclined his head towards a glass-walled cubicle beside the entrance door. Inside Patrick could see the tops of filing cabinets and an appropriately cadaverous middle-aged man glaring out at them. Mick, he assumed.

He wouldn't need to ask Mick or anybody else; he'd find out for himself.

'What's his name?' said the girl, nodding at the cadaver.

'That's confidential,' said Spicer. 'The important thing to remember is that he's Number 19.' He flicked a rectangular metal tag that was attached to the cadaver's wrist by a black zip-tie. In one corner was stamped the number.

'Anything and everything you take off or out of this cadaver gets bagged and tagged so it can be put back together again at the end of the course for burial or cremation. The fat and skin – what we call "fascia" – goes in the yellow bin marked nineteen in that refrigerator over there.' They all turned to follow his pointing blue finger to one of two big white doors in the far wall. 'And that fascia will also be reunited with Number 19 at the end of the course for burial or cremation.'

Patrick nodded. That all made sense, and followed nice strict rules.

Spicer clapped his hands and rubbed them together like a TV presenter. 'OK. We're all going to be meeting here around this gentleman twice a week for the next six months, so we might as well get acquainted.'

Introductions. Patrick hated this kind of thing, but the other students looked eager to be friendly.

The would-be obstetrician was Dilip, and the tall, beefy-looking boy with ruddy cheeks and thinning blond hair was Rob, who was considering surgery.

'Depending on how this goes,' he added, pointing at the cadaver with a wry smile.

The dark-haired girl's name was Meg and she was considering paediatrics.

Then there was Scott, who wanted to be a plastic surgeon.

'Boob jobs and tummy tucks,' he said, rubbing his finger and thumb together to denote money. 'You can all call me Scotty,' he added. 'Like in *Star Trek*.'

Patrick was confused. Scotty fixed starships, not breasts.

He noticed that Scott had the kind of uncommitted Mohawk made of gel and therefore easy to brush out for formal occasions. Then he realized that everyone was looking at him.

'You're up,' said Spicer, but Patrick felt himself closing *down*. Like an anemone snatching back its tentacles when touched.

'Patrick Fort. Anatomy.'

'Paddy,' said Scott.

'Patrick,' said Patrick.

'Just anatomy?' said Meg.

'Yes.'

'You're not going to be a doctor?' said Rob.

'No.'

'How about Pat?' said Scott.

'Patrick,' said Patrick.

'What are you going to be then?' said Meg.

He frowned in confusion. 'A graduate.'

They all waited for more, but he stared down at the corpse. He'd told them all he had to.

'Didn't expect the Spanish Inquisition, did you, Patrick?' said Spicer.

'No,' said Patrick. 'I don't even *speak* Spanish.'

Dilip and Scott laughed.

'Neither do I,' said Spicer. 'Anyway, you anatomists have lots of free time and you won't be joining us on hospital rounds, but the work you do here will be exactly the same as the med students, OK?'

Patrick nodded. The work here was all he wanted; the thought of being around real, live patients made him shiver.

'Right then,' continued Spicer. 'Pleasantries over. I'm going to show you how to handle a scalpel.' He touched the chest of the cadaver, where the curling, dark hair was going slightly grey towards the throat. As grey as it was ever going to get.

'We're going to make an H-incision here on the pectoral muscle to start with. When you do, imagine tracing rather than cutting, because these bastards are *sharp*, and if you get a bit Zorro you'll be down to the spine before you know it.'

As the blade touched the skin and a narrow door of blood opened in the chest, Patrick felt an unaccustomed buzz of pure optimism. This was the beginning of the end. Finally he could find his answers. Here was the place where his quest might reach its conclusion – in this very room, this cathedral to science, this white gallery of death—

Something heavy hit the back of his legs and he staggered slightly, then looked round to see Rob crumpled on the floor behind him.

'Shit,' said Spicer cheerfully. 'So much for surgery.'

9

I float, calm and disconnected. I feel as though I'm on drugs and I wonder why I've never tried them before if they're all this good. Mark Williams at work tried them all the time and had a ball. Until the college had to fire him, of course; then it wasn't such fun. But this is nice. This is like drifting on musical clouds. Maybe I *am* on drugs! This is a hospital, after all.

'He would just slip away,' says a woman very quietly.

'Would he be in pain?' That's another woman, also somewhere off to my left. They're discussing the man in the next bed. That means he's not dead, which is good and right. It was just a bad dream, like the giant crow and the masonry that fell on me from a crumbling building somewhere in Japan. Or Mauritius. Dreams are rarely geographically sound.

'Oh no.' The first woman again. 'We monitor his

medication very carefully. He wouldn't know anything about it.' She must be a doctor.

Through my haze I feel vaguely angry for the man who wouldn't know anything about it. How would *they* know? Maybe he'd know *all* about it; maybe he'd be scared, or in pain, down at the bottom of his own personal well.

'Is that what happened to the gentleman who used to be in that bed?'

'Mr Attridge? No, he died quite suddenly overnight. It happens like that sometimes.'

Oh, he *is* dead. Shit. His name was Mr Attridge and I watched him die.

'But what did he actually die of?'

I'm all ears.

There's a long hesitation and I can hear the doctor being careful.

'Sadly, coma patients die very easily. They succumb to infections, or have strokes, or asphyxiate on food or their own spittle, or sometimes the heart fails due to cumulative factors.'

Cumulative factors like being *murdered*!

'The longer someone is in a coma, the less likely they are to regain full consciousness. Such deaths may be sudden, but they are rarely unexpected or unexplained.'

'It's been two months now,' says the other woman, and someone touches my forehead with something that smells of rubber. 'But there's still a chance he'll . . . ?'

'Emerge.'

'Yes. There's still a good chance he'll *emerge*, isn't there?'

And all of a sudden I realize they're talking about *me*! Me, Sam Galen. Talking about *me* emerging – and talking about me *dying*!

I snap out of the cloud and get a bit frantic, which is difficult to do when you can't move or make a sound. I try to open my eyes. No lying doggo now! But they won't open. They won't bloody well *open*! I strain my brows upwards until it feels like my forehead will peel back like banana skin, but still my lids are dark maroon.

Maybe this is how it was for the man in the next bed – maybe somebody thought *he* should just 'slip away' while he tried to open his eyes.

'Every case is different,' the doctor hedges.

'All I want is an educated guess,' says the other woman. 'I understand it's not a diagnosis. *Please*.'

'In that case . . .'

Long silence. I can almost see the doctor tapping her teeth with the end of her pen as she takes an educated guess at my future existence. I stop straining to open my eyes and instead listen so hard that I feel the empty air swirl in my ears, while a smooth rubber finger drags over my cheek.

'I'm afraid,' says the doctor, her voice heavy with practised sorrow, 'it's getting to the point where *if* he emerges, it may not be in one piece.'

The finger leaves my cheek and there's no answer for a long time, and then only the sound of quiet sobbing.

I'm in one piece! I scream soundlessly. *Here I am! I'm in one piece!*

Aren't I?

10

Even when the streeets had been washed clean by rain, the malt rising from the Brains brewery made all of early-morning Cardiff smell like late-night Horlicks.

Patrick rode through the dawn, listening to the sound of his tyres hissing on the damp tarmac as he made a loop through the city.

In the Hayes, pigeons purred softly from the roof of the snack bar, and made him think of home.

It was an old city, despite the veneer of new wealth that made it shine in the wet Welsh sun. The buildings over the glittering shop fronts were all curled stone and soot, and the castle walls dominated the city centre, guarded by a strange collection of beasts, furred and feathered in stone. Victorian arcades linked the thoroughfares like secret tunnels, filled with shops that sold old violins, shoes, and sweets by the quarter from giant jars.

Cardiff was also a small city, and was easy to leave for the hills and forests and beaches that cupped it all round with nature. Sometimes Patrick rode west to Penarth and sat on the pier, which smelled faintly of fish, and which bore the scars of a thousand anglers who'd cut their bait on the salted wood. Sometimes he cycled beyond the narrow suburbs to the fairy-tale castle that guarded the city's northern approach; sometimes east across the flat, reclaimed land that bordered the sea so closely that only a grid of ditches kept it dry.

Ish.

Wherever he went, his route was guided by Welsh and by English – each road sign to *ildiwch* a reminder that the old oppressor had finally given way, after failing to beat the language out of the nation's schoolchildren.

The room Patrick was renting was the smallest in a small house that was distinguishable from its neighbours only by the white plastic '7' screwed to the front door. The back of it looked over the railway line where trains took passengers to and from the South Wales Valleys. One of them would have taken him halfway to Brecon if he'd caught it, but he had his bike, so he didn't need to.

His bed was squeezed between the wall at its head and the hot-water tank at its foot. He measured it and found it was six feet long – exactly one inch longer than he was. It took him a week to get used to sleeping on his side, with his knees bent, so that he wouldn't touch at either end. Even so, he was woken every morning by five thirty, when his feet grew warm as the heating kicked in. He slept in his sleeping bag because it smelled of grass and earth, and often he woke thinking he was on the Beacons.

A strip of chipboard under the windowsill served as a desk so small that he could only open one textbook at a time and still use his laptop. His books and disks had to go on top of the wardrobe. He had found a photo in his bag that he had not packed, and he left it there. The walls were woodchip, painted magnolia, and the carpet was brown, although Patrick wasn't convinced it had always been so.

The window had been modified so that it only opened about six inches. A deterrent to burglars, he guessed, although he doubted any burglar would brave the railway line, climb the tall garden wall and risk a drop into the thick brambles below, when it was plain from any angle that this grimy little terraced house must contain little worth stealing, and that easier pickings would surely be found almost anywhere else along the row. Even so, Patrick carried his bike upstairs to his room every night to protect it. It was a ten-speed Peugeot racer that was older than he was, but it was the only thing he'd inherited from his father, so he screwed two stout hooks into the wall and, while he slept, the bike hung over him like a sparkling blue talisman.

Two other students shared the house. Jackson and

Kim were both doing art degrees. Kim was a staunch lesbian – an elfin blonde who made lumpy ogres from plaster of Paris, with nuts and bolts sprouting at their genitals. Jackson made tedious video art that, to Patrick, looked like scenes where the cameraman had been killed and left the camera pointing at a dark corner of a dull room. Jackson had long, pale hands that flapped on slender wrists, and dyed black hair, so short at the back and so long at the front that Patrick itched to reach out and realign it with his head. He wore eyeliner, cowboy boots and a Yasser Arafat scarf, even when he was making toast.

They had all agreed to clean up after themselves, but Jackson was a slob, Kim not much better, and Patrick too nervous of germs to leave anything unwashed for as long as it might take either of his housemates to fulfil their promise. He simply got up earlier or stayed up later to clean the kitchen and bathroom. Kim occasionally left a dish of tasteless vegetarian food on his shelf in the fridge by way of thanks, but Jackson never mentioned the mess *or* the sparkling kitchen that was its mysterious corollary.

There was a TV in the front room that Jackson had brought from home, and which he controlled jealously – even taking the remote to the toilet with him. So Patrick learned all about the Turner Prize and *Hollyoaks*, and had to go to the bookies over the road to see any horseracing.

Sometimes they had parties in the house – not *him*,

but Jackson and Kim. At first they'd tried to involve him in the planning and the purchasing, but Patrick had no interest in parties and said he would stay in his room.

Jackson had narrowed his eyes suspiciously. 'Don't think you're going to come downstairs in the middle of it and eat our food and drink our booze then.'

'I don't drink,' said Patrick. 'And I wouldn't eat your food in case I got salmonella.'

'No need to be rude,' said Jackson.

'I'm not,' Patrick told him. 'You always have meat juice on your shelf; it's only a matter of time.'

'Don't come then,' Jackson said petulantly.

'OK,' said Patrick. 'Can I put the racing on?'

'Absolutely not. Cruel sport.'

Patrick was alone on the planet, it seemed, in being without a mobile phone. He'd tried one once but he could actually *feel* his brain being fried, and still flinched whenever a phone went off nearby. But it did mean that he had what seemed to be exclusive use of the public phone outside the bookies, although he always wore a stolen pair of the bright blue gloves when he called his mother every Thursday night, in case of germs on the receiver. She'd insisted he call once a week and Patrick did, only so that if he died he would be missed before his body started to smell too badly.

'Are you eating all right?' was one of the first questions she always asked.

'Yes,' he'd say. 'Monday I had toast and jam, then a cheese sandwich at lunch and pasta for dinner. Tuesday was the same but the sandwich was Marmite. Wednesday was the same but the sandwich was peanut butter. Thursday I ran out of peanut butter. And bread.'

'Did you get some more?'

'Yes.'

'Good,' she'd say. 'Don't forget to eat.'

'I won't,' he'd say, although sometimes he did.

Then, even though he never asked, she would tell him about the garden and the cat. It always went on for a lot longer than either of them deserved.

And then there were the silences. Patrick liked those bits of the conversation – the in-between bits that were so soothing and allowed him to think about things she wouldn't understand: adjusting the derailleur on his bike because first gear was clipping the spokes; the way fat looked like greasy yellow clots of sweetcorn under the skin; and Custom Lodge and Quinzi, who had died at Wincanton on Wednesday night.

'You are wearing your bike helmet, aren't you, Patrick?'

He nodded, his head elsewhere.

'Patrick?'

'Yes.'

'You are wearing your helmet, aren't you?'

'Yes. I told you already.'

'Sorry.'

The first death had been too quick, the second hidden from view behind screens, so neither had been useful to him.

'Well,' she'd say after a few more moments of silence. 'Thanks for calling. You take care of yourself and work hard.'

'OK.'

'I love you, Patrick.'

'OK.'

'Goodbye until next week then.'

'OK. Bye.'

Then he'd peel off the blue gloves and drop them in the bin on his way back to the house.

The click of disconnection always came so quickly after his last word that Sarah knew he was hanging up even as he said goodbye. Desperate to get away from her.

Could she blame him?

She often did.

Every week she thought of all the things she should ask him. But when Patrick wasn't around it was all too easy to forget how hard it was to keep a conversation going. As soon as she heard his voice, all the questions she would have asked any *normal* son died in her mouth.

Are you having fun in the evenings?
Who's your best mate?

Met any nice girls yet?

Patrick never had fun in the evenings. Not what most boys his age would call fun, anyway. He liked being on the Beacons, watching racing and collecting roadkill. The closest he had to a friend was Weird Nick next door, which said it all. And she could never imagine him even talking to girls, let alone allowing one to touch him or attempting a kiss. Asking Patrick those questions might not have upset *him*, but they would have upset *her*, because the answers would have reminded her of just how odd he still was – and possibly why.

And so every week they exchanged the same banalities and, instead of feeling relieved by them, his calls left her feeling guilty and resentful, even after all these years.

Or would it have been the same if Matt were still alive?

She'd never know now, she thought with a bitter dart. She stroked the cat too hard, so that it pushed off her lap with reproachful claws. It made Sarah think of trying to help three-year-old Patrick to unwrap a birthday gift – the way he'd squirmed away from her, and how she'd dug her fingers too deeply into his chubby little arm to keep him by her side.

But she'd lost him anyway.

And every Thursday she lost him again.

11

The flirting had worked. Now, whenever Mr Deal came to visit, he caught Tracy's eye and gave a little smile – and she always made sure she was looking her best and being her kindest. It was quite an effort.

It was all a little strange, of course, because the flirting usually happened somewhere close to the bed where Mr Deal's wife was lying comatose. Plus, it was not conventional flirting. Tracy had already resigned herself to the fact that she wasn't going to be able to flash her boobs or slide her bottom provocatively against the front of Mr Deal's trousers as he stood at the bar. No, this was secret flirting, using Mrs Deal as an unconscious conduit for their feelings.

'I've been putting extra moisturizer on her hands. I notice they get very dry in here.'

'Thank you.'

'Her wedding ring is lovely. Did you choose it?'

'We went together.'

'That's romantic,' sighed Tracy. 'Nobody's romantic any more.'

Mr Deal just nodded, as if he didn't have an opinion on romance one way or the other, so Tracy changed to a more professional tack.

'Did you know that the doctor upped her morphine?'

'No. Why?'

'I noticed she was frowning a lot. We discussed it and thought it might mean she was in distress.'

Jean had noticed, actually; Tracy hadn't noticed a thing.

'Frowning?'

'Yes. Like now. Look.'

'Oh yes, I see.'

Mr Deal stared at his wife thoughtfully. 'Does she ever say anything?'

'Oh no,' said Tracy. 'But when they frown, it can be due to physical discomfort, so we turn her more often and we thought it best to increase the dosage. The doctor did, anyway.'

'Which doctor?'

Tracy was irritated that Mr Deal wanted to know which doctor, when the point of her story was her own caring and observant nature, coupled with the life-or-death responsibility she bore as a nurse. She couldn't show the irritation though; irritation was an unattractive trait and to be kept hidden until at least a few weeks into a sexual relationship, along with nagging, and farting in bed.

'Oh, it begins with a B,' she giggled. 'There are so many doctors, and then there's juniors and students too, and I'm new on this ward, so I haven't learned them all yet.'

'Where were you before?'

'Paediatrics.'

'Did you like that?'

Did she? What would he want to hear? Tracy could have kicked herself for not checking whether the Deals had children. Even then there was no right answer. If they had children, maybe he'd rather have someone who didn't have baggage; if they *didn't*, then maybe that was *Mrs* Deal's fault, and he'd be keen to start a family with somebody new.

'Oh yes,' she enthused. 'But I like this just as much in a different way.' She hoped that covered both bases. He only nodded, which gave her no clue. But the next night, he brought a small box of chocolates and told her they were just for her. Sadly, they were truffles, but she was gushing in her thanks and promised to keep them a secret. She re-gifted them for her sister's birthday that very weekend, but took heart from the fact that she and Mr Deal were making progress.

Unlike her patients.

The most annoying bad patient had died and everything was easier without his thrashing and crying. They were all very relieved, particularly Angie, whose crooked finger was the only sign now that he had ever been there.

Still, all Tracy seemed to do was put food and fluids in at one end of the patients and clean up at the other. They were less people than simple flesh tunnels for processing calories into shit. It repulsed her.

The few patients who could communicate were painfully slow at the process. Between all her other tasks, Tracy was often required to sit and interpret their weird stretched moans, or their long-winded attempts to spell out pointless messages on the little Possum spelling gadgets.

'T . . . H. Is that an H? Or a G? Can you blink if it's an H? Was that a blink or a twitch? Try to be accurate, OK? I'm going with H.'

T . . . H . . . God, it took *for ever* and they never said anything interesting. It didn't help that one of the ward Possums was a bit dodgy and sometimes needed a good shake, or to be turned off and on again to avoid scrambling to gobbledegook.

While she waited for the patient to blink her way through the alphabet, Tracy's eyes wandered to the TV on the opposite wall. It was *Bargain Hunt* and the blue team were considering a hideous green vase. Her mother had one just like it, and Tracy made a mental note to admire it next time she was home; maybe her mother would give it to her. When she looked back the patient had laboriously spelled out 'T . . . H . . . I . . . R . . . S . . .'

Tracy smiled. 'Thursday? Aw, bless! No, it's Friday today, silly. TGIF! Off to Evolution tonight for a few drinks and a dance. Better get back to work now, though. No rest for the wicked.'

She put the Possum down beside the water jug, then went over to the nurses' station and slumped in the swivel chair. The coma ward was boring yet difficult. Like golf.

Then Tracy sat up and dug about and found a hazelnut cluster in the lower layer of the latest Terry's All Gold.

12

I surge up from the depths of the well like a killer whale, with everything going from dark depths to bright white as I break the surface, and open my eyes on a pair of breasts encased in blue with white trim, almost touching my nose. Her enormous name tag says, 'Tracy Evans, RN'.

She straightens up and looks at me and says, 'Oh!'

Help me, Tracy! Someone killed the man in the next bed. But my ears hear only 'Aaaaaaa waaaaa aaaaaaa,' like an annoying sheep.

'Oh,' she says again, 'you're awake.' Then she leans down close and looks into my eyes from about six inches away, so that I can see all the little flecks in her blue irises.

'*Are* you?' she says, suspiciously.

All I can do is blink slowly and hope she under-stands that I need to report a murder *right now*.

Instead she bustles away and I get so angry that I fall asleep . . .

I open my eyes again to find a woman old enough to be my mother, but who's not my mother, weeping at my bedside. She wears blue gloves and a surgical mask. Her hair is greying and her eyes are red, and snot from her nose has made a dark patch on the front of the mask.

Why is she crying? Has something gone wrong?

For a horrible second I wonder if *I*'ve gone wrong.

'Maaaaaa!'

She stops mid-sob and looks up, gasps, then chokes a bit. 'Doctor!' she croaks.

I flinch inside. A doctor is the last person I want to see, but what can I do? I have to show I'm awake and in one piece or they'll let me just *slip away* . . .

My stomach rolls in fear as a set of blue scrubs walks into my vision and looks down at me over an armful of clipboards. He's even younger than me.

'You awake again, mate?' he says – and this time I *do* cry with happiness – and relief – because that's such a nice friendly thing to say; not sinister or frightening.

I hope I'm nodding, but either way he turns and calls across the ward. 'Hello? Can we have some help?'

We. Can *we* have some help. I'm with *him* now; regardless of the scrubs, we're on the same side.

Tracy Evans with the big blue boobs comes over

and it's all bustle bustle bustle with people pinching my fingernails, requests to say my own name, establishing one blink for yes and two for no – while the young doctor announces each positive like a poo in a potty.

'Withdrawal from pain! . . . No comprehensible language, but that might come . . . Spontaneous eye opening. Very good!'

He makes a quick calculation, then tells the weeping woman that my Glasgow score is now ten. I have no idea what he means, but ten sounds pretty perfect to me. Then he gets all serious and lowers his voice – as if I can't hear him.

'But I need to warn you not to get your hopes up too high. He's not out of the woods yet. This may be as good as it gets, or he may even regress. We know so little about emergence; it's never straightforward, and he's still incredibly vulnerable.'

The woman nods and catches her mascara on the back of her fingers, her optimism tempered.

My optimism is sky high! He may or may not be a killer, but the doctor is my new best friend. He gave me a ten, didn't he? I feel like a traitor, but I'm so grateful to him that I don't care about the man in the next bed. I'll worry about him later.

Or maybe I won't.

He's dead and I'm not, and that's all that matters right now.

When Tracy Evans and the doctor finally go away,

the woman in the mask lays a rubber-gloved hand on my head.

'I knew you were in there. I *knew* it!' she says like a zealot.

Then she leans down and kisses me dryly through the blue paper mask. 'I love you, darling.'

Well, thank you, I think. *But who the hell are you?*

13

Patrick was disappointed by the heart. He wasn't expecting an on-off switch, but he'd hoped they'd find more than a mere pump made of meat and rubbery veins, and felt deceived by popular sentiment. So far people were almost as impenetrable on the inside as he'd always found them on the outside.

Other students had discovered scars and fused toes and numerous tattoos. Number 4 had one running around his ankle – *Diane and Maria, 1966* – that had provoked much speculation. The only vaguely interesting thing so far about Number 19 had been a small puckered hole in his side.

'Feeding tube,' Dilip had said with confidence. 'My grandmother had one before she died.'

'He probably died in hospital then,' said Rob. 'Unless it's old.'

Patrick had pushed his little finger carefully into the dark spot, and felt it travel easily through the skin and flesh. 'It hasn't healed.'

'Fucking *gross*!' Scott had laughed, and Spicer had given him a look that shut him up.

Now the hole had disappeared, along with most of the skin from the torso, and the body on the white table lay opened like a butterfly chicken in an Italian restaurant. In late October they had gone through the ribs with saws bearing the brand name TUFF®. They were tentative at first, but increasingly sweaty and workmanlike, with goggles to keep the bone dust and shreds of flesh from going in their eyes. They had allowed Scott to take the lead, and he'd proved as gleeful with a saw as Patrick was devoted to bagging and tagging every tiny fragment of Number 19 spat out by the metal teeth. Theirs was the cleanest dissection area in the whole room.

Table 22 became the first to establish a cause of death.

'They could hardly miss it,' said Scott sourly. 'The guy's heart is bigger than his head.'

Five others found signs of cardiac or vascular disease that enabled them to make similar diagnoses, and each was confirmed by Mick, who ticked them off his closely guarded list.

Patrick was not here for the cause of death, but he was still annoyed that they hadn't got there first, and now put his money on a brain tumour. He imagined finding the pink lump nestled in the grey matter, like a pearl in an oyster.

Meg stared down at the still-wrapped head of the dead man, as if she were thinking the very same thing.

'You know,' she said, 'in Thailand medical students bring flowers to their cadavers as a gesture of gratitude and respect.'

'OK,' said Rob. 'You call Interflora, we'll all chip in.'

'I'm not chipping in,' said Patrick quickly. He only had twenty pounds a week for groceries.

'Duh,' said Scott.

Rob hadn't fainted since the first day, and now he dug the handle of a spoon under one thick cord running from the wrist up the forearm, and levered it up. The cadaver's fingers curled in towards the palm. 'Look at that!'

'*Flexor digitorum superficialis*,' said Patrick, without looking at *Essential Clinical Anatomy*, which lay open on the table behind him.

'I think we should give him a name,' said Meg.

'Who?' said Dilip.

'Number 19.'

Patrick frowned. 'It's a corpse; it doesn't have a name.'

'Call him Stinky,' said Scott. 'He reeks.'

'*You* reek,' said Meg. 'This whole place reeks.'

It did. The strange sweetness of the dissecting room hung in the air and clung to their very persons. Patrick could smell a classmate five places away in the cafeteria line; he could smell it on his own T-shirt when he pulled it over his head at night and when he opened his drawer to get clean clothes; he could still smell it on his own skin as he stepped out of the shower every morning, red from scrubbing.

'Formaldehyde,' said Dilip.

'Nah,' said Rob. 'It's glycerol, I think.'

'It's dead flowers over shit,' Patrick informed them.

They all looked at him, then at each other – and screwed up their faces in fresh disgust.

Dilip said, 'You're right.'

Patrick didn't answer obvious statements.

'So Mr Shit it is then,' said Scott.

'No,' said Meg firmly. 'That's horrible. Table 11 called their lady Faith. That's nice. Something like that.'

Patrick sighed. He had solved the problem of the smell for them and wanted to move on. He pointed at a cord of pink muscle. '*Palmaris longus*.'

'That's a lousy name,' said Scott, weaving his forceps between the muscles and tendons of the other forearm. 'Even for a corpse.'

'Cadaver,' corrected Meg. Then, 'It's hard to think of a name without seeing his face.'

'So look at his face,' shrugged Dilip.

Meg didn't move. She glanced around: nobody else had yet unwrapped their cadaver's head. Dr Spicer was several tables away, talking to Dr Clarke.

Meg looked at the calluses on the palm of Number

19. Soon they'd be gone, along with the rest of the skin there. 'Maybe he's a builder.'

'More like a boxer!' said Scott, manipulating the tendons so that the hand curled into a fist.

'*Flexor digitorum profundis*,' Patrick pointed out.

Scott repeatedly raised and released the tendons.

'Or a professional lemon squeezer,' laughed Rob.

'Ssh,' said Meg softly.

'Ssh yourself,' said Scott and pulled the right tendons to make Number 19 give Meg the finger.

They all laughed, apart from Patrick, who had started to unwind the strips of cloth around the cadaver's head.

'What are you doing?' said Meg sharply, although it was obvious, so he said nothing.

They watched in silence as the man's head started to emerge, throat first – exposing a short, faded scar – then his chin, badly shaven.

'Don't,' said Meg nervously.

'OK,' said Patrick, and stopped.

'No, go on,' said Scott, and Meg said nothing else, so he went on.

The man's lips were parted over a slightly open mouth, as if the corpse was surprised by its sudden unveiling. The tips of the teeth were visible – reasonably white but a little uneven.

The nose was straight and short, with narrow nostrils and a few dark hairs.

Patrick felt suddenly nervous. He'd thought he'd

started unwrapping the head of their cadaver because he'd wanted to put an end to the chatter and get on with the dissection. Now he wasn't sure why he'd done it or what he wanted. He paused, the cotton strip draped over the bridge of the nose, feeling strangely shaky inside.

'Tease!' said Rob, and Dilip laughed.

'Let's see his eyes then,' said Scott and leaned in to push the cloth aside. Patrick knocked his hand away. 'Don't!'

'Hey, man, if I want to look at his eyes, I will! Don't fucking hit me!'

Patrick hadn't meant to. Hadn't even realized he was going to until Scott's hand had been *right there* over the man's face.

'Don't fight. It's not respectful,' said Rob.

'Neither is cutting his penis in two, but we did that last week,' said Dilip mildly.

'He hit me! You all saw it.' Scott glared at Patrick. 'Weirdo.'

Meg said, 'Shut up, Scott,' but Patrick ignored him. He'd been called worse.

Spicer was suddenly among them again.

'Handbags at dawn?' he joked.

None of them spoke and then Spicer noticed the partially exposed head. His smile disappeared in an instant.

'Cover that up,' he snapped.

Patrick started to wind the cloth slowly around the

cadaver's face again. The others looked at each other uncomfortably.

'It was my idea, Dr Spicer,' said Meg. 'I wanted to see his face so we could give him a name.'

'The ID is on the tags. That's *all*. And you will proceed with this dissection in the correct order and at the proper pace, under *my* direction, do you understand?'

'Yes,' said Meg, and the others nodded. Except for Patrick.

'What's the difference?' he said.

'Excuse me?'

'If we see his face now or later?' Patrick shrugged.

'What's your name again?'

'Patrick Fort.'

'Right,' said Spicer angrily, and walked out of the room.

The others watched him until he disappeared.

'Jesus,' said Rob. 'That's not like him to go off on one.'

Patrick said nothing. He carefully slid his scalpel under what he thought was either the *pronator teres* or the *flexor carpi*.

'You think we're in trouble?' said Dilip.

'No, I think *he's* in trouble,' said Scott, and jabbed a finger at Patrick. 'You ever touch me again, I'll take your fucking head off.'

'Oh, don't be a melodramatic twat,' snorted Rob.

Scott slapped his book shut and walked out, ripping off his gloves as he went.

'Too late,' said Meg quietly, and Rob and Dilip laughed.

'*Pronator teres*,' Patrick concluded.

It was six o'clock and already close to dark when Patrick unlocked his bike from the railings on the ramp outside the dissecting room. Students hurried past in the slow October drizzle, unaware that they were a slim brick wall away from thirty bloated bodies that looked as though bombs had gone off in their chest cavities.

As he wheeled his bike on to Park Place, Meg fell in beside him.

'Hi,' she said. 'Scott's not bad really. I think you just gave him a fright.'

Patrick was puzzled. Why was she walking with him? Why was she saying anything to him? Maybe she was just talking for her, not for him – the way his mother did.

His silence was no deterrent.

'So, why don't you want to be a doctor?'

Patrick had often noticed that the less he said, the more people wanted him to speak. But he had no idea what she wanted him to *say*. Meg wasn't his mother or the med school interviewing panel, so why was she interested in what he did or did not do?

'I'm just curious,' she said, as if she had read his mind. 'I mean, you're clever enough, so why not?'

She kept asking; he was going to have to answer her.

'Not interested,' he said.

'Not interested in what?'

Patrick was taken aback that she had a follow-up question – and so *fast*!

'What aren't you interested in?' said Meg, as if he hadn't understood her the first time.

'In making people better,' he said, and put a foot in his toeclip to show he was finished talking.

Meg wasn't finished. 'So what's the point of just doing anatomy?'

She frowned and Patrick thought she was angry but wasn't sure. He'd never been able to understand what people meant just from their faces. It was hard enough guessing from their words. She obviously wasn't going to leave him alone until he answered, so finally he did.

'I want to see what makes people work,' he said.

Meg wrinkled her forehead some more. 'But you don't want to fix them or help them work *better*?'

'No.'

'Oh,' she said. 'But you have such a great bedside manner.'

'No I don't,' Patrick said, and then saw she was grinning. 'Oh, you're joking.'

'You're allowed to laugh.'

'Maybe later,' he said.

'There's a party tonight. You want to come?'

'No.'

'Oh, come on. You'll have fun.'

'I won't.'

'How do you know?'

'I know I don't like parties.'

'What *do* you like then?'

He stopped talking and looked up the street to the traffic lights, wishing he was already there and that she was behind him.

'Do you like *any*thing?'

'Yes,' he said. 'I like some things.'

'Name your top five.'

He said nothing. He couldn't. He only had three.

Meg sighed theatrically, then held an invisible microphone under his nose. 'How does it feel to be a man of mystery?'

Patrick stared blankly at her fist. 'I don't know.'

She smiled. 'If you change your mind, here's my number.'

She took out a pen and lowered it towards his knuckles, so he tucked his hands into his pockets so she couldn't write on his skin.

She went red. 'All right then,' she said. 'It's 07734113117.'

'OK.'

She raised her eyebrows at him. 'You got that?'

'Yes.'

'See you at Number 19, Patrick.'

'OK,' he said, and swung his leg over the crossbar.

As he rode home he replayed the conversation in his head. It was the longest one he'd had with a stranger in ages. Now he tried to analyse it, the way his mother always nagged him to.

People say things for a reason, Patrick. If you listen carefully, you'll understand not only what they're saying, but why.

But while people were talking, he was always so busy wishing they would leave him alone that he found it difficult to think his *own* thoughts, let alone decipher theirs. Patrick didn't know what more he could have told Meg. Animals and photographs were two of the things he liked – and he didn't have to say *why*. But if he'd told her two things, she might have asked about the third – and the third was secret.

The third was his quest.

Patrick was not a liar by nature, but he had lied to Meg, just as he had lied to his mother and to the admissions interview panel.

He didn't care what made people work.

He was only interested in what happened when they *stopped* . . .

14

What have I done to deserve this? It seems like a logical question but the holes in my memory make it a pointless one too, because the answer is *I don't know*.

I keep looking for clues, but until I come up with something that justifies what's happening to me, I can't help feeling pretty short-changed in the karma stakes.

There's a photo next to my bed. I don't know the people in it and it hurts my eyes to keep them swivelled to the left for that long, so unless I'm on my left side, I only see it in snatches. A middle-aged man and a middle-aged woman. The man looks a bit like my father, but the woman is not my mother, that's for sure, even though she acts like it when she comes to visit me every day – stroking my hand, kissing my hair, massaging my feet the way the therapist told her to, and arranging bluebells and anemones in a jug she brought with her. I think I recognize the jug, but from where?

I don't know. Again.

The woman who's not my mother has stopped wearing the surgical mask, but she still wears the blue gloves.

'Apparently you can get the most dreadful infections if you don't take precautions,' she tells me conspiratorially. 'Upset tummy, you know.'

Sure I know, I think, and shit into my nappy some more, which makes her nose wrinkle. I don't care. It annoys me that she is here and Alice and Lexi are not. *Why don't they come?* It makes me sad – but also angry and suspicious. I hope they're all right, of course, but if they *are* then what would keep them from coming to see me?

Maybe they've been lied to. Maybe they've been told I'm already dead, and are even now getting over me, while I am here, hidden away, waiting for a fate that someone has designed especially for me. Sometimes I even wonder about the crash. Did I really hit ice while fiddling with the radio? Or did somebody run me off the road? Did somebody plan all this, to get me here, away from the people I love, where I can be experimented on – murdered! – without anybody knowing, anybody caring? It happened to the man in the next bed, didn't it? Maybe I'm just next in line.

Or maybe they don't come because of the same elusive reason why Alice has sad eyes. *That* fear is so great that sometimes it makes me cry, which is my only outlet for any emotion.

The nurses make up their own reasons for my tears. *I'm crying for my old life* is their favourite. They mean well, I suppose, but I still hate them for not bothering to understand.

When my eyes are open, I try to watch everything – not just the top of the TV. When I'm on my back, I can only see the top third of the screen anyway before my own cheeks get in the way, and that has to be the worst third of all. The top of *Bargain Hunt* is all squinting through jewellers' glasses at unseen treasures; the top of the rugby is only the stands and the occasional up-and-under, and the top of *Top Gear* is basically Jeremy Clarkson's head.

Every other day they turn me from my back on to one of my sides. On my left side I get a much better view of the ward. I watch the nurses eating chocolates at the station outside the door, and Tracy Evans making eyes at that tall, well-dressed man who comes in at night to ignore his wife. I follow the cleaner halfway round the room with my eyes. He's slow as treacle and misses loads, but the floor is still smooth and shiny enough to make me want to skid about it in my socks. I can see the fancy little white stereo I'm attached to by white wires. There are maybe fifty tracks that I used to love, and it takes about three hours to run through them. And start again. Three hours into twenty-four is eight. I listen to each track eight times every twenty-four hours, fifty-six times every week, two hundred and twenty-four times a month, until I feel I'm going mad.

When they turn me the other way – towards the window – I can't see anything but sky and wall, and it makes me so frightened I shake.

He's still incredibly vulnerable.

The doctor's words run through my head on a loop. Incredibly vulnerable. That's how I feel every second I spend on my right side. With my back to the room, the world sneaks around behind me. Anything could happen. A mad axeman could be slaughtering the other patients; a wolf might slink into the room and pad silently towards me; a nurse could inject something into my saline drip: insulin, or rat poison, and I would never know. Not until the agony started.

Incredibly vulnerable.

I stare at the wall and long for Jeremy Clarkson's repulsive head.

The only good thing about the right side is seeing the sky. Summer must be coming, and I count the days when the sky is blue instead of grey or white, or spitting rain. Once I get to three. Three whole days of blue! People at work would be making crap jokes about it by now. *Hot enough for you? They'll be banning hosepipes next. Did you enjoy the summer?*

Yeah, this is one hell of a summer – lying in my own shit, aching with stillness, fed through a cold tube in my side.

Sometimes Tracy Evans brings me a little alphabet screen called a Possum, so that I can write a novel. Ha ha – it takes me a week of blinking in time to her random pointing to ask her to turn off the *fucking music*. Then I feel bad because I should have been using that energy to tell her to call 999 and report a suspicious death, but now I'm exhausted, and she's gone all tight-lipped.

At least she turned the music off. And now that the babbling, crying man has been murdered, there's often a soft and wonderful silence like big powder puffs over my ears, so I can think of anything that floats into my head. Like the time Alice bought that slinky little green dress for the works Christmas party, and how I got a payrise a month later that she always claimed was *hers*. Or Lexi's fourth birthday party, when Cerys Jones from next door wet herself so badly during pass-the-parcel that three other kids had to go home in borrowed knickers. I remember bringing Patch home – so tiny that Lexi thought he was a hamster, and the time she ran inside shouting that there was a toucan in the garden, which turned out to be a magpie holding a cream cracker. The stuffy ward recedes for hours as I think of the Gower wind in my hair; laughing until we cried, and the pink kite's farewell tug.

I don't like Tracy Evans, but I get used to her and the other nurses, and to the therapist, Leslie, who tortures me grimly. The doctors don't have name tags and I hardly see the same one twice, so it's hard to keep track, but the nurses all have tags – as if they're domestic pets. Jean, Tracy and Angie. Fido, Rover and Tiddles. There are others, but not every day.

Jean is the best of them. Older, and thin and wrinkled with work. Angie is the shy, pretty one, who has two of her fingers taped from some old injury, but who never uses it as an excuse. Tracy is the worst. She cares – but only when the doctors are around. When they're not, she's lazy and slack. She never wipes the inside of my sticky mouth with water – even when I stare constantly at the jug. She does her nails at the nurses' station while call buttons buzz. She hides the chocolates they keep there. I see her. I know her. At school we had half a dozen Tracys every year – loud, orange, stupid. Flirts and bullies.

You got a girlfriend, sir? Is she pretty, sir? My friend fancies you, sir.

Then they were just a mild irritation.

Now a Tracy holds my life in her hands.

15

Meg still hadn't named their body, although several other groups had. Number 4 was Rufus, due to his red chest hair; Number 7 – the cadaver whose leg Patrick had touched on the first day – was called Dolly, because of her residual pink nail polish; and Number 2 had been christened Woody for his post-mortem tumescence.

'There's always a Woody,' Spicer told them with a rolling eye. He seemed to have forgotten Patrick's transgression and had reverted to his usual good humour.

The students had slowly become more casual about their work. The dissecting room was no longer nervously silent, but more like a factory where they all worked on a strange disassembly line.

There was also an air of competition now – to see who could make the finest incision, the most efficient dissection of the foot, the fastest removal of a hand.

Every time they came into the lab, there was still a low buzz of anticipation about cause of death. Now and then, Mick – the cadaverous lab technician – emerged from his glass box of an office to taunt them about it. At least, that's what it felt like, as he walked among them like the Grim Reaper, raising a bushy eyebrow here, tutting quietly there. He carried with him a sheet on a clipboard, and every time someone established a cause of death, he was openly disappointed – as if a secret that had once been his alone was diminished by being shared.

Table 22 had opened the floodgates. It seemed that suddenly everyone was finding tumours and clots and fluid-filled lungs. Cancers and blocked arteries were the order of the day.

'Had a suicide once,' Mick said suddenly one day as he stared down at Number 19. His eyes took on the misty look of a man remembering a romantic beach holiday.

'Hanging. Neck wasn't broken though, so we accepted the donation. Just some bruising and blood in the eyes.'

He sighed as if to say, *Those were the days*.

'Was it a woman?' said Patrick.

'Yes.'

'Is that why the neck wasn't broken?'

Mick nodded and looked at Patrick as if seeing him for the first time. 'She only weighed eighty-two pounds. So she strangled really.'

Meg grimaced. 'Poor girl.'

Mick shrugged. 'There are worse things than dying.'

'Really?' said Meg.

'Of course,' said the tech. 'Living badly.'

Patrick didn't actually care what their cadaver had died of, but he hated to give up on any puzzle. He'd always been that way – always insisted on working things through to their logical conclusion. He hated having help in these endeavours, and was as bent on solving the mystery of Number 19 as he had been about debunking the amateur magician at a school fête.

I can see the rabbit's ears sticking out!

Shut up, boyo.

Every time another organ was given the all-clear, Patrick's frustration grew. He dropped the perfect liver into a plastic bag, pulled the zip-tie tight with a loud buzz, and slung it under the table to join the rest of Number 19's innards.

Spicer winked at him. 'It's only a bit of fun,' he said.

Patrick frowned. He didn't answer pointless statements.

Turning Number 19 over was a messy business, with bits of him falling out of the chest cavity and on to the floor. At one point Patrick got his left hand caught in the sharp remains of the ribs, and almost panicked at the thought that the bone might tear his rubber glove and pierce his own skin the way *they*'d been invading the corpse's flesh for the past three months.

Payback.

He gritted his teeth and breathed hard and it didn't happen, and he was proud of himself for getting through the moment. He pulled his hands free quickly, though, and immediately scraped all the bits off the floor and into a clear plastic bag with yet another black zip-tie and yet another flat metal numbered tag. Patrick always cleaned up so diligently that he had used more than double the number of bags and tags of his nearest rivals. Mick had had to order more Number 19 tags specially. He had told Patrick this with a look on his face that Patrick felt sure must be approval for a job well done.

Months of lying prone without the benefit of circulation had left the body flattened on the bottom like a bag of sand. Now inverted, the buttocks remained oddly two-dimensional.

Rob started on the dissection, making long, assured incisions that showed how much they'd all learned.

'It's my birthday on Saturday,' said Meg. 'You're all invited.'

'Ace,' said Scott.

'Thanks,' said Rob.

'Cheers,' said Dilip.

'Coming, Patrick?' Meg asked.

'No,' he said. 'Again.'

He had told Meg his feelings on parties before and

thought she must have a very poor memory. He wondered how she was going to pass her exams with a memory like that. Dr Spicer had an endless supply of mnemonics – most of them dirty – to help stupid people. The bones of the wrist were the Scaphoid, Lunate, Triquetrum, Pisiform, Trapezium, Trapezoid, Capitate and Hamate. Spicer's aide was 'Slowly lower Tilly's panties to the curly hairs.' Scott had laughed long and hard, and kept repeating it, until Rob had told him to shut up. There were others much dirtier – especially between the forearm and the fingers, with all those flexors in between – but Patrick only found them confusing.

16

'Ah ah ah ah ah ah,' in a deep voice.

'Ee ee ee ee ee ee,' in a squeaky one.

This is what I'm reduced to. Ee-ing and Ah-ing like a crazed Northern mule, tended by strangers. It's not how I planned my life.

Leslie the therapist makes me do it. He's a thin, taciturn Scotsman without discernible humour, but with a grim determination to train my tongue as if it were a contender for the Olympic one hundred metres. Of course, he manhandles me too. Hangs me from the cross and pulls my legs. Pushes my head and holds it there, like a sadistic barber. Rolls tennis balls down my arms and tosses sudden bean bags at me, saying, 'Catch!' They flop on my chest or tumble off my legs on to the floor, and he just shrugs and picks them up and says, 'Better luck next time.'

But really, he's the tonguemeister.

Talking and eating are his goals in life – for me, anyway; I'm not sure he does much of either himself. Every few days he comes in and makes me stick my tongue out and waggle it, or puff up my cheeks, or blow through a straw, or struggle through an endless rota of farmyard noises.

'Aug!' as in August. 'Guh!' as in gun. I try so hard I fart, but he doesn't laugh.

What kind of man doesn't laugh at a fart?

'Ah ah ah—'

'Deeper,' he says.

'Ah ah ah—'

'Deeper. Dig down for it.'

'Ho ho ho,' I try for a joke. Dig. Hoe. You know.

But he just glances up from twisting my fingers and frowns. 'Not ho. *Ah.*'

Nobody gets a joke. Must be the way I tell 'em.

The bluer the sky gets, the harder I work. Nothing means more to me now than being able to talk and to eat. There are words I need to speak; questions I need answered. If my tongue works, then I have a future beyond the infuriating Possum screens and the coded blinks and the taste-free food, so I devote my half-life to its recovery. Even when Leslie's not here, I practise the exercises he gives me over and over and over, pursing my lips, straining my jaw. The nurses have stopped being impressed by me sticking my tongue out at them, although Angie will still sometimes stick hers out in return as she passes with a bedpan, or pushing a drip. Other patients' visitors see me gurning and grunting and avert their eyes.

I like the exercises. They exhaust me and so I sleep better. And when the doctors poke and prod me, or bring their baby-faced students to stand in a horseshoe around my bed and stare at the horror life can hold, I suck and blow like a whale in labour, to take my mind off the reason I am here and the people I have lost.

To take my mind off murder.

Christmas was coming, and someone hung the head of a laughing plastic Santa on the dissection room door, and his severed limbs around the room.

'Idiots,' said Rob.

'Yes,' said Patrick. 'They didn't put the tags on. How is anyone supposed to know they all belong together?'

Meg gave each of them a card with glitter on it. Number 19 gave them nothing but an empty stomach, full bowels and perspiration.

For the last week of term they worked on the back like navvies – stripping away the layers of muscle like old wallpaper, scoring either side of the vertebral column using handsaws, and finally breaking through to the shining river of the spinal column with hammers and chisels.

Patrick wiped sweat from his brow with the crook of his elbow and thought, *How can a human being die so easily when they're so hard to break?*

17

Patrick made the long ride home to the cottage outside Brecon that stood with a handful of others in a place too small for a name of its own. It was forty-five miles and rained all the uphill way, but it still felt good to be going somewhere real on his bike instead of making pointless circuits of the city.

December soon slid from sleet to bitter snow, but Patrick went out most days anyway. He preferred it to staying in the cottage with his mother.

Sometimes he went next door to Weird Nick's and they played Grand Theft Auto. Mostly he headed off alone across the Beacons, following the narrow impressions that marked sheep trails under the snow. Sometimes he went as far as Penyfan's flat peak. His favourite days were those where the sky was almost as white as the hillsides, so that it was hard to tell where one ended and the other began. In that dreamscape

Patrick's world narrowed to the exchange of warm air for cold in his nostrils, the crunch of crystals under his hiking boots, and the sting of his fingers and ear-tips. With a kind of nostalgia, he thought of all the dead things that would be revealed by the thaw. He didn't need them any more; he had something much better now.

Once he stood aside to let a small band of soldiers jog past him, laden with packs that would have bent donkeys.

'Lost?' said the last man, without stopping.

'No,' said Patrick. He had never been lost on the Beacons, and never expected to be. The soldiers jogged on and Patrick watched them until they disappeared over a rise and left him alone in his white world.

When he was in the house, Patrick spent most of his time in his room. When the TV reception wavered – as it often did up here in the mountains – Patrick cycled the five miles to Brecon, carving a deep scar in the snow behind him.

The bookies put memories into his head that he'd rather weren't there, but he didn't want to miss anything. Every time he wheeled his bicycle into the shop, he glanced under the counter. He knew the Labrador must be long dead, but he couldn't help himself. The same men were here though. Ten years older; fatter, greyer, poorer – just the way his father might have been. The Milky Way man always said hello, and Patrick always said hello back. That was all. He never joined in their coarse, friendly banter and never bet on anything, even when the woman behind the counter winked at him and called him 'Big Spender'. Patrick was no fool: the lino at the Bet window was worn through to the concrete, while at Payout it was as clean and shiny as the day it had been laid.

So he just sat down with his black notebook on his lap and watched, and waited for a glimpse of death.

Mr Deal kissed Tracy Evans. It was supposed to be a thank-you-for-looking-after-my-wife kiss, but his hand lingered on her arm and his lips on her cheek just long enough for her to know that it was actually an are-you-up-for-it? kiss.

While Tracy barely had the interest or patience to interpret even the letters of the alphabet for her locked-in patients, every fibre of her being was minutely attuned to any hint of sexual intent, and it was all she could do to stop herself from grabbing Mr Deal's crotch to let him know she was, indeed, up for it. That was for the clubs, and this was work, so she had to be smarter than that. So instead she asked him what aftershave he was wearing, and when he said 'None' – as she'd known he would – she fluttered her lashes and said, 'Oh, you smell like Armani,' even though she'd never smelled real Armani, only the knock-off stuff she used to buy at Splott market for Father's Day.

It was just the start. Flattery was everything with men. Nice cars, large biceps, money and – of course – big cocks. Those were the things you had to play to – had to admire – if you wanted them to remember you, to *choose* you. Tracy didn't know whether Mrs Deal had captured her husband that way, but she was certainly in no position to *keep* him that way.

Now that she had leaned into Mr Deal's kiss and started the seduction of flattery, Tracy knew that – finally – she had the edge on the woman in the hospital bed who was slowly twisting towards oblivion.

Sarah apologized for a chicken instead of a turkey.

'As there's just the two of us,' she explained, in case he'd neglected to notice that his father was dead.

Again.

At least chicken meant they could have trifle for afters without Patrick getting all alphabetical on her.

She gave him a book about the Cheltenham Gold Cup. He gave her nothing; he had no concept that giving might be reciprocal.

As they ate, Sarah asked Patrick how his studies were going and, to her surprise, he told her – haltingly at first, but then warming to his subject. He told her how difficult it was to scrape fat off muscle, of the way blood turned black and granular in embalmed arteries, and how some stomachs gave up gems such as the smooth, diminished carrot found in Number 11 or the gritty pips in Number 25 that turned out to be grape seeds.

'There was nothing in ours,' he added a little wistfully.

She tried not to listen, and wanted a drink. Christmas was always difficult. Christmas and New Year's Eve and Valentine's Day and Easter, and her birthday and Matt's birthday and their anniversary. Saturday nights and all day Sunday. Days with a Y in them.

It had started when Patrick was three. Her parents hardly drank – just a sherry on special occasions. If her father had a whisky, her mother started to mutter. So at first a glass of vodka and orange at critical moments had made Sarah feel independent and in control. By the time Patrick was five, she'd dispensed with the orange juice. By the time he was six, she didn't even need the glass. But after Matt had ... died, she'd stopped. Just like that. People said it was easier that way, but she couldn't imagine it being any harder.

Now she watched her son talk – his meticulous hands describing his work of the past three months, his eyes focused on the remains of the chicken. She thought of its cold, pimpled skin, and of how she'd slid her own hand into its cavity this morning and withdrawn the giblets in a juicy plastic bag. Her stomach felt uneasy and she burped quietly – and was punished by tasting the dead bird again.

When she became aware of his words once more, Patrick was explaining how Dilip had pierced the bowels, and how the smell seemed to be the most recognizably human thing they had yet found in the stiffened cadaver.

'Oh for God's sake, Patrick!' Sarah slapped the table, making the knives shiver. 'We're *eating*!'

'I'm not,' he said. 'I've finished.'

Sarah wanted to smack him. She could almost taste the vodka.

She stood up and banged the table again, less successfully this time – sending a fork clattering to the floor.

'It's not all about *you*. Dinner's not over, so we're still eating, OK?'

'OK.'

'And another thing. When someone gives you a present, the least you could do is say thank you! I don't expect anything in return from you, Patrick, but I do expect *manners*.'

'OK,' he said. 'Thank you.'

It wasn't enough. 'You're just so *selfish*. All you ever do is take, take, *take*!' She glared at him as if demanding an epiphany.

None came. He picked the fork up off the floor and

placed it back on her plate, nudging it repeatedly until it was parallel with her knife.

Sarah gave up. What was the point? Nothing ever changed. Nothing ever would.

'Sorry,' she said.

He looked at the fridge. 'What's for pudding?'

She sighed. That was the thing about Patrick – he didn't understand the sacrifices she made, but he also didn't understand the anger and the resentment. It was good in a way, she supposed; maybe for both of them.

'Trifle,' she said, and cleared the table while he read his book. He only looked up when she put the bowl in front of him and sat down.

'So,' she started again over the hundreds and thousands, 'this Scott and Meg and . . .?'

'And what?'

'Who are the other students you work with?'

'Oh. Rob and Dilip.'

'And Rob and Dilip. Are they your friends?'

'Yes,' he said through a mouthful of custard.

Sarah was glad she'd asked. This was new. Patrick had never openly acknowledged friends before – either his or those of other people – and it gave her that most resilient of emotions: hope.

Carefully she asked, 'What's Meg like?'

'Nervous with a scalpel.'

'I mean as a person.'

Patrick frowned hard and finally managed, 'Sentimental.'

'About what?'

'She wants to give it a name.'

'Give what a name?'

'The cadaver.'

'Oh,' said Sarah, surprised they hadn't done that on the very first day. 'Is she pretty?'

'It's a man.'

'No, I mean is *Meg* pretty?'

Patrick screwed up his face again and looked as if she'd asked him to summarize string theory.

'*I* don't know,' he finally managed.

She swallowed the urge to snap at him and said brightly, 'Well, it's nice to hear you have friends. What do you do when you all get together? Go to parties? Or to the pub?'

Patrick shrugged and ran a finger around his bowl to capture all lingering traces of raspberry jelly.

'Nothing,' he said. 'We just cut up the dead guy.'

18

WHARE IS MY WOFE?

Tracy Evans is an idiot. God knows how she passed her nursing exams, but she has the literacy skills and attention span of a toddler on Tartrazine. How can she mistake 'wife' for 'wofe'? What's a wofe when it's at home?

She stares at the little screen and moves her lips almost silently. 'Whare . . . Ismy . . .' Then she makes an unhappy face. 'What's a wofe?'

Exactly.

'Do you mean wife?'

I blink.

'Oh. She'll be in later.'

She says it breezily, as though my wofe comes to see me all the time, but my heart just about jumps out of my chest with excitement. Alice is coming! Alice is coming to see me! Will she bring Lexi? It's been so long! At least, it *feels* so long! I hope Lexi isn't wearing make-up or anything tacky. Kids start so young nowadays – and change so fast. Has she changed? Has Alice?

Have *I*?

I blink rapidly to get Tracy Evans's attention and spell out MIROR. Except I do it with two Rs and she ignores one of them.

'You want a mirror?' she says.

Sarcasm is *so* hard to do in blinks, so I play it straight.

She disappears. While I wait, I watch two nurses lift the woman opposite on to a special bed that can be tilted upright. I know now that Jesus on the cross in his pj's was just another patient. God knows what else I hallucinated back then! I've been on the tilt table myself now, and it's like a very low-grade funfair ride – the kind you could put a small child on without fear they'd be hurt. The ride my heart's on now is far more exciting. A rollercoaster of hope and fear and anticipation. I'll probably need a shave. Alice says facial hair makes everyone look shifty, and Lexi says it scratches when I kiss her goodnight.

Tracy Evans comes back with a mirror.

'There,' she says, and holds it so badly that I can only see a shaky image of half my face.

It's enough. My stomach cramps with horror.

That's not me. *That's not me!*

The face in the mirror is of a much older man. Ten

or twenty *years* older! I am the man in the photo beside my bed.

That's impossible. I'm not old! I'm thirty-five and Alice is thirty-three and Lexi is twelve and Patch is seven and the goldfish – well, they're rolling stock – but I *know* how old I am. I know I haven't been asleep *that* long. I'm sure of it. The woman who smells of rubber said I had been in a coma for two months. Not two *decades*.

This is impossible.

The shaky old man blurs as my eyes overflow, and I blink like a stutterer.

'All right?' says Tracy cheerfully.

Yes. No. I don't know. Call the police! *Call the police!* Someone has stolen great lumps of my life, and I feel the shock of its loss like an amputee.

Tracy lowers the mirror. 'You get some sleep now,' she says, 'and she'll be in later.'

I want to howl. I want to howl and scream and pound my fists on to tables and smash someone in the face. What's happened to me? *Someone* must be to blame. Someone has to take *responsibility*. This is *wrong*. This is *all wrong*. I've been changed; I've been cheated, and nobody seems to understand or to care.

In my head I'm a vengeful dervish, an angry Hulk; Godzilla tearing down civilization.

In reality I lie there like meat.

'Aaaaaaa! Aaaaaaa! Aaaaaaa!' That's not the sound of *me* crying, because I am not me.

And I don't know where I've gone.

19

It was a cold January, and the light in the dissecting room was flat and grey when they finally exposed the face of Number 19.

Hips and knuckles and stomachs were only 3D versions of *Essential Clinical Anatomy*. Once they'd overcome their natural aversion to cutting into a human being, those things were routine, even boring. But this was very different, and there was a long silence while they looked at the face of the person whose body they knew more intimately than a mother or a lover ever had.

He was the middle-aged man they'd long expected. Mick had shaved his head before embalming, but his straight nose had greying hairs in it, and his crows' feet were deep enough to have survived the swell of formalin and glycerol.

Patrick noticed with relief that his eyes were closed

– and that Scott made no attempt to open them. He also noticed that Meg's lower lip trembled, and he watched with interest the way it pulled her chin out of shape.

'Why are you crying?' he asked.

'I'm *not*,' she said. 'Shut up.'

'There are tears in your eyes,' he said.

'Shut up, Patrick,' said Rob firmly.

Patrick glanced around the table and realized that everyone felt something that he didn't. The students looked . . . angry? No, that wasn't right.

He suddenly thought of his father's face on the day Persian Punch had died, and his heart jolted at the sudden connection. Sad! The other students looked *sad*. Even Dr Spicer was pale and uncharacteristically quiet, and – for the first time he could ever remember – Patrick thought he knew the feelings of strangers. He was *sure* he was right. The excitement almost over-whelmed him. All he wanted to do was to drink in the clues on their faces so that he would know Sad if he ever saw it again.

'He looks like a Bill,' said Meg, adding snot to the sleeve of her paper coat, which was already disgusting with yellow fat and brick-brown blood.

'Yeah, he does,' said Scott, and was rewarded with a tiny smile from her.

Spicer stood at the head with his scalpel, and they joined him there with more than a touch of what felt like first-day nerves. Nobody looked as if they wanted to start. For all the incisions they'd made so far, there was something quite different about slicing into the throat with the face exposed; something executional.

Spicer was about to make the first cut, then changed his mind.

'Patrick can do the honours, I think.'

The others sighed with relief and glanced at each other. If this was Patrick's punishment for his previous infraction, they were in full support.

As Patrick took the scalpel from Spicer he noticed a slight tremble in the man's hand, and wondered if he was a drinker. Lots of doctors were, he'd heard – although his mother was a shop assistant.

He followed Spicer's finger to the starting place below the hyoid bone, and traced a murderous line across the throat, and then slid the blade boldly over the bumpy thyroid cartilage, through the old pale scar, down to the base of the neck.

'Well done, mate,' said Rob and patted him on the back. The touch was over before Patrick could flinch.

Under Spicer's guidance they all took turns at cutting and cleaning and scraping, peeling back flat layers of neck muscle until Bill's throat was spread about him like the flaps of a startled basilisk.

'There's something in the oesophagus,' said Dilip, and they all watched as he sliced and clipped back a six-inch gash in the tube of muscle. The pink membranes inside were thickly freckled with dark fragments.

'Pharyngeal debris is quite common,' said Spicer. 'Usually it's blood or vomit. Just clean it up using the swabs.'

'Is it relevant to the cause of death?' said Scott.

'Might be.'

'Ace,' said Scott. 'So he might have choked or had internal bleeding or something?'

Spicer smiled faintly; he was giving nothing away. Patrick hoped it was not the case; he was trying to be faithful to his pearl of a tumour.

Meg started to wipe away the debris to reveal the multiple folds of the throat. Unlike the flesh, which was made strangely orange by the embalming fluids, the membranes and organs remained pink and lifelike.

There were several nicks and cuts in the soft palate and back of the throat where Patrick could see Dilip had been clumsy with the scalpel, and a fragment of blue latex made him check his gloves feverishly. They were not infallible – especially around the sharp edges of ribs and teeth. Patrick was relieved to find his intact on this occasion, but he peeled them off and got a new pair anyway.

When he returned, Meg had finished clearing the throat, which was gleaming and alien. The root of the tongue was lumpy with tastebuds and larger papillae.

'What's that?' said Patrick.

'What's what?' said Meg.

Patrick was so focused that he brushed against her

shoulder without even noticing, as he leaned in and touched a particularly large, discoloured lump. It moved a little, so he plucked it out with his forceps and held it up to the light.

'What's that?' said Dilip.

'You pulled his tonsils out, idiot!' said Scott.

'No I didn't. It wasn't attached.'

Patrick turned the lump slightly in the afternoon light. It was pale tan and about half the size of his smallest fingernail, domed on one side, flat on the other, with a single groove running down its length.

'You think it's a tumour?' said Meg, looking as concerned as if the corpse would have to be told the bad news.

'Looks more like a cyst,' said Scott.

'Or a nodule,' helped Rob. 'You get them on the vocal cords.'

'It's a peanut,' said Patrick.

They all laughed, even though he was serious.

Dr Spicer came over and confirmed Patrick's diagnosis. 'Probably brought up from the stomach with the rest of the debris.'

'There was nothing in the stomach,' Patrick reminded him.

'Maybe that's why,' said Rob.

'I bet he choked on it,' Scott insisted.

'It's too small, isn't it?' said Dilip. 'Something that size couldn't block the airway. It would just be sucked into the lungs, wouldn't it?'

'What are the post-mortem symptoms of choking?' said Spicer.

'Blood in the eyes?' said Meg.

Scott leaned over the face and Patrick looked away as he checked the sunken eyes.

'Nada,' said Scott. 'Shit. I give up. I'm asking Mick.'

He walked away and Patrick dropped the peanut into a fresh bag.

'I don't really think that's necessary,' laughed Spicer.

'Anything and everything you take off or out of this cadaver gets bagged and tagged so it can be put back together again at the end of the course for burial or cremation,' said Patrick, and Spicer looked stunned to hear himself quoted verbatim.

'Are you being funny?' he said carefully.

'I don't think so,' said Patrick, and fastened the bag, tagged it, and then put it under the dissection table along with Bill's left arm, both feet, and that day's skin and fat. Spicer shook his head and turned his attention to the table again.

Scott came back from the office, frowning, and they all looked at him expectantly. 'It's not choking, but he wouldn't say what it was. That bastard *likes* watching us suffer.'

They all turned towards the glass-walled office. The bald lab tech gave them a wave, looking as cheerful as they had ever seen him.

When five o'clock came round the students started to peel off their gloves and leave.

'See you tomorrow, Bill,' said Meg.

Patrick didn't go.

Instead he slid his fingers into the cadaver's mouth and ran them around the inside of the stiff lips and under the leathery tongue. Then he checked from the other end too, wiggling his index finger up behind the soft palate and into the nasal cavity.

'What are you doing?' said Meg, wandering back to the table.

'Looking for vomit.'

'Any luck?'

Patrick glanced at her over the corpse. 'Would it be lucky or unlucky to find vomit with my finger in the mouth of a dead man?'

She paused and then smiled. 'You're joking.'

'You can laugh,' he said.

She shrugged. 'Maybe later.'

Patrick checked thoroughly, then held up a clean blue finger.

'Luck,' he said, and she laughed.

20

Today I closed my mouth until my teeth touched. I strained and sweated and groaned and grimaced, and when I felt enamel on enamel, I cried with joy. Cried like I haven't since Lexi was born. Cried so hard that Jean had to come over and suck the snot out of my nose with a turkey baster – or something very like it.

'Well done!' she said, dabbing at my eyes and cheeks, and smiling like she meant it.

It means so much. If I'm to find out what's happened to me, I have to be able to speak. I have to understand how long I have been here, and what has happened since the accident. Maybe what happened before the accident. Or even *during* it. Can I even trust my memory of that?

The woman who says she's my wife keeps coming to see me, and keeps being a stranger. Alice and Lexi keep *not* coming to see me. Maybe because of something I did wrong? I keep feeling that I've done something wrong, but I just don't *know*.

And I'm not going to find out by blinking.

The more I can do, the more I realize I *need* to do. Opening my eyes was the first thing, but that got old quickly. Then sticking out my tongue took precedence. Now closing my mouth to help to form words has become critical too, and the touching of teeth leaves me euphoric.

I don't even feel embarrassed by my tears; that's how happy I am.

Leslie was unimpressed by my joy, of course.

'Big babby,' he snorted, then tossed a bean bag at my heart.

Patrick rode down Park Place with his head full. It had been a red-letter day.

He had recognized sadness in his fellow students – actually *understood* something about people instead of feeling only disinterest and confusion. It was a strange progression – tinged with unease by the memory of his father – but he could not shake the feeling that it had been a special moment.

He also felt that although they still didn't know the cause of death, they must be getting closer, simply by a process of elimination. The brain tumour was looking more and more likely, and the prospect of being right was always good. More than that, he had been allowed to make the difficult first incisions in the throat, which meant Dr Spicer must think he was the most capable of the group – better than Scott. The idea of winning the prize for the best dissection student was an attractive one.

Then Rob had touched him and he hadn't panicked, even though his shoulder had crawled from the contact. And he'd ascertained that there was no more vomit in the cadaver's mouth. Patrick wasn't sure why he'd done that, but he'd felt compelled to check.

Finally – unexpectedly – he had made Meg laugh. That had surprised him and, more than that, it had given him another interesting feeling that he took a while to identify as pleasure.

He was too excited by it all to go home. He cycled round the city aimlessly for hours as the shops and offices dimmed, before turning into the castle grounds and racing along the dark paths between dormant roses, until all he could think about was the burning in his lungs and limbs. Then he leaned his bike against an oak and sat on the grass beside it. Once his breathing had slowed, he rested his back against the trunk and enjoyed cooling down.

He closed his eyes and listened to the sway of branches and the rustle of small animals all around him. In the darkness, and with the smell of grass and earth in the air, he almost expected the polite cough of a sheep. Quickly he fell asleep, cross-legged, with his head tilted backwards and his hands upturned in his lap, as if seeking enlightenment from the rising moon.

He woke shivering, just before the grey malt dawn, to find a young man in a white tracksuit sitting facing him in an almost identical position, but with a long screwdriver in his upturned hands.

'I could have killed you while you slept,' he said, not unpleasantly.

Patrick stood slowly and got on his bike and rode away. When he looked back, the young man was nothing but a pale blob facing the empty trunk.

Back at the house, he'd missed a party. Someone was passed out behind the front door and Patrick took five minutes to force his way in, and another two to ascertain that the girl on the floor was not dead.

The hallway was strewn with plastic cups and empty bottles, and halfway up the stairs there was a bowl of popcorn with a shoe in it.

Kim was on the living-room sofa, eating toast with a man in his forties who was wearing nothing but her short kimono.

'Hi, Patrick,' she giggled. 'This is my boyfriend, Pete.'

Patrick was confused. 'I thought you were a lesbian.'

Kim giggled again and Pete winked at Patrick. 'So did she.'

'OK,' said Patrick. This morning was starting to be the weirdest one he could remember.

Pete leaned in and licked butter off Kim's cheek, and Patrick looked at the television.

'Don't be embarrassed,' said Kim.

'I'm not embarrassed,' said Patrick. 'But I can see Pete's bollocks.'

He left his bike in the hallway and went upstairs to shower. At the top of the stairs, Jackson accosted him.

'Have you seen him?' he demanded in a stage whisper.

'Seen who?'

'*Pete.*'

'Yes, all of him,' said Patrick.

'She's supposed to be a *lesbian*!' hissed Jackson. 'If she was going to chop and change, she could have told *me.*'

Patrick didn't see why Kim should tell anyone anything. Personally, he'd rather *not* have known about her lesbianism, her vegetarianism, her lumpy art *or* her hairy-balled boyfriend. It was all just mental clutter to him.

'Why do you need to know?' he asked.

In answer, Jackson just huffed and flapped a slender hand at Patrick. 'You wouldn't understand.'

They were words Patrick had heard a thousand times throughout his short life, and he'd always believed them. But suddenly, for the first time, he felt they might not always be true. Perhaps he didn't understand *now*, but what if he *might* at some future point? He'd understood sadness, hadn't he? He'd made Meg laugh. What if understanding living people was something that could be learned, like anatomy or the alphabet?

'Maybe I could,' he said carefully; he didn't want to commit himself to anything too drastic.

'Yeah,' snorted Jackson. 'Maybe you could.'

Patrick's spirits lifted even further. Jackson agreed with him! Maybe he *could* learn! And if something could be learned, then Patrick knew he could learn it.

All it took was motivation.

21

Patrick didn't go in the day they did the eyes.

He went to the museum instead and stared at the leatherback turtle, swimming forever in the air. Even the turtle knew the secrets that he craved. A long scaled flipper hung down and Patrick tentatively reached up.

'Don't touch the turtle please!' A woman in a blazer and a bun glared at him from the doorway.

'I'm not going to damage it,' he said.

'Touching exhibits is not allowed. Otherwise you will be asked to leave.'

Slowly Patrick withdrew his hand. He went back to the ground floor. Then, for the first time, he continued all the way down the stairs and found a café, where women with pushchairs picked up juice boxes and cappuccinos, while pensioners made shared crumbs in rheumy silence.

He hadn't planned to buy anything, but he saw they had Coke in hourglass bottles in the chiller, and handed over £2 for what he estimated to be less than a penny's worth of fizzy brown liquid.

The bottle was smaller than he'd remembered; he could make an easy ring around it with his finger and thumb. But it tasted the same, and in a second he was back at the Rorke's Drift, feeling the clink of his father's glass against his bottle, knowing that sudden, unexpected closeness to another human being.

To Persian Punch.

Although he'd never eaten in a restaurant, Patrick sat down at a table in the corner of the café to finish the bottle. Before he left, he spent all morning and almost half his week's food budget on three more.

When he went back to the dissection room for the next session, it was to find that the top had been sawn off every cadaver's skull.

Thirty brains were exposed like giant walnuts, and the smell of fresh bone dust hung in the air. The circular saw was sitting where Mick had left it on the counter by the door, like a horror film prop, with skin and frayed flesh still clinging to its jagged teeth.

The final stage of dissection was under way and Patrick felt giddy with anticipation. He was suddenly acutely aware of his own head, and imagined all the things going on inside it. All the electricity and connections and creativity. Something from nothing, bursting out of the darkness and lighting the way to the universe.

How did all that just *end*?

Where did it all *go*?

And once it was switched off, could it ever be switched back on?

So far, Number 19 had been thoroughly dead. But if any spark remained – or any promise of more than a mere spark – then it would be found in this most tantalizing of organs.

Over the course of a morning, they prised the brain out with spoons, and it flopped into Patrick's hands like a water-filled balloon. He shook a little as he turned it, his eyes and his fingers probing the jelly-mould mind for clues, while the others peered over his shoulders and prodded at it with their blue fingers.

Patrick felt his excitement morph seamlessly into disappointment. Not the disappointment of a child denied a treat, but the kind of disappointment that makes the chest ache and the belly roll with nausea at the loss of all hope.

There was nothing.

The tightly packed convolutions were wrapped in dura, decorated with a network of nerves, and fed by thick arterial passages like mineworkings in blanc-mange. The pink-grey folds taunted Patrick with their perfect mystery. Whatever had made Number 19 the person he had once been was now lying *right here* in his hands, and yet there was no trace of him left, nor any clue as to how he had disappeared. No pearl, no tumour, no secret passageway to the beyond.

Patrick felt hope desert him.

Death was an inverse Big Bang; an impossible magic trick where everything had become nothing in the very same instant, where one state had been replaced so completely by another that no evidence of the first could be detected, and where the catalyst had been vaporized by the sheer shock of the new.

Patrick felt his face grow hot, and he stared stupidly down at the perfect practical joke overflowing in his palms.

If there were no answers here, then he no longer knew where to look for them.

He fumbled the brain to Dilip and walked out of the dissecting room in a blur.

Patrick was in the cafeteria, not eating chocolate pudding, crisps and a tuna sandwich, in that order.

Outside the window he always faced was the rack where he always locked his bike. He could get on it and ride away. There was nothing here for him now; now that he knew a dead man was no better than a dead bird. A dead father.

If he had kept hold of his hand, would that have anchored him to life?

Would the car have missed him?

Or hit them both – and revealed the truth to two instead of one?

'Can I sit here?' said Meg, and then sat there anyway before he could do anything about it.

'Penny for your thoughts,' she said.

'What?'

'Penny for your thoughts.'

Patrick stared at her blankly and she went a little pink.

'My grandma used to say it. I'll give you a penny, and you give me your thoughts.'

Patrick didn't like the sound of this game. 'Do I have to?'

'No, of course not.'

'You haven't even given me a penny.'

'It's just a silly saying. You don't take it literally.'

But Patrick was still perturbed by the whole concept. 'And a penny is nothing. You can't get anything for a penny. You'd have to pay a lot more than that.'

Meg sighed. 'You don't have to tell me anything.'

'I know I don't.'

'I just wondered if you were OK, that's all.'

'No, I'm not,' said Patrick.

'What's wrong?'

Patrick stirred his chocolate pudding mechanically, the spoon grating on the china.

'There's nothing there,' he said. 'It's just meat. Meat and shit.'

'Oh,' she said carefully. 'What did you expect?'

'Something else. Something *more*.' He felt weirdly like crying, and his stomach knotted and ached the way it had that day. The day of the punch in the back, the bat in the face. He knew now what Sad *looked* like; was this how it *felt*? He didn't like it.

'But there *is* more,' she said, grabbing the salt cellar for emphasis. 'Just because we don't know doesn't make it any less . . . amazing. Can't you *feel* it?'

'No, I can't,' he said. 'If someone dies and you don't *see* it, how do you know what really happened?'

'See what?'

'That thing that changes between *here* and *there*. Between life and death. I can't feel it; I want to *see* it. I want to know what it *is*.'

'We'll all know that one day.'

'I want to know it *now*!' he snapped.

There was a long silence while Meg stared into the crusted hole where the salt lived.

She cleared her throat. 'You're different, you know.'

'Only different from *you*,' he said. 'Not different from *me*.'

'That's true.' She smiled. Then she poured a careful little pyramid of salt on to the table.

'What's it like to be you?' she said.

Patrick was surprised. Nobody had ever asked him what it was like to be him, not even his mother.

What *was* it like? He'd never even examined it himself before. Never been asked to come to a conclusion about it and share it with another. But Meg hadn't called him names, and she wasn't rushing him, and so, for the first time in his life, he reached into himself in the hope of finding something to tell her – something to show her – in the same way that Number 19 had submitted to being opened and deconstructed.

'It's . . .'

He scraped slow chocolate patterns in the bottom of the bowl while he struggled to corral his feelings and put them into words.

Meg waited for him.

'It's very . . .'

He gritted his teeth. This was crazy. There was so much *in* there – he could feel a million things coursing through him, and yet he kept coming up empty. It was like putting his hand into a tank filled with goldfish and trying to grab one. He'd done that in a pet shop once and it hadn't worked, *and* his mother had slapped his legs.

Still Meg waited, and suddenly Patrick was filled with a tight, burning frustration at his inability to explain what it was *like*.

'It's *very*,' he said forcefully. 'Very very.'

'Very what?' she asked quietly.

But he had nothing to give her, even when he tried.

He dug his spoon so hard into the bowl that it rang, and spewed chocolate across the table.

'*Very*,' said Patrick.

People looked at them in a sudden hush. Then the faces turned away and the low drown of voices and echoes and cutlery resumed.

Meg simply nodded. 'It must be.'

22

They're trying to kill me.

I don't think it's my imagination, although that's what the doctor is telling the woman who says she's my wife. My wofe is how I think of her now – not the same thing.

'Paranoia is common ... emerging coma ...' he whispers, trying to keep me from hearing, but I get the gist. 'A normal response ... situation.'

They both glance at me with the same expression – concern and pity, and the need to keep things from me for my own good.

Maybe I wouldn't be paranoid if they weren't out to get me. The idiot Tracy Evans who regularly unplugs my heart monitor so she can plug in the electric razor; the cleaner who bumps my bed with her mop and glares if I wake; and the doctors who stand over me – too close, too watchful – and make covetous notes that they hang on my bed for everyone to see but me. Every time one of them stands over me, the sweat runs into my eyes and stings a warning.

Even my wofe. She's supposed to be on my side. She doesn't seem to notice that I'm an old man now. She says she loves me; calls me Darling.

'SOMEONE KILLED THE MAN IN THAT BED.'

She'd looked at the Possum screen, then looked at the bed, frowning – as if the fact that the man was no longer there somehow cast doubt on my claim.

Secret, I'd begged her with my eyelids. *Secret*.

Doesn't she understand English?

Now the doctor looks at me but whispers to her, '. . . infection . . . several days. Sometimes . . . sudden cardiac episode . . . vulnerable.'

There it is again. *Vulnerable*.

The thing that makes me feel most vulnerable is you bastards whispering in a corner about me! That doctor might even be the one! He might be the killer! Now he knows I saw something. Now he knows! And what will he do about it?

Anything

he

likes.

Fuck you, doctors. Fuck you, nurses. Fuck you, wofe. That's the last time I trust you. The last time I confide.

She comes back over and starts to repeat the lies.

'Sam, sweetheart, the doctor says—'

'Ah ah ah ah ah. Ee ee ee ee ee . . .' Deep and squeaky.

'Darling, I'm trying to—'

'AH AH AH AH AH EE EE EE EE. Guh! Guh! Guh!' I want my *wife* back. I want my *child*. I want to speak and eat and move my own feet. I want to know what happened to the man in the next bed and I want to know what happened to *me*. If I have to do it all myself, I will; I can't rely on anyone else – I see that now.

'*Guh! Guh! Guh!*' I put everything I can into it, to let her know how angry I am.

'Sam, please . . .'

She takes my hand and I close my eyes; I know that hurts her.

She starts to cry and I don't care.

23

The more Patrick scrubbed his bedroom carpet, the more he felt betrayed by the corpse. Number 19 was not a rabbit or a crow; Number 19 had been a man, just like his father, and Patrick felt the cadaver had somehow reneged on a species-specific agreement to give him the answers he sought. Instead of revealing what happened when a person stopped working, Number 19 had only *added* to the confusion with his elusive cause of death. And Meg had only rubbed his nose in it, going on about how ignorant they all were. As if Patrick didn't know *that*.

He was sick of being confused. About *everything*.

Losing his father had at first seemed to be a kind of confusion – like losing a glove or a sock. Those things didn't cease to exist just because you couldn't see them; they were always *somewhere* – under the bed, in the machine, down the back of the sofa – and eventually they turned up.

Sooner than eventually, if you actively looked for them.

So Patrick had actively looked. Ever since the school counsellor had told him about the one-way door, Patrick had tried to find some sign of where it was and how it might be opened. First he'd sought it in the animals and birds he brought home off the Beacons, then in the faces of the dead that he found on macabre postcard collections, or of the dying in African aid stations on the *News at Ten*. Finally he searched the eyes of racehorses as they waited patiently for the bullet on snapped legs, in the only sport where death was routinely televised. With every crashing fall, Patrick felt the shock of the inevitable, and then a tingling in his belly – a bubble of anticipation in case *this* was the one, *this* was the horse, *this* was the moment when all would be revealed to him, when the door might open just a chink and allow him to glimpse a deathly Narnia on the other side.

He had never come close.

Upinarms, Malaga, Freezeout, Luckbox. Each now knew the secret he was so desperate to share, but watching them die only left him feeling more empty than before. Still, Patrick wrote their names in quiet pencil lists because who else would mark their passing? His father had remembered Persian Punch with a pint and a bottle of Coke; it seemed only right to do *something*.

The carpet was filthy. He'd already emptied his bucket of dirty water twice, and only properly cleaned a patch a foot square. Under the dark brown it was a vile ginger. Patrick didn't like it, but he was determined to reveal it anyway.

He emptied more blackened water into the bath, refilled the bucket and added another dollop of bleach.

'What are you doing?' said Jackson.

'You wouldn't understand,' said Patrick.

'Huh?' he said, and Patrick showed him the scrubbing brush.

'I'm cleaning.'

'Ha ha, very funny,' said Jackson, then followed Patrick back to his bedroom and hung around in the doorway as if cleaning were a spectator sport.

'Have you seen Pete lately?'

'What's lately?'

'In the last couple of weeks?'

'No.' Patrick realized he wasn't going to be able to do this all in one go, so he mentally divided the visible carpet into squares.

'I think maybe they broke up,' Jackson went on.

Patrick didn't feel that required an answer. Not that he *had* an answer. Or an opinion – although he did hope Kim had washed the kimono.

'Do you think I have a chance?' said Jackson.

Patrick sat back on his heels and thought about it. He wasn't quite sure what Jackson was talking about, but horse racing had taught him that *everything* had a chance – of death *and* of glory.

The idea invigorated him, and suddenly he felt his

determination surface again from the mud of betrayal. He was employed in solving a far bigger mystery than Number 19's cause of death, so he shouldn't let something as simple as that get the better of him! Patrick knew exactly where to get the information he was entitled to.

'Yes,' he said. 'I do.'

Jackson said, 'Thanks!' Then – in a rare burst of generosity – he added, 'Your carpet looks great.'

Not yet, thought Patrick, but it would. He got to his feet and dropped the brush into the bucket with a plop. He was newly filled with hope, and his head and nose felt suddenly clear again. He wondered briefly whether it was the bleach.

He lifted his bicycle off the wall and started down the stairs.

He wasn't going to be beaten by a carpet *or* a corpse.

4017.

Patrick prickled at the need for the offensively random code.

The door of the anatomy wing clicked shut behind him, damming the flow of other students and leaving him alone in the quiet corridor creek that led to the dissection room and, beyond that, the stairs leading down to the embalming room, where Mick spent most of his time.

His Pumas made a low squeak on the scuffed tiled floor.

The white double doors of the DR were not locked. It wasn't a dissection day, and so the cadavers lay patiently on their tables, looking lost without their attending students. Patrick picked out Number 19's domed form from across the room. He felt a sense of adversity that had not been there before.

You can't keep secrets from me.

Mick was not in his office and a note on the half-glazed door told Patrick that he would be back at three thirty p.m. Patrick looked at his watch; it was only eleven a.m. but he was on a roll and had no interest in coming back at three thirty. Three thirty was light years away.

He tried the door handle and it opened, so he went inside.

Mick ran a tight ship. There were uncluttered shelves, a well-swept floor, a single pot-plant on a filing cabinet. The desk was clear, but for a tidy with two pens in it and a three-tier letter tray that held only a few donation and cremation forms. Patrick approved of the tidiness, even if it meant the clipboard which held the Cause of Death checklist was not just lying around.

There were two pale-grey filing cabinets beside the desk. Patrick tried the drawers of both, but they were locked. He rattled them, but this time it didn't work.

His determination became frustration in a heart-beat. The cadaver was still trying to cheat him. Still guarding its mysteries, even though it was dead and had no use for them itself.

But Patrick had waited so long, and worked so hard. He *deserved* to know the answers. It wouldn't be wrong; he was *entitled*.

He had seen TV shows and films where people did things like sneaking into villains' headquarters to uncover top-secret information, so he knew it was possible, but the movies made it look like a major operation that was unlikely to be achieved without satellite communications and a grappling hook. A black turtleneck sweater, at the very least. He had none of those. He looked around the bare little office, then went back out to the dissecting room and selected a robust carving fork from the white tray near the door.

He inserted the tines into the metal drawer to lever it open. As he did, he noticed that the plant on top of the cabinet was tilted at a slight angle. He couldn't leave it like that – he knew that the moment he saw it. He couldn't even concentrate on the task at hand until it was righted.

He put down the fork.

Under the pot was a saucer, and under the saucer was the key to the filing cabinet.

Inside the top drawer of the first cabinet he opened was the clipboard.

Easy.

On the board was the form he'd only glimpsed before as Mick walked among them, wishing them ill. Patrick's eyes were drawn directly to the last column, labelled 'COD'. Cause of Death.

Number 19 had died of heart failure.

That couldn't be right.

Patrick had held that heart in his hands. There had been no stenosis, no clots, no aneurysm. He had come in here to uncover a secret, only to find that the secret was a lie. He glared at the form, feeling cheated, wanting *more*, and noticed that the very first column was headed 'NAME'. He ran his eyes down the list.

'What are you doing here?'

He turned; Mick was in the doorway.

Patrick looked at his watch. 'What are *you* doing here? The note said you'd be back at three thirty.'

Mick opened his mouth and raised his eyebrows so high that they almost touched the place where his hair would have been if he'd had any. He closed the couple of paces between them and snatched the clipboard from Patrick's hand. 'That's confidential information.'

'I wanted the cause of death. That's not confidential. Dr Spicer said we could ask any time, and this is any time and you weren't here to ask, so I looked.'

'You broke into a locked filing cabinet.'

'I used the key.'

'The hidden key.'

'If it was hidden, I wouldn't have found it, because I wasn't looking.'

Mick brushed past him and put the clipboard back in the drawer, then slammed the drawer and locked it. He dropped the key into his pocket.

'What's your name?'

Why did everyone always want to know what his *name* was?

'Patrick Fort.'

'You're in a lot of trouble,' said Mick.

'What for?'

'I just told you what for.'

'Why?' Patrick was confused; he had explained everything.

'Don't play stupid games with me. I'm going to speak to Professor Madoc about this.'

'OK,' said Patrick.

Mick seemed disappointed that he wasn't more worried by the prospect. 'All right, you can get out now.'

'OK,' said Patrick, but didn't go. 'I think the cause of death is wrong.'

'What cause of death?'

'Number 19. You've got heart failure but the heart is not diseased.'

'If that's what's on the death certificate, that's what it is. I'm not a doctor, and neither are *you*, by a very long way.'

'I know that. But—'

'No buts. This conversation is over.'

'OK,' said Patrick, so started a different conversation. 'When the people die, you embalm the bodies, right?'

Mick looked at him but didn't answer, so Patrick went on, 'Where do they go afterwards?'

'They come up here,' said Mick. 'Then when you lot have finished with them I put all the bits in a bag and they go back to the families for funerals.'

'Not the bodies. The people.'

'Excuse me?'

'Is there an exit?'

'A *what*?'

'An exit. In their heads. Like a door they go through.'

'Like the one I should have kept locked?'

'Yes,' said Patrick, 'like that. Some kind of *barrier* that people go through when they die.'

Mick squinted at Patrick; he shook his head; he made a face. 'No,' he finally said.

'Then what happens to them? Where do they *go*? Can they come back?'

Mick stood and stared at Patrick for a long moment, then reached down and lifted up the phone. 'Hold on a second,' he said, 'I'll see if the police know.'

'OK,' said Patrick, and waited to see if the police knew.

Mick stabbed the first two nines with a flourish and a glare, but then sighed and hung up.

'Just get out, will you?'

'OK,' said Patrick.

In his excitement he'd forgotten his gloves, and by the time he'd cycled back to the house, his fingers were red and numb. He ran hot water into the kitchen sink and held them under, then stared out of the window that faced next door's fence and let his mind drift like kelp on a turning tide. The window was dirty; he would have to wash it. He was hungry and he was out of bread. Once his hands had warmed up he would put on his gloves and go over the road and get chips. His mouth tingled in anticipation of vinegar, and he thought of all the twists and turns the chips would have to take as they dropped into his stomach. All the places they'd have to avoid; all the choices his body would make for them, all the chemistry it would employ to break them down; how his peristaltic muscles would guide them along the conveyor belt of his guts until he passed them some time tomorrow morning.

Patrick took his hands from the water and dried them on the tea towel, while his brain turned its inevitable wheel to what had killed Number 19.

The list on the clipboard was almost as disappointing as the brain had been. He had gleaned only one piece of additional information, and that felt like a very minor victory in a failed war of secrets.

The corpse's name was Samuel Galen.

24

'Not bad, Sam,' Leslie tells me, filled with gloom. But it's praise indeed from him, and I redouble my efforts to retrain my tongue – stretching, sucking, blowing and braying.

'Have you eating and drinking soon,' he adds grudgingly.

This turns out to be a big fat lie, but I *do* make progress. The tongue is a magnificent thing. I think about it a lot, now that all my hopes and dreams depend upon it, and less than a week after my wofe betrayed me to a possible killer, Jean and Tracy prop me up in bed and spoon orange juice down my throat.

Elixir of the gods. I know everything is relative, but it tastes so good to me that I actually start to cry.

'Ahhh, look how happy!' says Jean.

'Ahhh,' parrots Tracy Evans, but I can see she's not interested. She barely looks at me and keeps clattering the teaspoon against my teeth. She's looking for the man she's trying to . . . well, *seduce* is too elegant a word. She thinks we don't see. I suppose she thinks we're all vegetables, but *I* see; I know what she's up to. I knew girls like her at Hot Stuff in Merthyr. All the lads knew them – sometimes twice a night.

She puts the juice in too fast and I feel the strange and horrible sensation of it going down the wrong way.

'Ah!'

Jean notices – bless her. She jumps up and rushes to get a machine I've seen them use on other patients. It's like a vacuum cleaner and she feeds it down my throat and sucks stuff out of my airway with a nasty rattling sound, while Tracy stands there with her arms crossed, as if I'm making a fuss about nothing and had better not blame *her*. But in Jean's eyes I can see how serious this could be.

She puts the horrible tube into me twice more, and collects watery orange mucus in a kidney bowl while my eyes stream with something similar, and I fight to keep breathing.

Finally she stops and takes Tracy away. For a bollocking, I hope.

I lie there panting, feel as if I've been punched on the inside, all my fresh hope scrunched into a stupid ball and tossed away.

Even if they're not *trying* to kill me, they might yet succeed.

And all I can do is lie here and wait for it.

~

'Patrick Fort!' said Professor Madoc, as if he were a long-lost friend. 'Have a seat.'

Patrick sat down and looked around. Professor Madoc fiddled with a Rubik's cube behind the vast wooden desk that held two silver-framed photographs – one of a smiling young woman, and the other of a boat. There was another photo of the same boat on the wall behind him, with the professor himself looking tanned and rich, waving from the puffy red depths of a life-jacket. Patrick could read the name painted on the prow: *Sharp End*.

'Damn thing,' said Professor Madoc at the cube. 'You ever done one of these?'

'Yes,' said Patrick.

The professor put it down and cleared his throat. 'I hear you've had a few run-ins, Patrick. A few problems.'

'No,' said Patrick. 'No problems.'

'That's not what people have told me.'

'OK.'

Professor Madoc looked at a piece of paper in front of him.

'Inappropriate attitude to staff, a near-physical alter-cation with a fellow student over a cadaver, ignoring procedure during dissection, and unauthorized access to confidential donation details.'

'I wanted to know the cause of death; that's not confidential.'

'That's not the point,' said Professor Madoc. His hand strayed towards the cube but he caught it in time and drummed his fingers on the desktop instead. 'You broke into a locked filing cabinet.'

'I used the key.'

'It was locked for a good reason.'

'What reason?'

'For reasons of confidentiality.'

'But the cause of death isn't confidential.' How many times did he have to say it?

'But the identity of the donor *is*.'

'But I don't *care* about the identity of the donor. I only wanted to know the cause of death.'

'Listen,' said Professor Madoc more sharply. 'This is a medical school, not a kindergarten. We won't tolerate this kind of disruption from our students, even ones with *issues*.'

'What issues?' said Patrick.

Professor Madoc took a moment to adjust to frankness. 'We understand about your Asperger's, Patrick, and we certainly have made allowances for it, but I have formally to advise you that we cannot make *endless* allowances. If I have further reports of incidents of this nature, I will be forced to suspend your studies here at Cardiff. Do you understand?'

Patrick pursed his lips.

'Do you *understand*?'

'Yes, I *understand*,' said Patrick. 'I'm trying to decide whether I *care*.'

Professor Madoc raised his eyebrows the way Mick had. 'What do you mean?'

'I might not care. I might have finished here. I don't know if there's any point in going on.'

'No point in going on? What does that mean?' The professor's hand twitched again towards the cube.

Patrick thought that Professor Madoc might have a touch of Asperger's himself, because he didn't seem to comprehend anything he was saying.

'I think the cause of death on the sheet is wrong. What's the point of going on if I'm basing judgements on bad information?'

'Cause of death is certified by a doctor.'

'Doctors get it wrong all the time. You see it on TV.'

Professor Madoc's hand flinched, and this time he followed through with a pick-up and started to twist the cube's little coloured blocks – frowning at them disapprovingly as he went on.

'The DR technician told me you asked him about a . . . doorway in the brain? Does that have anything to do with all of this?'

'Yes,' said Patrick, and stared at the cube turning in the man's long, elegant fingers. 'I want to know what happens.'

The professor sighed deeply and put down the cube. 'You know, Patrick, all we see in the dissecting room is the physical aftermath of a life. A medical student starts his journey with the dead and works backwards.'

Patrick pursed his lips. 'But I want to start with the dead and work *forwards*.'

Professor Madoc gave a small laugh. 'The dead can't speak to us, Patrick, although our lives would be immeasurably simpler if they could. While doctors might discover the mechanics of *how* someone died, they are privy to neither *why* they died nor to what happens to them *after* they die. To solve *those* puzzles I think you'd need to consult a detective . . . and a priest.'

He smiled, but Patrick didn't.

'And how do *they* solve those puzzles?' said Patrick, leaning forward.

Professor Madoc looked a little taken aback by the sudden interest in a throwaway remark. He spread his hands in new uncertainty. 'Well, I imagine a priest doesn't actually *know*. That's a matter of faith.'

'Superstition,' Patrick corrected him. 'How does the *detective* know?'

The professor gave it serious thought. 'Well,' he finally said, 'I suppose that to find out why somebody died, a detective would have to consult the living.'

'What kind of living?'

'Friends and family. Witnesses. Attending medical professionals. People like that, I suppose.'

Patrick sat back in his chair and Professor Madoc blew out his cheeks in relief. He wasn't sure how this conversation had turned from him issuing a formal warning to a student firing awkward philosophical questions at him. He needed to get back on track.

'You know, Patrick, Dr Spicer tells me that despite these difficulties, you're a real talent in the dissection room. He says you're a leading candidate for the Goldman Prize. It would be a shame to give up now, wouldn't it?'

Patrick remained still for an uncomfortably long time. Finally he nodded silently and rose to his feet, then paused and reached across the desk. The professor withdrew slightly, but Patrick picked up the Rubik's cube.

Professor Madoc watched as the matching colours spread quickly up the six sides until the puzzle was complete and Patrick laid it back on the desk.

'It's not difficult,' he said. 'I can show you, if you like.'

'Thank you,' said Professor Madoc, and Patrick left.

25

The orange juice has gone to my chest.

Pneumonia. They don't say it, but I know that's the fear. People die of pneumonia – even healthy people. But I'm *incredibly vulnerable*. Phlegm rattles in my throat and my back is agony every time I breathe, so I try not to do that.

It doesn't work.

Jean and Angie use the vacuum on me almost constantly. It's disgusting and painful. Two doctors come. I wonder if one of them is the killer. Who knows? *I* would, if only I'd kept my eyes open that night. Would it be better or worse to know whether a killer was standing over me, taking my pulse, checking my drip? Right now I don't care if one of them killed the man in the next bed, as long as they help *me*.

'Blink twice if it hurts,' says one, tapping my chest in that creepy way that doctors do – as if they're trying to find a secret passage in a smuggler's wall.

I blink lots and they exchange worried looks.

Without warning, tears roll out of my eyes and into my ears. I'm going to die, and I will never have seen Alice or Lexi again. I'll never have told them how much I love them or why I never came home that day, or where I've been since.

'Es!' I say.

'Don't try to talk,' says the younger doctor. 'It will only hurt.'

He's right, but I don't care. I don't want to slip into unconsciousness and die without doing my best to leave something behind, even if it's a single word.

'Es,' I say. 'See.'

'Ssssh,' says Jean, holding my hand and looking nervous. I reckon she and Tracy will get it in the neck if I die. Leslie will be furious – in a monosyllabic sort of way. All that work wasted. Even now my tongue curls away from where I want it to be, and I have to think of everything he taught me. I make an enormous effort, full of grunts and phlegm.

'Egh. See'. I can't do the L.

'What's that?' says the older doctor, then turns to Jean. 'Do you know what he's saying?'

'I'll get the Possum,' she says, but I don't want it. I want to hear my own voice.

'*Ek. See*,' I say as my lungs protest, my back spikes, and sweat and tears pour down my nose and cheeks.

'*Ekseee.*'

173

There! I did it!

'Sexy?' says Jean.

Not sexy, for Christ's sake! *Lexi!* But it's all I can do and it really doesn't matter whether they understand or not. Whether it's just the first word of thousands, or the last one ever to pass my lips, at least I've named the most important thing in my life.

'He must mean Angie,' smiles Jean. 'I'll get her to come by and say hello', she pats my hand encouragingly. 'You'll be ordering us all about by lunchtime.'

Another big lie.

Who cares? I don't even know what's true any more. If you can't trust a mirror, what *can* you believe?

Jean bustles away with the older doctor. The younger doctor takes my notes off the end of my bed. I can't see it happen – I just see the top of his head – but I know the feeling and the sound like my own breathing. The gritty little metal noise and the tiny vibration it makes in the steel frame and through the mattress. The princess had her pea; I have my notes.

He moves slightly so that I can see him as he reads them intently – I wonder what's written there: just the injuries from the flying Ford Focus? Or everything from childhood measles onwards? He reads them like they're instructions for a bomb disposal. Then he comes over, jabs a needle into my hip and I close my eyes, exhausted by the effort and the pain of living.

If I wake up dead, so be it.

26

There were only two Galens in the Cardiff phone book, and only one with the initial S.

The house was up Penylan Road – a large red-brick home set towards the back of a broad, unimaginative garden, where the only flowers were snowdrops and primroses in a narrow stripe either side of the wide gravel driveway. Everything else was shrubbery made of laurels and conifers. Patrick was allergic to conifers and regarded them all with suspicion. If he lived here, he'd dig them all out and have a bonfire.

He wheeled his bike past a late-registration BMW. This was how Number 19 had lived: well. It was a start, but to find out how he had died, Patrick guessed he needed more than he could gather from noting what kind of car the man had driven. He wasn't sure *what* he needed, or how he was going to get it, but

Patrick also knew that there were too many variables for him to have formulated a watertight plan of action. The front door might be opened by anyone – a wife, a mother, a son, a cleaner – and each of them would require a different strategy.

But he only had one strategy.

Therefore the only concrete opening he had prepared was *My name is Patrick Fort and I want some information about Mr Samuel Galen*. He assumed everything would fall into place from there.

Patrick put down the kickstand on his bike and knocked on the door. He could see his silhouette in the glossy black paint, and his face in the chrome letterbox.

'*Go away!* I've called the police!'

Patrick blinked in surprise. It was a woman's voice, high and screechy. And illogical. Why would she have called the police before he'd even knocked? She didn't know why he was there.

Even so, he was wary. He took a step backwards. Maybe he'd done something wrong; something he couldn't understand. It happened all the time. Once when he was fourteen he'd almost been arrested for walking out of Asda wearing jeans and a blue striped T-shirt so his mother, who was in the car, could approve the purchase. Patrick had tried to explain to the security guard that he had left his own clothes in the fitting room, so how could he be stealing these ones? Especially with the labels still swinging off them.

Maybe this was like that. Somebody not under-standing things.

The faint sound of breaking glass drew him and his bike around the side of the house to the back garden. He flinched as glass broke much closer to him this time.

A girl stood in the garden. A girl or a woman; Patrick was never quite sure when one became the other. She was as slim as a girl, but as angry as a woman. She had startling white-blonde spikes of hair, and – despite the late-winter chill – wore a white T-shirt, black leather mini skirt and motorcycle boots.

She drew back her arm and hurled what looked like half a brick through a downstairs window.

'*I've called the police!*'

'So have I!' the girl/woman screamed back at the house. 'You fucking old cow!' She turned away and Patrick thought she was going to run, but instead she started to look around for something else to throw. It wasn't easy; the garden was as well-tended as the house – apart from the broken windows. Even the soil in the shrubbery looked stone-free. Patrick couldn't see where she'd got the half-brick from.

'Hi,' said Patrick.

The girl/woman looked at him for the first time. 'Who are *you*?'

'Patrick Fort,' said Patrick. 'Are you Mrs Galen?'

'No, I'm fucking *not*,' she spat vehemently. 'And neither is *she*.' She parted the shrubbery. Patrick noticed a smallish stone next to his foot.

'Here,' he said, and held it out to her.

The girl looked at him suspiciously, then came over and snatched it from his hand like a wary monkey. 'Cheers,' she said, and threw it through an upstairs window. It made a neat black hole and a web of white cracks.

'The police are coming,' he pointed out, and she cocked her head at the sound of approaching sirens.

'Bollocks.'

'I thought you called them?'

'Yeah, right,' she snorted, and walked over to the six-foot wooden fence that surrounded the garden. 'You going to gimme a leg up or what?'

Patrick wheeled his bike across the lawn and edged his way through the shrubs. He hesitated, then went to put his hands around her waist so he could lift her up.

'Watch where you're putting your hands, mate!' she said, and he took a step backwards. 'Like *this*.' She made a stirrup with her fingers.

He flinched as she stepped into his interlaced fingers, and then almost slung her clean over the fence, she was so light, and he was so keen to be rid of her. He wiped his hands hard on the seat of his jeans.

'You coming?' she said from the other side.

Was he? Patrick stood for a moment, weighing up his options and objectives. He wanted information. The woman in the house wouldn't speak to him, whereas the girl in the garden had. She was probably his best bet.

'OK,' he said.

He'd never escaped over a fence before and wasn't quite sure of the procedure. He propped his bike against it, then stepped on the crossbar and lay precariously along the fence, with the planking digging a long line of discomfort from his shoulder to his balls, while he gripped with one hand and his feet. He teetered there, and stretched an arm back down to grip the crossbar. He should have put the bike over the fence first.

'Come *on*!'

'I'm getting my bike,' he explained.

'There's no *time*!'

Two uniformed policemen walked briskly round the side of the house and Patrick realized too late that he'd chosen the wrong team. They saw him and started to jog across the lawn.

'Oi!' shouted one. 'Stay right there!'

A rush of adrenaline took Patrick completely by surprise. It fired a stream of white-hot excitement through his body. No video game had ever made him feel this way, and he laughed at the policemen as they speeded up across the grass.

But the bike anchored him on the wrong side of the fence. He should really leave it.

He didn't. He hauled it up, one-handed – his shoulder burning with effort and his chest and balls shrieking to be allowed off the narrow wooden ridge. He would have overbalanced back into the garden, except that the girl who wasn't Mrs Galen grabbed two handfuls of him – his jeans and his hoodie – and provided a counterweight as he lifted his bike up to join him, until his weight shifted and they both rolled off the fence and dropped on to the ground, only missing the girl because she jumped out of the way with a shriek.

He lay in the alleyway, winded and staring at the same sky that had been there the day of the monkey bars and the swing.

The first of the policemen hit the other side of the wooden fence with a grunt. The girl yelled, 'Run! Run!' then took her own advice and disappeared from his field of vision.

Patrick was on his feet in an instant, running alongside his bike until he had the presence of mind to jump into the saddle, like a Dodge City bank robber on to a getaway pony.

He heard the police shouting something behind him, but never looked back, and very soon his pedalling took him to a calmer, quieter place – as it so often had.

He caught up with the girl in the park down at the bottom of the hill. She was walking now, not running, and staying close to the shadows of the rhododendrons.

He slowed his bike beside her and said, 'Hi.'

She put a hand to her chest. 'Shit! You nearly gave me a heart attack!'

But she started laughing then, and didn't stop until she was crying.

'Shit,' she said again. 'That *bitch*!' She wiped her eyes, leaving dark streaks from her eyes to her temples. Patrick waited until she'd finished.

'You want to get a drink?' she said.

'I don't drink,' Patrick told her.

'Don't be stupid,' she said.

They went into the Claude on Albany Road. 'You got any money?' she said, so Patrick bought her a rum and Coke, and himself a Coke without the rum.

'You really don't drink,' said the girl. 'Why?'

'No reason,' he said.

'Liar.'

He wondered how she'd known, but said nothing else. They sat at a table near the door and she clinked his glass with hers. 'Bottoms up,' she said.

She drank half her rum and Coke in one go. 'What was your name again?'

He was practised at the answer now and told her with barely a pause.

'Thanks for the leg up over the fence.'

He nodded. 'What's yours?'

'My what?'

'Name.'

She said, 'Lexi,' and drained her glass. 'Want another one?'

'I haven't finished this one.'

She hid a burp behind her fist, then reached over,

took his Coke from his hand and swallowed it in three swift gulps.

'Want another one now?'

He bought her another one, and a coffee for himself, because he thought it would be cheaper, but it wasn't.

'You're not Samuel Galen's wife?' Patrick said as he sat down with the drinks.

She took a gulp and shook her head. 'He was my dad.'

'But she's not his wife either?'

'She's just a fucking gold-digger,' she said. 'You got a fag?'

'No.'

Lexi took out a pouch of tobacco and rolled her own.

'Sitting there in a bloody *mansion* with bloody great Beemers out the front, while I'm kipping on a mate's *couch* above a fucking *pet shop*. Got a light?'

'No.'

Lexi went to the bar to ask for one and the barman told her there was no smoking in the pub.

'Jesus *Christ*!' she said, and yanked the roll-up from her lips and stormed back to her seat.

'Bastard says there's no smoking! In a fucking *pub*!'

'It's the law,' Patrick pointed out.

'I *know* it's the law.'

'Because of passive smoking.'

'Thank you, Chancellor of the Exchequer.'

'I'm not the Chancellor of the Exchequer.'

'You don't say.'

Patrick was confused because he plainly *had* said.

'Stupid fucking rules,' she said and poked the roll-up into her cleavage. 'What's wrong with your hand?'

Patrick looked at his knuckles, which were red, with long yellow blisters already coming.

The shrubbery.

'Conifers,' he said. 'I'm allergic.'

'Allergies fucking *blow*,' said Lexi enthusiastically. 'I have a million of them. Fish, cats, eggs – you name it. Not trees though. Does it hurt?'

'It itches.'

Patrick was finding it hard to keep up with Lexi's flood of words and emotions and expletives. She seemed to say anything and everything that popped into her mind. All Patrick had to do was try to sift the gold from the grit. But he wasn't sure which was which, and so let her stream of consciousness wash over him in the hope that he could sort it out later.

'What was going on at the house?'

'Oh, *that*,' she said with a scowl. 'All I did was ask for my own money, and she goes bonkers.'

'What money?'

'That my dad left me in his will. I need it *now*, not when I'm twenty fucking five.'

'No need to swear,' said Patrick.

'Of *course* there's a need to swear!' she said, slapping the table and making him flinch. 'Swearing's the only thing that keeps me going! What kind of world do *you* live in where there's no need to fucking swear? A world where you don't drink and don't smoke and nothing ever pisses you off? I bet there's no sex either. Fan-fucking-tastic.'

Patrick felt his face growing hot and he stared into his coffee cup. He had never thought much about sex, but all of a sudden not having had it seemed like a very stupid oversight for someone of his intellect.

There was a long gap in the conversation while the scratchy pub speakers played 'Wonderwall' by Oasis. *1995*, thought Patrick. *Before everything went wrong.*

He finished his coffee.

'I'm sorry,' Lexi said. 'I'm such a fucking big mouth. I just get so *grrrrr*! You know? And then I say all kinds of stupid shit.'

'OK,' he nodded.

'Seriously,' said Lexi, ducking her head to try to meet his eyes. 'I'm an idiot.'

She reached for his hand across the table. He saw it coming and fought his instincts. What had his mother said? *I don't expect anything back from you, Patrick, but I do expect manners.* That meant she *did* expect something back. She'd given him a gift and Patrick was apparently supposed to say 'Thank you.' Gifts came with strings attached, even if they weren't always obvious. Lexi's father had allowed five strangers to cut him to pieces and put him into yellow bins and plastic bags. The string attached to that gift was right here, right now, coming at him across the scar-and-varnish pub table.

He couldn't do it; he moved his hand and sat on it. 'How did your father die?'

Lexi picked up her glass instead. She didn't seem surprised by the question. 'He was in an accident, and then a coma for a few months, and then he just died. They said he might. They said it happens all the time.'

'Who said?'

'I dunno. The doctors, I suppose.'

'Were you there?'

She shook her head and knocked back what was left of her drink, even though it was mostly ice now. 'I only went to see him once. It was shit. He was crying. I held his hand but he didn't even know it was me.'

Patrick nodded. 'Altered states,' he said. 'You know, there have been cases where people woke from comas with previously unknown skills. Thinking they're Abraham Lincoln, or with an Italian accent. Things like that.' He'd always found those accounts fascinating, but Lexi stared across the pub as if he hadn't spoken.

'I don't care,' she declared. 'He was an arse anyway. Arse isn't swearing, is it? I mean, it's what he was.'

'OK,' he said, then remembered about working backwards and added, 'Why? Was he an . . . arse?'

Lexi gave an exaggerated shrug and toyed with her glass.

Patrick noticed that the dorsal metacarpal arteries showed sky blue up the backs of her pale hands. He wondered whether she and her father would be identifiable as relatives if they were laid out side by side and peeled of skin. He knew that he himself had a strange twist to his thumbs that his mother had given him, and that when he shaved he could see his father's mouth and eyes in the bathroom mirror like a ghost in the glass. How deep did such bonds go? Was it all about eyebrows and lips? Or were there veins and kidneys that had similar familial quirks?

'He didn't give a shit about me,' said Lexi. 'I fucking hated him.'

Then – before Patrick could ask her why – she put her glass down firmly and said, 'You got a couch?'

Once she was on the couch, Lexi was impossible to dislodge. She watched *Hollyoaks* and *EastEnders* with Kim and Jackson, while Patrick went upstairs and cleaned another three squares of carpet.

When he came down at ten o'clock she was still there, watching something full of guns and noise, with the remote control in her hand.

Jackson and Kim cornered him in the kitchen.

'She has to go!' hissed Kim.

'Kim's right,' hissed Jackson. 'She has to go.'

'OK,' said Patrick, and started to make a peanut-butter sandwich while they both watched him.

Kim said, '*You* brought her here. *You* have to tell her!'

'OK,' he said, and cleaned up after himself. Then

he put the sandwich on a plate that had a cartoon zebra in the middle and the alphabet around the outside. It was a child's plate but the alphabet had always calmed him so he'd brought it with him from home and Kim had dubbed it 'retro-hip'. He took it through to the living room, where Lexi had now spread herself down the length of the sofa.

'You have to go,' he informed her.

'What are you eating?' she said. 'I'm quite hungry.'

'Peanut-butter sandwich.'

She made a face. 'Have you got some cheese?'

'Yes,' he said. 'Kim and Jackson say you have to go.'

'Can I have a cheese sandwich?'

He stood for a moment, uncertain of what to do next. He had told her she had to go and she'd ignored that and asked for a cheese sandwich. He didn't understand how the two were connected. But he didn't mind giving her a cheese sandwich; maybe she'd go after that. Things wouldn't happen in the expected *order*, but they'd happen.

'OK,' he said, and went back to the kitchen.

'Has she gone?' said Jackson.

'No. She wants a cheese sandwich.'

'Shit,' said Kim. 'Jackson, tell her she has to go!'

Jackson looked unsure, but left the kitchen. Patrick was considering whether to cut the sandwich square or on the diagonal when he came back.

'Has she gone?' demanded Kim.

'She wants a blanket.'

'Oh for fuck's sake, Jackson!' Kim stormed out and Patrick went for square because he always had *his* sandwiches cut square, so if Kim made Lexi leave now, he could take this one with him for lunch tomorrow.

'She just ignored me,' said Jackson, biting his nails.

'Me too,' said Patrick.

'Now Kim thinks I'm a wuss.'

Patrick nodded his agreement.

'Shit,' said Jackson softly.

They listened to the low voices from the front room, and then heard footsteps ascending the stairs and coming down again. Then more low voices.

Then Kim came back into the kitchen and didn't look at them. She opened the fridge and pushed things around her shelf for a long time.

'Has she gone?' said Jackson.

'Did someone eat my yoghurt?' said Kim.

'No,' said Jackson and Patrick together.

'Oh,' said Kim and shut the fridge door and went upstairs. Jackson followed her.

When Patrick took the sandwich through to the front room, Lexi was wrapped in a red blanket on the couch.

'Thanks,' she said as she took a bite. 'Have you got anything to drink?'

He brought her a glass of water and she said, 'Have you got anything else?'

He knew what she meant. He also knew there was a half-bottle of white wine on Kim's shelf in the fridge.

'No,' he said.

'Not very good students, are you?'

'I'm the best in dissection. Jackson says Kim's good, but I don't know about art. It just looks lumpy to me.'

She fidgeted and ate half her sandwich while he watched, then asked where the toilet was.

She was gone for ten minutes and came back with the wine.

'I found this in the fridge. I'll replace it tomorrow.'

He said nothing.

'You want some?'

He shook his head. Lexi poured her water into the puny rubber plant, and filled the tumbler with wine instead. She drank it the way she had the rum and Coke, in rapid, repeated draughts – as if she was impatient to see the bottom of the glass – then she refilled it.

'You drink too much,' said Patrick.

'You talk too much,' she snapped back.

They watched something about driving trucks on icy roads. Every time a truck skidded off, Lexi giggled and glanced at him.

She checked the empty bottle twice. Patrick knew it wouldn't be the last time and couldn't bear to watch.

'I'm going to bed,' he said.

'Hey, Patrick,' she said. 'I know when I've had too much. I've been drinking since I was, like, fourteen or something. So I think I know what I'm doing by now.'

'OK,' he said.

'Everybody's so judgemental. Gets on my fucking tits.'

'OK.'

'Oh I'm sorry. Didn't mean to swear. Sorry.'

Sorry. The word meant nothing to him. It was like static, and he'd learned to ignore it.

'Thanks for the sandwich,' she said. 'See you in the morning.'

'OK,' he said, and went upstairs.

Around one a.m., he woke to find Lexi worming her way on to his narrow bed alongside him.

'That couch is made for midgets,' she said, all elbows and bottom. She was still wrapped in the blanket and he was in his sleeping bag, but the thought of her body pressed along the entire length of his galvanized him. He stood up and stepped over her as if crossing an electric fence, and picked up his sleeping bag.

'Where are you going?' she said.

'Downstairs. Don't bang your head on the bicycle.'

'What?' she said, but he didn't answer her.

The couch *was* made for midgets, so he settled down on the carpet, on his side, and with his knees tucked up just enough to avoid touching the water tank that wasn't there, and thought about Lexi.

There was so much to think about. She was like a tornado that had picked him up, whirled him high and dumped him, dazed, in a foreign field. It was scary, but it was also exciting.

It was hard to separate *her* from the information she'd given him. The gold-digger in the big house, the half-brick through the window, the frozen inheritance, the rum and Coke. Those things told him lots about Lexi, but all they told him about Samuel Galen was that he was rich, mean and dead.

Patrick frowned into the darkness and felt the familiar itch of an unsolved puzzle. Maybe he should have stuck with the gold-digger; maybe she'd have been more . . . coherent. Almost certainly she wouldn't have followed him home and demanded a couch, a blanket and a cheese sandwich; almost certainly he'd be asleep in his own bed now.

Patrick sighed and blinked against the crook of his elbow pillow. His eyes grew used to the night until he was able to see a pale curve under the couch. He tried to work out what it was but finally had to touch it to discover the plate on which he'd brought Lexi the sandwich. She had left her crusts, even though he'd put the cheese right up to the edges. Patrick made a good sandwich; he liked them because their structure meant he could put almost anything in them that didn't start with A. Bread was always on the outside, then Butter. Then, as long as the fillings continued from the outside to the inside in strict alphabetical order, the world was his oyster. Peanut butter was his favourite filling, but he had a soft spot for cheese and chutney – as much for their economy of alphabetical progression as for the taste. He wondered floatily whether Lexi would have eaten her crusts if he'd put chutney on her sandwich. But she hadn't asked for chutney, and had made a face at peanut butter, and he had been too flustered to offer her Marmite or—

Patrick rolled on to his back, his breath suddenly shallow and his stomach fluttering with tension. He held his twisted thumbs up to the dark ceiling and thought again of the delicate blue veins in the backs of Lexi's hands. Her skin was so fine and pale – nothing like Number 19's tough orange dermis. Making an H-incision in *her* throat would be completely different. There would be no scrape of old stubble against his knuckles, no Adam's apple to teeter up and down again, no smell of lilies and shit. Only the pliable tracheal rings, dipping gently into the jugular notch at the base of her smooth neck. Nothing about it would be the same as the cadaver's, even if her veins and kidneys *did* give away the family connection.

But what if . . .

What if family was about more than a visual match? What if it was also about the speed at which her neurons fired, or the rate at which her glands excreted, or the way her blood responded to chemical changes?

Patrick stood up and kicked himself free of his bag, his own blood squirting powerfully through his heart, and a light sheen of sweat making his skin prickle in the cold room.

He went upstairs and turned on his bedroom light with a bright click. Lexi was asleep on her back, with her hands clenched loosely on the pillow beside her head, the way a baby sleeps. She stirred at the light but didn't open her eyes.

Patrick put out a tentative hand, then withdrew it.

'Are you awake?' he said clearly.

Her forehead creased. 'What?'

'Are you awake?'

'No.'

'You must be or you couldn't say "No".'

'What do you want?'

'Are you allergic to nuts?'

She squinted one eye open, then shielded it from the light. 'What?'

'Are you allergic to peanuts?'

'Yes. If I have one I could die.'

'Was your father?'

'Yes.'

'OK,' said Patrick. He opened his wardrobe and put on his T-shirt and hoodie.

Lexi sat up, hair awry, and hugged her knees through the red blanket. 'Why? What's going on?'

He didn't tell her because he didn't hear her. He was overwhelmed by a looped image of his own blue finger dipping into Samuel Galen's puckered flesh, like Doubting Thomas peering into the side of Christ, while a question buzzed through his being.

If Number 19 was being fed through a tube, what was he doing with a peanut – that might kill him – in his throat?

Lexi watched him pull on his jeans, then flinched as

he reached over her head and took his bike from the hooks on the wall.

'*You*'re nuts,' she said.

He hoisted the bike on to his shoulder and hurried down the stairs; she scrambled off the bed and hung over the banisters to call after him, 'And your room stinks of bleach!'

27

I wake with a start in the dark, and the shadow beside my bed flinches too. I gave us both a fright, and if I could laugh, I would.

It's the doctor who gave me a perfect ten, come to tap my chest. He does that with warm fingers, then breathes on the stethoscope. It's the little things that show they care. You'd never know, otherwise.

He listens to my lungs, staring past me at my pillow to avoid embarrassingly close eye-contact.

I wonder drowsily what he hears in there; whether my lungs have passed their orange-juice crisis. My breathing still hurts, but nothing like it did a week ago. I'm on the mend.

He stares intently at the linen beside my ear. Then he straightens up and looks in the direction of the nurses' station. I turn my head with a little surge of athletic achievement and follow his gaze.

There is nobody there.

It was going to happen.

Tracy Evans could feel it in the air. She was on three nights in a row. She'd got a spray tan, her eyebrows threaded, her legs waxed, and her pubic hair ripped agonizingly into a dark little heart. It didn't match her blonde hair, but nobody had ever complained. She was wearing underwear that matched and wasn't grey, and she'd bought that perfume by Britney – not fat, bald Britney, but slutty Britney in school tie and knee socks. Now she wore her ugly blue tunic with new sensuality – her smooth new wonders sliding beneath its utilitarian starch.

On the first night, Mr Deal had sniffed the air around her, but hadn't gone for it immediately, which was slightly annoying. But at least it had given the pimples on her pubis time to calm down.

This was the second night. Angie had swapped shifts with Monica, who was new and easily bossed about, and even more easily deceived. Tracy had already been through the Quality Street and eaten all the big purple ones while Monica was helping someone with a bedpan.

She heard the lift doors open and felt a delicious twitch as Mr Deal came round the corner, silhouetted against the harsh fluorescents.

Tracy hid *Rose Budding*, which she was re-reading, then picked up a sheaf of random paperwork, pushed out her chest, sucked in her tummy, and composed her form and her features into their most flattering aspect.

'Hello, Tracy,' he said quietly, and she turned as if surprised and gave him the demure but promising smile she'd practised so long in the mirror. Slutty Nun, she called it. She was rewarded by seeing his brooding face soften into a look of being pleased to see her.

Men were so easy!

But he'd better make his move before she had to go through the hell of waxing again, or she'd make him suffer.

For an hour Mr Deal stood with his back to his wife with a cup of machine coffee. At nine p.m. he had another. Tracy knew that nobody *chose* to have two cups, so he was obviously killing time. She went into the ladies' bathroom and threw away the cardboard bedpans that she routinely left stinking on the windowsill. Made the place a bit nice.

At ten thirty p.m. Mr Deal put another pound into the coffee machine and Tracy Evans's nipples responded.

Just after eleven, she told Monica to go out for a cigarette. As they were on the fourth floor, Tracy knew that that entailed a fifteen-minute round-trip for a two-minute smoke, and so Monica usually had a couple while she was outside the ambulance-bay doors. Which took it up to twenty minutes.

Plenty of time, in her experience.

'You sure?' said Monica.

'Course,' said Tracy. 'You go. I'll be fine.'

The lift doors closed and Tracy got up and hitched up her bra straps.

The dance had been slow and frustrating but she knew that the end of it would be as familiar to her as her own reflection.

The doctor looks back down at me and clears his throat.

'I'm very sorry, Mr Galen,' he says softly.

My mind turns slowly around the pivot of his words. He *does* sound very sorry. *What for?* I start to worry. Maybe he heard something in my lungs. Maybe I'm not as on the mend as I thought I was. Maybe—

Then he leans over me again and I see that in his right hand he holds a pair of tweezers.

And that between their glittering points is a peanut.

My heart spasms with electric terror and in an instant I understand everything.

He's the one! He's the killer!

And he knows how incredibly vulnerable I am . . .

My panicked hand flaps like a fish on a bedspread beach as my memory detonates: I'm four years old and my throat tightens and my eyes swell shut, even while the traitorous treat still seasons the inside of my mouth. My mother screams somewhere, and my head bounces on my father's arm as he runs from the stalled car into the hospital, shouting, 'He can't breathe! He can't breathe!' I'm jostled and tossed and snatched from my father's arms by other arms in white sleeves, and the lights jiggle overhead as the doctor runs down the corridor to save my life with a scalpel and a tube in my throat, so that I can grow up to bring the stubby hands to the marital table. The stubby hands and the allergies listed on my medical notes for everyone to see . . .

The doctor lowers the peanut towards my lips.

'*Guh!*' I cry. '*Guh!*'

I'm more scared now than when I was a child. No one is going to help me this time.

I feel a knuckle against my chin, the nut nudging my lip – and I jab out my well-trained tongue, my only defence. It knocks the peanut from the grip of the tweezers and for a split second I'm triumphant.

And then I feel it drop instead into the back of my throat . . .

Dying is far easier than it looks in the movies.

There are no flashy cuts, no explosions, no speeches – just a clumsy doctor, swearing and fumbling between my teeth, digging the sharp tweezers into my palate and tongue, even as my throat swells jealously around the evidence he wants back.

The terror. The panic.

The *sorrow* for all I'm leaving behind.

I can't die! I have people to hold, to love; to make it up to—

Too late. *Too late.* Pain cleaves me. My jaw clamps in agony and I slither back down the well. There's no tunnel, no light, no return.

Darkness snaps shut and truth spills from my dead heart – *I love you I love you I love you*—

A small hand takes mine.

'Look at it *go*, Daddy!'

28

4017.

The ugly code had its uses.

Patrick took a while to find the switches, then blinked as the lights shuddered awake to banish shadows from the dissecting room.

The cadavers were just sickly-sweet leftovers now. Missing limbs, gaping chests, with their skin peeled off them in dirty brown folds, and their pale brains gleaming with wetting solution beside their empty skulls.

Yet they seemed more alive to Patrick now than they had at the start. More *real*, now that he understood them better.

As he passed them, his sense of excitement grew. He knew the cause of death. He was *sure* of it. The list was wrong; Mick was wrong; Spicer was wrong; his fellow students were wrong; and whatever doctor had signed the death certificate was wrong. None of them knew what he knew – that Lexi Galen had an allergy to peanuts. And Patrick would bet the bicycle he'd inherited from his father that she had inherited that allergy from hers.

He couldn't wait to tell them all that he'd solved the puzzle. Especially Scott.

Patrick looked down at Number 19, whose one remaining eye stared through him dully. He looked away quickly, and hunched down beside the table. Underneath it were the scores of bags they'd slowly filled with the dead man's lungs, his liver, his small intestines – all pressed against the clear plastic like the cheap mince his mother bought from the wagon at Brecon market. More of Number 19 was now under the table than on it.

Patrick sorted through it all but couldn't find the peanut.

He frowned. That made no sense; he had bagged it and tagged it himself. He was too impatient; it was small; he must have missed it. He went through the process again in slow reverse, sitting on the cold floor, loading the shelf under the table more carefully this time.

The peanut was not there.

Patrick sat very still. One of the others had got there first. Scott? Dilip? But *how*? How had they known about the allergy when he'd only found out by accident? Had he missed something obvious? And if they didn't know about the allergy, why would they take it?

The lights went out and he was blind. He quickly squeezed his eyes tightly shut. It was a trick his father had taught him on night walks in the Beacons.

Too late he registered that the main door of the Biosciences block had been open. He'd not noticed it because he'd never seen it closed, but in the middle of the night it would have been; *should* have been – unless someone was already inside.

Idiot!

He opened his better-adjusted eyes. A black figure was framed in the charcoal doorway.

Patrick started to get up to leave but, before he could, the man entered the room.

Strangeness rippled up the back of Patrick's neck. Turning off the lights *before* entering a room made no sense. So, instead of standing up and asking why the lights were off, Patrick stayed put on one knee and one spread hand, his stomach knotting with a fear that was all the more fearful because he didn't understand it.

The man walked confidently between the bodies, as if he did so in the dark all the time. There was no fumbling, no banged shins or muttered expletives. Between the struts of the tables and the remains of the ruined bodies, the figure walked swiftly towards him, announced only by the small squeak of shoes on polished linoleum.

He was coming straight for him.

Without thinking, Patrick crawled silently on to the shelf below Table 19, along with the bags of meat and bone and offal.

Lexi's cold father gave a little under his body, and he almost cried out with the idea of the cold flesh cushioning him.

Only the plastic between them stopped him screaming.

He bit his own lip as the shadow stopped beside him. In a moment that rushed him back to the bookies and the Labrador, Patrick watched the knees and the thighs of the man's black trousers turn slowly, as if scanning the room, looking for something.

Patrick stopped breathing; if he could have stopped his heart pounding, he would have.

The moment seemed endless. Then the legs walked away and back towards the door.

For a second Patrick was relieved – then he realized that if the man left the block, the outer door would be locked, trapping him inside.

He rolled off the bags of cold meat and one of his trainers squealed on the floor. He froze again, then quickly pulled the shoes off his feet and slid swiftly across the floor on his socks to Table 21, and from there to Table 13.

The man was still ahead of him. He had to catch him up. Or slow him down.

Patrick wasn't a spy. He didn't have a grappling hook or satellite communications, or even a black

turtleneck sweater. He had his trainers – that was all –
so he hurled one of them into a dim corner of the
room, where it landed with a slap and a clatter.

He almost laughed when the man stopped, turned,
and then followed the noise to the back wall like a
stupid dog, while Patrick skidded out of the door in his
socks.

He couldn't ride properly with one trainer, so he
walked. Ran. Half walked, half ran, pushing his bike,
and with his socks wet and stretching and tripping him
up until finally he peeled them off and dropped them
in the gutter. His foot was shockingly white under the
streetlights.

A police car passed and Patrick pressed himself into
a garden hedge, even though he'd done nothing
wrong. Something told him that this was one of those
occasions when people might not understand what
he'd been doing. And he had no answers tonight – only
questions that made his head ache to think of them.

Before, Patrick had only thought about the peanut
in relation to *how* Number 19 had died, not *why*. Why
was a far tougher puzzle, and now that it was gone, the
peanut seemed to be a critical piece of that jigsaw.
How did Number 19 ingest a peanut that could kill
him? And why would somebody steal it now?

Cold rain trickled under his T-shirt and down
his back, and still he stood there. For the first time that
he could ever remember – and he could remember

almost *everything* – Patrick knew he needed help.

Patrick didn't have his blue gloves with him, but he stopped at the payphone outside the bookies and dialled with a wet sleeve pulled over his shivering index finger.

It took thirteen rings before the mechanical rhythm was halted by the sound of sleepy mouth-breathing and a croak that might have been *hello*.

'If there was something that proved how someone had died,' he said, 'why would you want to hide that?'

There was a long silence and then his mother said shakily, 'Who *is* this?'

Why is he asking? What's happened?

Sarah Fort's head asked the questions her heart didn't want answered. She had been expecting the worst for years – ever since Patrick was a small boy – and yet time hadn't dulled the sharp panic she felt pricking her chest and starting to turn her stomach.

'What do you mean?' she asked him. Anyone but Patrick would have noticed her voice shaking.

'Say someone dies,' he said again. 'And then, if someone *else* – not the dead person – someone *else*—'

He was obviously getting muddled, but she didn't help him out. She was in no hurry to hear what he wanted to say. She would wait all night – all her life – rather than help him to reach the point where everything she had done for both of them would fall apart.

But he persisted. He was always so bloody *persistent*.

'If that someone hides something that might show *why* the other person died.'

'Yes?' she said faintly.

'Well, what does that mean?'

Sarah paused. 'I don't understand the question.'

She knew she was being obtuse. Things would be so much simpler if she'd just said, *What are you trying to tell me, Patrick?* She didn't ask because he would tell her – and she didn't want to deal with whatever might happen after that. She would rather play this precarious game of denial.

'Why are you calling tonight? It's not Thursday.'

'I know,' he said. 'I need help.'

'Are you all right?' She was surprised to hear a sharp note of concern in her voice, despite everything.

'I lost one of my trainers and I need help to understand the *actions*.'

'What actions?'

'Hiding the *thing*,' he said in a tone that revealed his frustration, 'that might show why something happened. What does that *action* mean?'

She thought carefully of the best way to answer him, and then did.

'People hide things because they don't want anyone to know about them.'

'Why?'

You tell me, Patrick! Rotting animals under your pillow,

and pictures of dead children and crazy lists of weird words!
YOU tell ME!

Instead she said, 'I suppose . . . because they feel guilty.'

'About what?'

Sarah felt sick. 'Doing something bad.'

'Like what?'

'I don't know, Patrick! Something bad! Something very, very *bad*!'

There was a pause.

'So what must I do about it?'

What indeed? She felt emotion start to clog her throat.

'Do whatever you think best,' she said hoarsely.

'Best for who?'

Sarah could barely whisper. 'For you.'

There was a long silence and then Patrick said an abrupt 'OK' in a tone she knew meant that, for him, the conversation was over.

She didn't press him, even though it was three in the morning and any other mother would have done. *Should* have done. Any mother of a different son.

But she was only relieved that he'd stopped asking questions that made her fear him, even as she feared *for* him.

'Good,' she said, and then 'Goodbye.'

She sat in the kitchen with the phone in her lap long after Patrick had rung off. It was a harsh February and the kitchen fire had long since gone out, but she shivered for other reasons too. The cold from the stone floor seeped through her socks and crept achingly up her ankles and her shins, and still she sat there, thinking about her strange son calling her on a strange night to ask a strange question.

The splinter of progress she thought she'd seen at Christmas – away from the obsessive past and into a more normal future – now seemed like a cruel deception. She wasn't a religious woman, but she wanted a sign. A single, solid indicator that Matt's life – and hers – had not been wasted.

She couldn't think of one.

Not one.

On another night – a warmer night; or if the fire had not gone out; or if the cat had been sitting on her lap – habit alone might have been enough to keep her going.

But this night was cold and this night was dark, and the cat was outside killing small things.

So there was nothing to stop her standing up and staring out of the kitchen window at the Fiesta outside the old wooden shed. Nothing to stop her pulling cold rubber boots on to her bare feet and crunching across the gravel under the slitted moon in her towelling robe; nothing to stop her driving six miles to the twenty-four-hour service station and buying two bottles of Vladivar.

One for now and one for just in case.

29

When Patrick got home it was four a.m., so he was surprised to see the lights were on. The minute he opened the door and pushed his bike inside, Jackson appeared at the top of the stairs in fake silk pyjamas. Patrick knew they must be fake because silk was expensive, but Jackson's TV was a piece of junk.

'Where the fuck have *you* been?' Jackson yelled at him.

WHERE the fuck have you been?
Where the FUCK have you been?
Where the fuck have you BEEN?

Patrick said nothing. He wiped his bike down with a towel he kept in the hall, then carried it upstairs and hung it on its hooks, while Jackson harangued him from the doorway.

'I told you she had to go, didn't I? She's *your*

fucking guest and *you* should have kicked her out. Then none of this would have happened!'

'None of what?'

'Oh Jackson, shut *up*!' Kim shouted from her room, and Jackson stomped down the short corridor to her door, and they yelled at each other for a bit, using words like 'whore' and 'slag' and 'control freak' and 'arsehole'.

Patrick almost said something, but then reserved judgement on whether or not there was a need to swear. He used the time alone to strip off his sodden clothing, wring it out of the window and pile it on top of the hot-water tank. He stared at his single trainer and wished he'd had something else to throw. He only had one pair of shoes with him at college; now he only had half a pair.

'Don't pretend you give a shit!' yelled Kim.

'I won't!' Jackson shouted back. 'I *don't*!'

Patrick pulled on dry shorts and a T-shirt, turned out his light and got into his sleeping bag, shivering with delayed cold, and feeling again the paintwork of the old door, pressed against his cheek as his parents fought behind it. Over him. This felt just like that.

'Oh, for Christ's sake!' said a voice he recognized as Lexi's. 'Some of us are trying to *sleep*!'

A dull thumping on the wall beside Patrick's head told him that some of the people trying to sleep lived next door.

Kim's door slammed like a gun.

'Fuck you, too!' Jackson yelled, then came back to Patrick's room and stood in the doorway.

'*Bitch*,' he said. 'Fucking *bitch*.' And then he walked in, sat heavily on Patrick's legs and burst into tears.

Patrick stared at the ceiling. He hoped that soon Jackson would tire of crying, get off his legs and go back to his own room. But when none of those things happened, he asked him what was wrong.

Apparently what was wrong was that after Patrick had left, Lexi had crawled out of his bed and into Kim's bed instead – where it turned out that Kim *was* a lesbian, after all.

A loud one.

'If you hadn't brought her home, none of this would ever have happened,' sobbed Jackson.

That was self-evident, thought Patrick. But then, if he hadn't brought Lexi home, he would also never have found out about the allergies. He would still have two trainers, he wouldn't have called his mother without gloves and on the wrong night of the week, and he would not now understand that the missing peanut might mean that *someone* was hiding *something bad*.

Cause and effect was a funny thing.

For the first time since he had come to the city, Patrick felt his need to complete his quest vying for space in his head with this new mystery. He had spent more than half his young life seeking answers about what had happened to his father, but suddenly it was

Lexi's rich, mean, mummified parent that excited his mind.

And the new mystery did not involve the intricacies of reaching out to a life beyond this one, only the simple question of who was guilty, and why.

PART THREE

PART THREE

30

JEAN BOTTI HAD worked on the neurological ward for seven years, so she'd seen it all. Miracles and murders. Oh, they happened – both of them – although neither was ever acknowledged by the hospital.

Since starting work on what was commonly known as the coma ward, she knew of three reliable miracles and two less reliable murders. The miracles were not of the walking-on-water, feeding-the-five-thousand variety. That would be silly, even to a staunch Catholic like Jean. But, in Jean's eyes, they *were* events of such startling recovery that they would have challenged the story of Lazarus.

There was sixteen-year-old Amy Russett, who spent a year frozen in a coma and then, one chilly March night, got up, walked down the corridor and took herself to the toilet – marking the start of a rapid and unexplained recovery.

Then there was Gwilym Thomas, a sixty-six-year-old farmer, who had never been beyond the Welsh border but who, after being gored by his own prize bull, awoke speaking only French. Even more bizarrely, the only English he seemed to remember was the name of the bull. Jean could recall it even now: Barleyfield Ianto.

Mrs Thomas had proved to be a stoic, and hadn't taken it personally. After a brief flurry of confusion, she had armed herself with a Linguaphone course and started a new, more Gallic life.

Jean's personal favourite was Mark Strickland, who crashed his car as a drunken lout, and emerged from his coma six weeks later quoting a Bible he'd never read, and humbly asking the Lord for help as he sweated through the agony of physiotherapy.

Miracles all, in Jean's eyes.

Then there were the murders.

Jean couldn't help thinking of them that way, even though she knew they were not malicious. She would have preferred to think of them as 'mercy killings', but in her heart she knew that God didn't agree with her.

Of course, just as the miracles were never official, neither were the murders.

Just a few months after she'd first started work on the ward, a boy named Gavin Richards had come in after being mugged. He had been hit so hard in the head that the shape of the claw hammer was clearly outlined in his shaven skull.

At first his family hoped for a miracle. They *all* did; it was only natural. But, as the days started to pass into weeks, and the weeks into months, it became apparent to everyone that seventeen-year-old Gavin was never going to make it. Everyone except his mother, that is. Gavin's mother came in every day and spent hours holding his hand, clipping his nails, putting cream on his raw bottom, and singing childhood songs to him in a gentle, quavery voice barely above a whisper, while her other children – a boy of nine and a girl of fourteen – suffered the twin loss of a brother *and* a mother. Tragedy upon tragedy.

Despite the best care, Gavin slid slowly downhill towards death. Soon the doctors would start to speak to his family about withdrawing life support and allowing him to slip away.

But then, one terrible day, Gavin inexplicably opened his eyes and said, 'Mummy.'

Immediately he'd sunk back into the hinterland of unconsciousness, but the damage was done. His mother redoubled her efforts – and her neglect. She started to bring in a sleeping roll and spend nights under his bed. 'Don't mind me,' she told Jean as she crawled out every shivery morning. 'I just want to be here when he wakes up.'

But Gavin was *never* going to wake up. That was the trouble. And even if he did, so much of his brain had been pulverized that his future held nothing but animal needs in a shell of a human body. But however often the doctors showed her the scans and explained the extent of the horrible damage the single hammer blow had caused, Mrs Richards would have no truck with the idea that he might not come back to her just the way he'd left on that fateful night. *Mummy* had been an aberration, a false dawn, a cruel neurological hiccup that would hold Gavin's family captive forever unless something was done.

And so a senior consultant did something.

He suggested that Gavin was ready to go home.

Gavin's mother cried with joy; Gavin's father cried because he understood what that really meant.

With a bravery Jean was humbled to witness, the family made preparations for young Gavin's home-coming. They altered their home with ramps and rails. They bought medical equipment and an optimistic wheelchair. They hired nurses. And they were not rich people.

Gavin left hospital with his mother alongside the trolley, beaming and waving as though she were leading in the Derby winner.

Five days later, Gavin was dead from the expected complications, and his family was reunited in grief – as they should have been months earlier.

Jean had received the news with a sudden welling of tears, but they were of relief – and of guilt. If he had not gone home, Gavin would still be alive.

In a manner of speaking.

And there was the rub. She'd hated the consultant

for making a decision she would never have been able to make herself. She still had sleepless nights about it. Nights when she would sit up in bed and read trashy novels by the dim circle of a booklight, to avoid waking Roger.

The second murder – just last year – was more straightforward. An elderly woman, hospitalized after a massive stroke, who was being kept alive by means of a ventilator.

Her large, sweet-natured family had trooped in and out of the ward twice a day to suffer the slow, heartbreaking erosion of everything they had loved, while the nurses struggled to keep her alive when it was plain she would be better off dead.

Once more, it was left to a doctor to make the decision – this time a young man only recently qualified, but with a kind heart and a caring way with people.

On the fifth night of their vigil, he had suggested that the family might like to take a break in the coffee shop downstairs.

'You're exhausted,' he said. 'It's important that *you* remain strong.'

They had been reluctant, but had finally nodded and left.

'You look as if you could do with a coffee too, Jean.'

'Oh, I'm fine,' she'd smiled.

'*I'm* not,' he'd said. 'I'd love one. Would you mind? I'll hold the fort here.'

He'd insisted on giving her two pounds, and she'd left. It was only when she'd been halfway down in the lift that she'd wondered why he hadn't simply asked one of the family to bring him a coffee.

Jean had returned to the ward just as he'd switched the ventilator back on.

Her heart had jumped so hard that she'd slopped the coffee on her hand. She'd heard of this before but never seen it – this kind of simple, final intervention that was undoubtedly in the best interests of the patient, and just as undoubtedly murder.

In a manner of speaking.

Jean had swallowed her heart and her shout, and backed away from the door of the ward. With shaking hands, she'd mopped up the spilled coffee and wiped down the half-full cup. Then, in a moment that would define her for ever, she'd re-entered and handed it to the doctor, along with his two pounds.

'Mrs Loddon has passed away,' he'd said, and Jean had noticed that he was holding the old lady's hand.

'Oh dear,' she'd replied. And then, 'Shall I go and get her family?'

'No. Let them have their break.'

Jean had nodded and they had sat there together in silence in the semi-darkness until Mrs Loddon's family had come back, refreshed.

There had been deaths since then, but deaths were expected on a ward like this, where patients prevaricated between living and dying, and frequently did one or the other against medical expectation.

Jean had not seen anything she could call murder since – but then, she no longer looked too hard. When Mr Attridge died last March she was relieved enough for all of them not to question it. When Mr Galen died just a few months later it had been more unexpected, but the pneumonia had not cleared entirely from his lungs, and it might only have taken some panic over a bit of phlegm to cause the heart attack that had killed him.

At the end of the day, it was almost always a merciful release for patient *and* family, and that sense pervaded all who worked on the neurological ward.

So, after all the good and bad she had seen, Tracy Evans was nothing to Jean. Her type had come and quickly gone over the years. Only the really good ones stayed. Angie had been here for three years, but Monica would be gone by summer, Jean would bet her housekeeping on it.

The only sad thing about Tracy leaving was that Mr Deal's visits became shorter and less frequent. Jean had no indication of whether Mrs Deal had ever been aware of her husband's presence, but the idea that she might suddenly be aware of his absence pained her. She tried her best to spend a little more quality time with Mrs Deal, telling her world news and ward gossip, but knew Angie was picking up her slack on meds and bedpans, and finally just had to give up and suffer the guilt.

Then, five months after Tracy had left, Jean made a last-ditch effort on behalf of Mrs Deal. She put an index card on the noticeboard: WANTED: KIND, RELIABLE PERSON TO READ TO PATIENT.

She then brought in three books from home, put them on Mrs Deal's nightstand, and hoped for another miracle.

Meg saw the notice after finishing her ward rounds for the day. The rounds were exhausting and exhilarating all at the same time. Especially the current placement – paediatrics. Meg had always wanted to be a paediatrician, but now wondered whether she might change her mind. Children – even sick ones – were such hard work. Every task had to be made entertaining, or painless, or explained in such a way that a screaming youngster would allow her access to his broken arm or her sore tummy.

Today – after being kicked repeatedly by a five-year-old boy with appendicitis – Meg had even considered switching to veterinary science, where the patients could be tethered, muzzled and caged.

She stopped at the noticeboard on her way out. It had become a habit that had started when she was looking for a bicycle. Watching Patrick Fort swing his leg over the bar of his shining blue bike had reminded her of how much fun it was to get somewhere fast and glowing with blood, with the wind in your hair.

She never did see a bike on the noticeboard, but instead became addicted to the randomness of the messages there.

Kittens free to good homes, only boys left.

Lift offered daily from Newport. Share petrol and wine gums.

Come whitewater rafting in Scotland! Under which some wag had scribbled 'indoors if wet'.

Kind, reliable person . . .

The words caught Meg's eye. She felt herself to be kind. She felt herself to be reliable. She read on.

Meg loved reading. The thought of someone not being able to read for themselves was horrible. The poor patient. But she had so much to do! Everybody knew that med students didn't have time for anything but studying. There were hospital placements and the mountains of books, and she only allowed herself two nights a week away from her work as it was. Fridays and Saturdays, when she went to the pub or the cinema with her housemates, or to the occasional party. But she was entitled to *some* time for fun, wasn't she? She was only twenty years old, for God's sake!

Meg walked away from the board, feeling defensive without ever having come under attack.

She stopped suddenly as she remembered that the dissection would soon be finished. There was barely anything left of poor Bill to be sliced and diced now, and soon he'd be off to the crematorium or the cemetery. That would clear two days a week for the rest of the term. She had planned to devote one to further study and the other to relaxation. TV, sleeping, reading; stuff like that. She'd determined to work her way through great literature she'd been told she should read. She already had *Our Mutual Friend* and something by James Joyce on her shelf, threatening to remain unopened for ever.

Would it really make any difference if she read them out loud – to someone who might be desperate to hear them?

Meg went back to the board and took down Jean's number.

31

The dirty blue-and-white trainer sat on the polished desk like a trophy.

'This is very serious,' Professor Madoc said and Patrick laughed because he thought that was funny, but nobody else did. Not Mick *or* Dr Spicer.

Patrick looked at the faces of the three men and tried to guess what they were feeling. He guessed at angry and thought he was getting better at this. He was certainly getting lots of practice.

Now Professor Madoc pointed at the trainer. 'This *is* yours, isn't it?'

'Yes,' said Patrick. 'Can I have it back?' He was wearing Jackson's trainers and they were killing him.

'So you admit you were in the dissection room last night?'

'Yes,' said Patrick again. 'Can I have it back?'

Nobody said he couldn't, so he took the shoe off the desk and held it in his lap.

'I'm glad you admit it, Patrick, because we also have the record of your code being used to gain access.'

Patrick didn't answer pointless statements. He'd already said he was there, hadn't he?

'You threw your shoe at Mr Jarvis.'

'Who's Mr Jarvis?'

'I am,' said Mick.

'No,' said Patrick. 'I threw it *over* him.'

'Why?'

'I didn't want to be locked in.'

'Wouldn't it have been easier to simply let him know you were there?'

Patrick said nothing. Technically the answer was *yes*, but he had no words to explain why that hadn't happened. No words for the clamminess of his skin or the shallowness of his breath. Those things didn't seem logical now; only foolish – like not having had sex yet.

But you had to get so close!

'What was *he* doing there, anyway?' Patrick said.

'Not that it's any of your business, Patrick, but Mr Jarvis frequently works unsociable hours in the embalming room. When he came upstairs and found the dissection room lights on, he became suspicious.'

'But why switch them off?' asked Patrick.

'Because it gives me the advantage over an intruder,' said Mick. 'I know that room like the back of my hand. Doesn't make any difference to me whether the lights are on or off.'

'But if you'd left them on, you'd have seen me.'

'Maybe. Maybe not.'

'Yes, you would have,' said Patrick enthusiastically, 'because I was right under your nose.'

Dr Spicer made a little noise that turned into a cough, and Professor Madoc frowned at him, and looked back at Patrick.

'At our last meeting I told you that we could not overlook discreditable behaviour simply because of your other issues. Do you remember that, Patrick?'

'Of course I remember,' said Patrick testily. What kind of goldfish did the man think he was?

'Good,' said Professor Madoc. 'Because I'm afraid I'm going to have to ask you to leave.'

Patrick started to get up and then hesitated. 'You mean leave the room or leave the whole ... college thing?'

'The whole college thing.'

'Oh,' said Patrick.

He remained hovering over the seat of the chair. Now that this was actually happening, he found he *did* care about leaving. He was quite surprised by how much. He decided against getting up, and instead sat down more firmly. 'That's a poor decision,' he said.

'Oh, *really?*' said the professor, leaning back in his chair and steepling his fingers. Patrick also noticed that he went a little redder in the face.

'Yes, very. It's inconsistent. You said discreditable behaviour was inappropriate attitude to staff, a near-physical altercation with a fellow student over a cadaver, ignoring procedure during dissection, and unauthorized access to confidential donation details.'

Professor Madoc just looked at him with his mouth a little open, so Patrick patiently explained his point. 'You didn't say anything about throwing a shoe.'

'I'd have thought that was implicit!' snapped the professor.

'I don't think so.'

'It would have been to any normal person!'

'We're getting off the point,' Spicer interrupted smoothly. 'The point is, Patrick, that you entered a restricted area at night without permission.'

'Nobody said I needed permission,' Patrick said. 'I didn't break in; I got in using the code I was given by *you*. I was not trying to hide from anyone, which is why I turned on the lights. When someone turned them *off* it wasn't logical, so I *did* hide then. When I thought I might be locked in, I created a diversion and left. I didn't hurt anyone, I didn't damage anything, I didn't steal anything. I was there to try to establish the cause of death, which is what we were told to do by Dr Spicer, and which I strongly suspect has been incorrectly recorded as heart failure, when in fact it is anaphylactic shock caused by the ingestion of a peanut.'

Patrick ran out of breath. His heart pumped and his jaw ached from saying so many words. The three men were staring at him so intently that it made him squirm, so he looked around the room for relief. He noticed that the Rubik's cube was on the bookshelf, and that Professor Madoc had messed it up again. Even from here, he could see where he'd gone wrong.

'A peanut,' said the professor.

Dr Spicer spoke slowly. 'There was a peanut in the cadaver's throat, but it bore no relation to the cause of death.' He looked at Mick, who nodded his own confirmation.

'You *were* told,' Mick said.

'*Scott* was told. I'm not Scott.'

The silence around him resumed, and went on for some time, and Patrick felt himself growing calm once again. The three men exchanged looks and he was grateful that at last they were taking him seriously. Now that they realized the importance of the peanut, and why it was critical that he find it, everything would be all right.

Instead Professor Madoc sighed and said, 'Nevertheless' – and then expelled him on the spot.

Patrick left the oak-panelled office in a tight ball of confused shock.

He couldn't believe what had just happened. Instead of doing the thing that made sense, Professor Madoc had expelled him! It was turning out the lights all over again. For a full minute he stood in the centre of the corridor, holding his trainer to his chest, as other students bumped and brushed past him. He didn't even feel them.

Then he started to walk briskly to the end of the corridor. By the time he reached the stairs, he was running.

They were behind him. Not *right* behind him. But not in front of him, *that* was the point.

It meant he had a head start.

Patrick felt the adrenaline coursing through him once more – just as it had when he'd climbed the fence. He'd never had it before meeting Number 19, but he recognized it now and liked it.

One last look at the cadaver – that was all he needed. But a look through more suspicious eyes; eyes that were seeking clues from the past, not to the future. He would go straight for the throat, where the peanut had been. That was the logical thing. The throat, the mouth, the tongue. He thought of the cuts and nicks that Dilip had made – that he'd *assumed* Dilip had made. That was where he would start. He would find something. More chunks of black blood, another scrap of blue latex. Another thrill passed through him. He didn't know what, but he would find *something*.

Still holding his trainer, Patrick ran past the porter at the entrance to the block – through the doors that were always open – and feverishly jabbed his code into the keypad on the anatomy wing door.

It didn't open.

Patrick rattled the handle, then put his code in again. 4017.

Nothing. 4017. 4017. 4017. Nothing, nothing, nothing.

Patrick banged the metal door so hard with the side of his fist that it rang.

'Oi!' said the porter, but Patrick didn't hear him. He kicked the door hard, not even feeling it in his toes.

The porter grabbed his arm and Patrick shook it off, struggling to keep calm. 'Don't touch me!' he said. 'You have to let me in. I need to get in.'

'No, you need to leave,' said the porter. Patrick had never seen him standing up before, but now realized that he was quite burly.

'I'm allowed to be here. I'm doing anatomy. I'm allowed to be in the dissection room.'

'Not today you're not, sunshine. Today you're going home to sleep it off.'

The porter took his arm more firmly this time, and Patrick punched him in the face. The man was well built, but he still staggered backwards like a drunk – and then sat down and rolled comically on to his back with his legs in the air.

Patrick left before they came down.

He ran straight to the police station; it was only down the road behind the museum and City Hall.

'I want to report a crime,' he told the desk officer, who sat behind the thick glass window as if she were selling train tickets.

'What kind of crime?'

'I'm not sure. It might be murder, but I can no longer gather evidence myself, so I think the police should get involved now.'

She said nothing, and looked at his hands. Patrick noticed a smear of blood on his left knuckles.

The porter's nose.

He quickly withdrew his hand from the counter and wiped it on his jeans. 'That has nothing to do with it,' he told her.

'What *has* it got to do with?' she said.

'Something irrelevant. Are you going to take my report or not?'

The young woman stared at his face so he had to blink and look away.

'Take a seat,' she said. 'An officer will be right with you.'

Patrick took a seat that faced the glass front wall of the foyer. The rain had left the air outside clear, the trees washed, and the pink gravel avenue sparkling in the February sunshine.

A police van pulled up at the kerb and an officer opened the back doors. Patrick expected to see a dog jump out, but instead a man did – the young man in a white tracksuit that Patrick had met in the park.

His sleeves were soaked to the elbows with blood.

Two policemen walked him up the wide steps to the foyer. His wrists were cuffed in front of him but he still had a casual bob to his gait and a faint smile on his face.

The trio came in and walked straight through to an inner door. One of the officers tapped in a code on the security pad. 1109; he made no attempt to conceal it. Patrick wondered whether the exit code was the same.

The young man, meanwhile, stared around the foyer and caught Patrick looking at him. He raised his chained, bloody hands as if pleading – or praying. 'I didn't do it,' he said.

'I doubt that,' said Patrick, and both policemen laughed, even though it wasn't meant to be a joke, and then ushered the young man through the door.

'What's your name?'

The desk officer was talking to Patrick, leaning forward, with one splayed hand against the glass.

He was suddenly wary. 'Why?'

'We can't file a report without a name,' she said.

Patrick was puzzled. He'd watched enough TV to know about anonymous tip-offs. Therefore the officer's words made no sense. Therefore they couldn't be true.

Therefore, thought Patrick, she was lying.

But *why?*

She'd looked at his knuckles. Patrick thought again of the porter's nose spreading under his fist. Blood on his knuckles, just as the young man in the white tracksuit had blood up his sleeves. And how the police had laughed when that young man had turned to Patrick and said *I didn't do it*. Even Patrick hadn't believed him. The guilt was there on his sleeves for all to see.

And the blood was there on his own knuckles.

Nobody had seen the porter grab hold of him first, or Mark Bennett punch him in the back, the day his father had died.

So instead of giving the officer his name, Patrick stood up and walked out.

She came after him, but he was already running, and by the time he stopped on the steps of the war memorial, Patrick had only his ghostly breath for company in the pale winter sunshine.

The rare ringing of the phone woke Sarah Fort for the second time in twelve hours. This time it was daylight – a stabbing glare that made her wince and hate the world.

At least she didn't have to get out of bed this time. This time she was already at the kitchen table, where a small puddle of spit marked her spot.

She snatched up the phone and said '*Hello!*' far too loudly, so she said it again more carefully. 'Hello?'

Silence. Someone was there; she could hear them breathing.

'Hello?' she said more forcefully.

Breathing.

'Are you going to say anything, pervert?'

The breathing stopped.

Sarah put the heel of her palm in her eye and held

it there to push the dull pain further back inside.

She hadn't felt this way for years. Years and years. Years when she'd had to be strong because it was just the two of them, and she'd had to do everything all by herself.

Wasted years now. It had been so easy to stop being strong that she couldn't believe she hadn't done it before. She looked down at her cream nightdress with the little blue flowers on it. She hadn't even got dressed before throwing herself off the wagon – apart from the boots, of course. It didn't matter; she had no one to get dressed *for*; no one who cared. Who would have her with a son like hers in the house? She should have done this years ago and saved herself the empty hopes.

She remembered she was on the phone and put it slowly back to her ear.

'Patrick?'

The line went dead.

Patrick stared at the receiver in his shiny blue hand and knew that he could not go home. His innards vibrated like a ribbon in a storm. It was ten years since he'd felt this way, but it felt like ten minutes.

It was like riding a bicycle: the sound of his mother when she was drunk.

32

In the over-mascara'd eyes of Tracy Evans, a written warning for leaving the nurses' station unattended on the night Mr Galen had died was a small price to pay.

Mr Deal had proved to be an adequate lover that night and on several subsequent occasions – and a more than adequate provider of gifts, whose worth grew in direct proportion to the sexual acts Tracy was willing to perform. She'd already had meals, a Burberry scarf and mid-priced trinkets, despite being uncharacteristically coy with her favours. There was no point in showing off all her wares at once, she reasoned; Mr Deal might be a once-in-a-lifetime cash cow and she was determined to milk him correctly. She would soon have her overdue rent paid, and they'd barely moved beyond the missionary position! Her grand plan was pregnancy – and a fiscal bond that would last a generation.

Plus, there was something about Mr Deal that she couldn't quite put her finger on. Despite their short, frenzied couplings, he remained quite aloof. He was pleasant but not fawning; his gifts were given casually and without sentiment. He took her to restaurants with tablecloths, and sent back the wine. He didn't call her and rarely answered his phone, even though she knew he had caller ID. In short, there was nothing of the puppy in Mr Deal – nothing of the doormat – and Tracy found herself thinking of him at odd moments, even when she *didn't* need twenty quid for the gas.

All in all, it was working out even better than she had imagined.

Of course, Tracy was *sorry* that Mr Galen had died. He hadn't been a bad coma patient – no worse than any other – and his wife had been OK, despite the bacon-frying. If she'd heard the alarm that had accompanied his demise then Tracy would almost certainly have responded. It had simply been Mr Galen's bad luck to go into cardiac arrest just as she was suffering her own little death astride Mr Deal in the ladies' loo, behind a sign that read – aptly – OUT OF ORDER.

She'd explained her absence that night by saying she had a pelvic inflammation which required frequent toilet breaks. Her explanation was accepted and, ironically, proved to be true a few days after the sealing of Mr Deal's fate.

Jean and Angie were disapproving. They said

nothing to her face, but *everything* behind her back. Monica, on the other hand, was a staunch supporter of anyone who covered for her fag breaks, and nodded vigorously when Tracy told her, 'They're just jealous.'

Tracy honestly believed this to be true. Jean was a dried-up old martyr, whose pot-bellied husband wore a moustache with bits in it, and Angie had snagged herself a junior doctor and a ring, but was still empty-ing bedpans – so obviously didn't understand the rules of engagement in the war of the sexes.

In August, a month after Mr Galen's death, Tracy transferred to the geriatric ward, where people dying was even less unexpected than on neurological, and where few of them could reach the buzzer – or even remember that they *had* a buzzer.

Monica gave her a tiny white teddy bear holding a big red heart that said 'We'll all miss you'.

But Jean and Angie didn't even say goodbye.

33

This was only her second time, but already Meg wondered how much longer she could read to Mrs Deal.

She was normally a fluent reader, but here she was too aware of her mute listener, too distracted by the still horror of the situation to give her all to a book – even when it was *The Da Vinci Code*, which she'd found beside Mrs Deal's bed and which had sucked her in so fast that she'd abandoned any pretence she'd ever had of tackling *Ulysses*. She would be going along just fine, then Mrs Deal's finger would twitch and she would have to re-read a sentence three times until it made sense. Or she would turn a page and a machine would gurgle – then would wonder if she'd skipped a page, so would go back and start again – only to realize three-quarters of the way down that she was indeed repeating herself.

Meg stumbled over the prose for the umpteenth time, and saw Mrs Deal's hand judder in apparent response. Was that how coma victims expressed annoyance? By flicking a finger and hoping that everyone understood how pissed off they were?

The finger flicked again. It drubbed a little, then stopped.

Meg sighed. Jean had warned her about imagining communication where none existed. There was no understanding in Mrs Deal, she said; no control.

Meg looked at Mrs Deal's face. She wondered whether she'd been pretty once. It was hard to tell now; she was so ashen and thin, and the bottom half of her face was covered by the thick white plastic of the ventilator that kept her breathing. Sometimes her eyes opened and they were a pretty hazel colour, but mostly they were closed or showed only slim crescents of white, like now.

'Are you OK, Mrs Deal?' said Meg, and stroked her hand. Under her palm, the finger twitched again several times, then stopped.

It gave Meg the creeps. What was going on inside Mrs Deal's head and fingers? Was the twitching a desperate attempt to communicate? Or just the sputtering leftovers from a failed electrical system?

She picked up the woman's loose hand.

'I could do your nails. Would you like that, Mrs Deal?'

The finger stayed still.

'Would you like pink?'

The finger stayed still.

'Or red? Go for the vamp look.'

The finger stayed still.

Meg sighed and placed Mrs Deal's hand gently back on the pale-yellow cover. Immediately the finger juddered again, then stopped.

Meg frowned. 'Can you do that again, Mrs Deal?'

She did it again.

'Can you give one tap for yes, two for no?'

Meg held her breath. Mrs Deal's finger started to tap, but kept going – five, six, seven, *eight* times, and Meg picked up the book again. She wondered whether she was just wasting her time. For the first time, she realized that her actions were not entirely altruistic. Deep down, she had hoped that reading to a coma victim would spark a recovery for which *she* would be responsible. It was humiliating to confess such a motive – even to herself. She was a kind person, sure, but was she also a glory-seeker? A show-off? Meg didn't like the new light by which she found herself examined. It was not modest or selfless and it made her ashamed.

Chastened, she found her place again and resumed reading. From the corner of her eye, she saw Mrs Deal's finger tapping and stopping, tapping and stopping.

Angie came over to check one of the machines beside Mrs Deal's bed, and smiled at Meg.

'Why does she do that?' asked Meg, nodding at Mrs Deal's juddering finger.

'It's just something that happens – a patient twitches or speaks, or opens their eyes, even when completely unconscious.'

Meg nodded slowly.

'Does it bother you?' asked Angie.

'A bit.'

The nurse smiled sympathetically. 'I know it's upsetting at first, but after a few weeks you won't even notice it.'

She smiled a goodbye and moved on to the next bed.

A few weeks!

With a sour ball of dread in the pit of her stomach, Meg stared slowly around the ward, at the bedridden lumps that had once been real people.

The idea of this clammy vigil becoming part of her future for weeks or months to come sent a shiver down her spine.

34

Tea was a curious time.

Kim made toast for herself and for Lexi, who wore the kimono. Patrick hoped that that meant she was Kim's guest now, not his. Everything had gone so horribly wrong all at the same time, and he had neither the time nor the inclination to make cheese sandwiches or to sleep on the floor.

The three of them sat in the front room and watched some bright, noisy show with glove puppets and a robot, while in the kitchen Jackson slammed the cupboard doors. Patrick flinched at every bang.

'Jesus Christ.' Kim rolled her eyes and yelled, 'Could you make any more noise in there?'

'Sure!' he yelled back and threw what sounded like cutlery into the sink.

'Child,' muttered Kim, and ate her toast.

'Where did *you* go last night?' Lexi asked Patrick.

She had her feet tucked up beside her on the couch and Patrick noticed that the kimono – although a better fit on her than it had been on Pete – still showed an awful lot of thigh.

'Out,' he said.

'Out where?'

'He won't tell you,' said Kim. 'Patrick likes secrets, don't you, Patrick?'

Kim was an idiot. Patrick didn't like secrets at all – especially today. The thought of never knowing the secret of Number 19 made him want to kick the TV.

'Ooh, I love secrets!' said Lexi. 'I want to know. Tell me!'

He didn't tell her. Let her find her own secrets at the bottom of a bottle. Someone – probably Scott – would stumble on 'heart failure' and claim they'd established cause of death, and then probably win the Goldman Prize for best student, when it should have been *his*. He hadn't found his answers. His quest had failed, and without it he was lost.

More than lost.

Emptied of hope.

From the corner of his eye he could see Lexi crane her neck to try to make him look at her. 'Tell me,' she sang. 'Tell me tell me tell me tell me tell me . . .'

Kim tutted. 'He won't; he's such a killjoy.'

'Nah,' said Lexi. 'He's just playing hard to get.'

'He's playing it very well,' said Kim and they both

shrieked with laughter, showing soggy toast in their mouths, like washing in a machine.

Patrick glared at the robot on the TV. It was trying to take a cake out of a cardboard oven, but it kept crushing the sponge with its metal fingers. The glove puppets were giggling and pointing, but the robot didn't understand what it was doing wrong, or why the cake kept crumbling through its hands.

Like meat crumbs falling out of the flesh-cake that was Number 19.

'I went to see your dead father,' Patrick said.

Kim giggled, but Lexi stopped laughing and said, 'What?'

'Last night, I went to see your dead father. That's my secret. We've been cutting him up for months. He's all in little bags now.'

'That's sick!' said Kim, and giggled uncertainly.

'What?' said Lexi again. Her face had become ashen, and the toast she held in her hand had flopped sideways on to her bare knee and stuck there, Marmite side down. Patrick had the sudden, uncomfortable notion that being knocked unconscious off a swing with a broken nose was nothing compared to the shock drawn so nakedly on Lexi's face that even *he* could read it.

'What do you mean?' she said through trembling lips.

'You wanted to know.' He shrugged, somehow wanting to make it *her* fault. He picked up a magazine from the arm of the chair. *Art Forum*.

Lexi turned to Kim. 'What does he *mean*?'

'Nothing,' she said uneasily. 'I mean, he's a med student, but . . . Nothing, I think.'

'What do you *mean*?' said Lexi again. 'What the fuck do you *mean*?'

Patrick didn't look at her and wished that she would stop looking at him. He wished now that he hadn't said it, but the glove puppets were so cruel! Why not just *help* the robot? Why did they have to laugh?

He threw *Art Forum* at the TV and walked out.

He was at the foot of the stairs when he heard Lexi coming, making a noise like a cat in a bag being thrown from a train. He turned and she slapped his face so hard that he fell backwards on to the stairs. She didn't stop. She was a crazy animal flailing on top of him, slapping, scratching, gouging – and all the time howling with rage and profanity, while Kim screamed '*Jackson! Jackson!*' over and over again.

Patrick covered his head and drew up his knees. He planted a foot in Lexi's stomach and shoved her away from him. She crashed backwards into the front door, then curled into a ball and started to cry in huge, open-mouthed gasps.

'Jesus Christ,' said Kim. 'Jesus *Christ*.'

'What the *fuck* is going on?' said Jackson, running from the kitchen.

'I don't know,' said Kim, and started to sob too. Jackson put an arm around her and she turned into him, pressing her toast into his shoulder.

Patrick sat up slowly and touched his nose; there was blood on his fingers and his heart was beating so hard he could see the pulse twitching under the skin of his thumb.

This felt bad. *He* felt bad, although it brought him no satisfaction to recognize it. He frowned at Lexi, hugging herself on the dirty hall carpet, and – out of nowhere – thought of his mother the night the policemen had taken him home and made him beans on toast. Wailing on the floor.

The two things felt connected but he didn't understand why.

Why? That was the question. That was *always* the question, and always would be unless he took control and solved the puzzle.

To find out why somebody died, you have to consult the living.

Professor Madoc's words came back to him unbidden, and cleared his head in an instant. He got up and went over and squatted down beside Lexi.

'Just leave her!' said Jackson, and Kim echoed him. 'Leave her alone, Patrick!'

But he didn't leave her. He needed her.

And maybe she needed him.

He didn't know how to start, so he started awkwardly. 'My father's dead, too.'

'Good!' yelled Lexi, and a string of snot swung from her nose and attached itself to the carpet like an escape rope.

'He was hit by a car,' Patrick continued.

'Good,' said Lexi again, but with a lot less feeling.

'I don't know what happened to him or why,' said Patrick. 'I've tried, but I just can't understand it. But *your* father—'

He stopped to think.

Slowly Lexi sat back on her heels to look at him, her arms clamped around her midriff and her face streaked with black tears and silver snot.

'What? What about him?'

Patrick closed his eyes. He rarely spoke without knowing what he was going to say, but here he'd set off without a map, unsure of the footing ahead, or of where he might be heading. He had no evidence. He had no expertise. He had nothing but a missing peanut and the strangest feeling in his gut that was so strong he couldn't ignore it, despite its lack of logic.

'What *about* my father?' Lexi insisted.

Patrick opened his eyes and they were all staring at him, so he looked away from them and at the grubby woodchip wallpaper before he could speak again.

'I think *your* father was murdered.'

35

'I'm pregnant,' said Tracy Evans.

Her reflection looked perturbed by the news.

'We're going to have a baby,' she tried again, and flashed her teeth, but it wasn't the same as smiling.

Her face was getting round. She turned sideways and stood on tiptoes so she could see her stomach in the bathroom mirror. She stroked the gentle swelling there, frowning at her reflected hands. Even though it had been nearly four months since she'd peed on a stick, it was hard to believe there was a baby inside her. A tiny stowaway, riding her belly, stealing her food and pumping her blood . . . Even harder to imagine that whatever was growing inside her now was going to come out of her some time next June, come hell or high water . . .

Frightening.

Tracy chewed her lip.

She hoped Mr Deal would be happy. Raymond. His name was Raymond, but she couldn't get used to it. Raymond, not Ray – he was quite firm about that – but the name rarely came easily to her lips, and never to her mind when she thought of him.

Which was often. Too often – she recognized that, but she couldn't help it. She wasn't sure why it was; she only knew she had never felt this way about any of the over-eager youths she'd slept with before, but – strangely – now felt no desire to sleep with again.

She saw Mr Deal three nights a week. He picked her up from work and took her to his home. Sometimes she stayed over. The house was like something from a magazine – white and spotless, with real art on the walls, where you could see actual brush marks if you cocked your head in the right light.

There was a steep spiral staircase and a bidet in the bathroom. On her first visit it had given her the opportunity to ask about whether they had children.

'Why would you say that?' Mr Deal had frowned.

'Because there's a kiddy's toilet,' said Tracy, and Mr Deal had laughed at her on and off for the rest of the evening. When Tracy had pressed him to explain how it worked, he'd told her to Google it.

Then they'd had sex. As usual.

Tracy looked into the mirror now and wondered when it was that she'd stopped thinking that an evening without a quick shag was an evening wasted. Now there were moments – just moments, mind you –

when she took just as much pleasure in watching him eat food she had cooked, or smelling the side of his throat when they embraced. He didn't use aftershave but he used coal tar soap, which reminded her that sometimes childhood had not been such a bad place to be.

On the four nights she didn't see Mr Deal, she had no idea what he did. When she asked he just said, 'Nothing much.' Those were nights when Tracy had started to wonder, and to worry. Men were very easily led, and she didn't want some slut luring Mr Deal away from her . . .

She'd begun checking his phone and his laundry when he was out of the room.

She'd stopped taking the pill at the end of August.

And *this* was the consequence.

Tracy stroked her belly again. She would have to work faster than she'd initially planned.

But she thought that if Mr Deal felt the same way about her as she might be starting to feel about him, then everything would be just fine.

36

'I don't want to go in.'

Lexi stalled at the bottom of the driveway of the house on Penylan Road.

'OK,' said Patrick, and started up the gravel by himself.

'Wait!'

He turned.

'Are you going in anyway?'

'Yes.' Of course he was. Why would he *not*? It was what they'd come here for, wasn't it?

'Well, what am I going to do?'

'I don't know. What?'

'I don't know.'

Then why was she asking him? Patrick shook his head in confusion. 'OK,' he said again, and carried on to the front door. By the time he lifted the heavy brass knocker shaped like a lion, Lexi was beside him again, biting her lip nervously.

'How do I look?' she said suddenly.

Patrick looked her up and down, then shrugged. '*I* don't know.'

She glared, but it was wasted on him.

The door was opened by a dumpy woman in jeans and a big cardigan.

'Alex,' the woman said warily.

'Hello,' said Patrick firmly. He had prepared his opening lines and didn't want to be diverted. 'I need information about Mr Galen. Can I come in?'

The woman looked at Lexi. 'Are you going to cause trouble?'

'No,' said Patrick.

'I was talking to Alexandra.'

'Who's Alexandra?'

'She is.'

Lexi crossed her arms and fidgeted, and Patrick leaned away from her to avoid accidental contact.

Lexi finally said, 'No,' and the woman opened the door and let them both in.

The house was about ten times bigger than any house Patrick had ever been in.

The dumpy woman looked at him and said, 'I'm Jackie.'

'I know,' said Patrick. 'Your ceilings are very high.'

'Yes, they are,' she agreed with a strange look.

She led them into the front room, and an old

mongrel hauled itself off the rug in front of the blazing fire and gave a token bark.

'Ssh, Willow. Friends.'

Willow wagged apologetically and came over to lick Patrick's hand.

Patrick smoothed the dog's head. 'Soft,' he said.

Jackie smiled and pointed to the couch. 'Have a seat.'

Patrick sat down, but Lexi didn't. Instead she wandered around the room, looking at things as if taking an inventory.

The room was like something from a magazine. *Art Forum* or something else. It had decorated ceilings and pale-pink walls, and a big white fireplace.

On the mantelpiece was a photograph of Jackie and a man with a snowy mountain and blue sky behind them. The man was smiling with teeth Patrick knew very well. It was Number 19, on holiday.

Patrick tried to imagine him in this room now, but couldn't make him alive. Every time he tried, a cadaver clicked bonily into the room on zombie legs, or lolled, stiff and orange, on the couch, leaking fluids on to the chocolate leather.

'How are you, Alex?'

Lexi shrugged.

'You look well.'

'What's that supposed to mean?'

'Nothing.'

'Yeah, right,' said Lexi.

'Are you going to introduce us?'

Lexi shrugged again, but said, 'This is Patrick.'

'How do you do?' said Jackie.

'Do what?' he said.

'Excuse me?'

'Ignore him,' said Lexi. 'He's . . . you know.' And she made her fingers whirl around the side of her head.

'Oh,' said Jackie. 'Well, I'm glad you came, Alex.'

'Are you?'

Jackie flinched and Patrick noticed that Lexi had picked up a small china ornament – a shiny stag on a knoll of purple heather. He also noticed that the French windows at the back of the house had a pane of cardboard where the glass had been broken. It looked uglier from the inside than it had from the garden. He wished now that he hadn't handed Lexi the stone. He didn't know why she had done it; Jackie seemed nice – not what he'd expected. Somehow he'd thought she'd be wearing leopardskin.

'How have you been?' Jackie asked.

'I've been poor,' said Lexi.

Jackie's lips went tight and Lexi pointed the stag at Patrick. 'He thinks my dad was murdered.'

'*What?*' said Jackie.

'He said he needs to insult the living.'

'*Con*sult,' said Patrick. 'To find out why somebody died, you have to consult the living.'

Jackie stared at them both, apparently lost.

'You're the living,' he explained to her. 'I'm consulting *you*.'

'What's this all about murder?' she said. 'Your father died because of a car crash, Alex. His car skidded on ice. You know that. You came to the hospital.'

'But they said he was getting better. Then he just died.'

'He got pneumonia and that led to heart failure. You'd know that, too, if you'd been there, like I was, twice a day, every day for months. He was so *vulnerable*.'

'That's not what Patrick says.'

'I don't give a *shit* what Patrick says! He wasn't there. Who the hell is Patrick, anyway? Why is he here?' Jackie turned to him now; her voice got louder and her throat was going red.

Patrick guessed she was definitely upset about something.

'Tell her, Patrick.'

'Yes, *tell* me, Patrick!'

Patrick said, 'Can you stop shouting? I can't think while you're both shouting.'

'Oh, for God's sake!' snapped Lexi. 'Patrick found a peanut in Dad's throat.'

'*What?*'

'There was a peanut in his throat. We're allergic to peanuts.'

'I know that.'

'I *know* you do.'

'What's *that* supposed to mean?'

Lexi shrugged balefully.

Jackie looked at Patrick. 'How did he—'

'He's a medical student—'

'Anatomy,' Patrick corrected her.

'Whatever. He found a peanut during the . . . thing.'

'Dissection.'

'Yeah, during that. Patrick says that's what killed him, not *pneumonia*.'

'*Could* have killed him,' said Patrick, but she ignored him and stood over Jackie.

'I didn't even know he'd left his body to science or whatever the fuck it is they do. Is that even *true*?'

Jackie nodded silently.

'How could you let them just . . . cut Daddy up?' Lexi's voice broke.

'Why are you shaking?' Patrick said. She didn't answer.

Jackie stood up, but didn't go anywhere. She crossed her arms, then uncrossed them, then crossed them again. She bit her lip and Patrick saw her eyes go shiny.

'It was *his* choice, Alex. He made it years before we met. I could only respect it.'

'Did you give him the peanut too?'

'Of course not! Don't be disgusting! Nobody did; he was being fed through a tube.'

'I don't know,' said Lexi. 'Maybe you got sick of visiting him *twice a day, every day*.'

'Yes, I got sick of it! I won't lie. It was horrific. Someone you love gurgling and crying and wearing a *nappy*. The *smell* in that place! I held his hand and stroked his hair and chose his favourite music and he never even knew who I was! I spent two hours a night with him and another two crying in the car park. I cared about Sam every second he was alive, which is more than *you* can say!'

'You fucking *cow*!' Lexi hurled the deer against the pink wall. It burst into white shards that rained down on the dog, which leaped to its feet and started to bark.

'Get out!' said Jackie.

'*You*'re the one who should be getting out! This is my dad's house! *You*'re the fucking gold-digger keeping everything for yourself!'

Patrick felt they were getting off the point. 'What about the peanut?' he said, but nobody seemed to hear him.

'Is that what this is really about?' said Jackie. 'The money? Because you're wrong. We bought this house with *our* money.'

'And what about *my* money? I would have had it by now if it wasn't for you!'

'And you would have drunk it, too!' yelled Jackie. 'Sam knew that! We both did!'

'That's none of your business!' Lexi screamed at her.

'You're hurting my ears,' said Patrick, which was true. He covered them with his elbows.

Jackie ignored him. 'How is it none of my business? You did nothing but make him miserable. Running about God knows where, drinking God knows what, sleeping with God knows who.'

'It's *my* life,' yelled Lexi.

'You were fourteen! That made it his life, too.'

'Bollocks. He never cared.'

'He *always* cared.'

'He cared before *you* came along. *That*'s when everything went to shit.'

'I'm sorry your mother died, Alex, but don't you dare blame me for something that happened before we even met! Our door was *always* open for you. It's not my fault if you were too blind drunk to find it.'

Patrick stood up. 'You're too noisy,' he said. 'I'm going.'

Nobody noticed. He left the room and Willow followed him gratefully to the door.

He heard them yelling at each other all the way down the driveway.

When Patrick got home, Jackson and Kim were sitting together on the couch, watching *Grand Designs*.

'Where's Lexi?' asked Kim.

'With her stepmother.' He couldn't be bothered to go into details.

'Hey,' said Jackson, 'have you been wearing my shoes?'

'Yes,' said Patrick. 'But they're too small.'

'Not for *me*, they're not!'

Kim said, 'Did you find out who murdered Lexi's dad?'

'Not yet,' he said, and went upstairs.

He sat at the window with *Netter's Concise Neuroanatomy* open in front of him and watched the Valleys Line trains pass through the darkness in short, illuminated worms. He wondered whether Lexi and Jackie were still shouting at each other over the dog's cowed head. Shouting about love and money, when death was all that really mattered.

Finally, at around midnight, Patrick curled up on his bed. Tomorrow he would have to come up with another way to find out what happened to Number 19.

Consulting the living was a big fat waste of time.

37

It had been almost a week, but everyone was still talking about Patrick punching the porter.

'Remember that time he punched me?' said Scott, with the point of his scalpel in Bill's cerebellum.

'He didn't *punch* you,' said Rob.

Dr Spicer said, 'Watch what you're doing there, Dilip; you're going to sever the artery.'

Scott shrugged. 'All I'm saying is he's the violent type.'

'He's not,' said Meg. 'The porter grabbed him first, apparently, so that's why he couldn't press charges. It was self-defence.'

'It wasn't self-defence that time he punched me.'

Rob sighed. 'He didn't *punch* you, he *deflected* you. Stop making such a bloody meal out of it.'

Scott sulkily wiggled the scalpel back and forth in

the grey matter. 'He should be in prison, not here with normal people.'

'Very compassionate,' said Rob. 'Remind me never to get the flu around *you*.'

'Or a boob job,' said Spicer.

'Has anyone seen him?' asked Meg.

'Patrick?' said Dilip. 'No.'

'I hope he's OK,' said Meg.

'Whatever,' said Dilip, then sighed. 'I'm glad we're almost finished with the dissection; I have never seen such a boring brain.'

Meg wondered idly what Patrick's brain would look like. She imagined thousands of convoluted little boxes with locks and labels on them, and smiled to herself.

'What's so funny?' said Rob.

'Nothing. Just thinking.'

'How's the reading going?'

'OK, I suppose. I think she likes it.'

'How can you tell?'

'I can't really. Sometimes her hand twitches, but . . .' She ended the sentence on a shrug.

'What's this?' asked Spicer, so Meg explained about Mrs Deal.

'If she's aware of anything at all,' Spicer said, 'it must be the highlight of her week.'

'Do you think they *are* aware of what's going on around them?'

'I'm sure some are,' he said. 'But I'm not sure that's always a good thing.'

Meg nodded. She knew what he meant. They'd all done rounds in the neurological ward, shocked into silence by the horror of both the endless inertia of those who might never emerge, and the rage, pain and frustration of some who already had.

'What are you reading to her?' asked Dilip, bringing her back to the present.

Meg reddened slightly. 'Well, I did start *Ulysses*, but neither of us liked that, so now we're on some rubbish that I found on her bedside table.' She didn't tell them that it was *The Da Vinci Code*, or that she could hardly bear to put the book down between sessions, even if it did make her feel intellectually dirty.

She also didn't tell them that when the book was finished she hoped never to go back to the coma ward.

'I'm sure it's not easy,' said Dr Spicer, as if reading her mind. 'Good for you.'

'Shit,' said Dilip, 'I've gone through the artery.'

Talk of the devil, thought Meg. At the foot of the long ramp down to Park Place was Patrick.

'Hi,' she said. 'How are you?'

'I got expelled,' he said.

'I heard. For hitting the porter?'

'No, before that.' He then cut her off before she could ask a follow-up question. 'You have to do something for me.'

Meg arched a sarcastic eyebrow. 'Of course I do.'

'Good,' he said. 'You have to take photos of Number 19's mouth and oesophagus.'

Too late she realized her sarcasm had been wasted. 'I can't do that, Patrick. We're not allowed to take phones or cameras into the DR. You know that.'

'Then give me your code and I'll do it.'

'I can't do that either.'

'Why not?'

'Because then I'd be expelled too.'

'It's an emergency.'

'How can it be an emergency? Bill's already dead. You'll be asking me to do CPR next.'

'That would be stupid,' said Patrick. 'This is not.'

'Why?'

'Because I think he was murdered.'

'Who? Bill?'

'Yes.'

'*Murdered?*'

'Maybe.'

'I don't understand.'

'OK.' He shrugged.

'No, I mean, explain to me why you think that.'

'OK,' he said again. 'He was allergic to peanuts and was being fed through a tube, but he had a peanut in his throat when he died.'

'OK,' said Meg, nodding agreement.

'That makes no sense unless someone gave it to him,' said Patrick. 'Anaphylactic shock could have led to a heart attack, which is what's been listed as the cause of death, but that's just *how* he died, not *why*.'

Meg frowned at him. 'How do you know all this?'

'I found out his name and spoke to his daughter. She's inherited the nut allergy; that's what made me think of it. But when I went to look at the peanut, it had gone. Someone took it and *that* means they're hiding something. There's only one dissection class left – then the bodies will be taken away and then I'll never know what happened. That's why it's an emergency. That's why you have to help me.'

Meg stared at Patrick in amazement. 'You found out his *name*?'

'Yes. Samuel Galen.'

'And you spoke to his *daughter*?'

'Yes.' Patrick wondered if she was hard of hearing. 'How?'

'It's not important. I can't get in to do it. You have to help me.'

Meg was astonished into silence. *How* had he found out the cadaver's name? *How* had he spoken to the dead man's daughter? She shuddered at the thought of *that* social interaction. It all sounded crazy and, from anyone else, she would never have believed it. But Patrick was compelling. Not his words, but *him*. His usually blank expression was gone. He was flushed and alive. Even his eye contact was better as he begged her – in his own way – for help.

Looking at him, Meg felt her defences slipping. Still she stalled. 'What is it you're looking for?'

'There were cuts in the mucous membranes of the throat, remember?'

'Yes.'

'At the time I thought Dilip had made them because he's so poor with incisions. But now I think perhaps they were made ante-mortem.'

'So you think the person who took the peanut could be the same person who put it there in the first place?'

Patrick stared at her so intently that Meg mentally kicked herself for sounding keen and involved when she was loath to be either. She looked into his eyes and felt a little shiver – before she realized that he wasn't even seeing her. He was looking right *through* her to the solution on the other side.

'Maybe,' he said. His face split into the first smile she'd ever seen from him, and Meg knew with a sinking heart that she was about to do exactly what he asked. She made a last-ditch effort to get something out of it for herself.

'I'll do it on one condition.'

'OK,' he said.

'You have to go and read to Mrs Deal.'

'Who's Mrs Deal?'

'She's a woman in a coma. There's nothing to it.'

'What do I have to do?' he said warily.

'Only read to her.'

He frowned. 'Out loud?'

She smiled. 'If you want her to hear you, yes, you have to read out loud.'

'Read what?'

'A book.'

'Does it have to be a *long* book?'

It flitted through Meg's mind to say, 'It doesn't matter,' but then thought of poor Mrs Deal at the mercy of Patrick's choice of reading matter.

'It has to be over two hundred pages. It must be fiction and it must be popular. Off the bestseller lists or a classic. But it can't be about war or some boy-rubbish like that. Or sci-fi.'

'No war, no sci-fi.' Patrick nodded sombrely, and Meg realized she could give him specific instructions and he would carry them out with the precision of a computer. For a cruel second she almost demanded *Pride and Prejudice* from him, but pushed it aside with an inner giggle.

'If I do that, you'll take the photographs?'

'I will take the photographs.'

'OK then,' he said reluctantly.

'Do your best,' said Meg.

'I always do my best,' he said seriously.

She laughed and stuck her tongue out at him and he blinked.

38

'I'm pregnant,' said Tracy, and Mr Deal finished chewing a mouthful of steak, leaned back in his chair and looked at her.

Tracy felt her smile falter and worked at it harder, despite the shaking inside her.

Mr Deal – *Raymond* – was a meticulous man, who felt no need to gush or to pander. She found him hard to read, but she also knew that if she pushed, he would take even longer to give. It was annoying, but strangely exciting, too.

He cleared his throat and sipped his red wine. 'How far along are you?'

'Far enough.'

'Are you going to keep it?'

Of course I'm going to keep it! This is the plan!

'If that's OK with you?' she said carefully.

He cut another piece of steak. He ate his meat

270

blackened and bloodless. 'Of course,' he said. 'Are you sure?'

Why are you checking? she asked herself. *Why are you giving him another chance to say no?*

Mr Deal finished that mouthful, then dabbed his mouth with his napkin and leaned across the table to kiss her cheek. 'Of course I'm sure,' he said. 'It'll give us something to put on the kiddy toilet.'

Tracy felt a giddy rush. Suddenly she couldn't have stopped smiling if she'd tried.

They went to his bed after *Newsnight* and she did things to him she'd never done before. Not only because she thought she should, but because she *wanted* to.

Later – back at the house she still shared with less fortunate girls, she lay awake half the night with excitement. And when she went to work the next day, she was astonished to find that it did not seem quite so repulsive to wipe old Mr Cutler's pooey bottom, or so arduous to tip cold soup between Mrs Aldridge's drawstring lips.

Of course, she couldn't wait to give it all up and never work another day in her life, but in the meantime, it felt almost *rewarding*.

When a buzzer sounded just as a few of them had sat down with a cup of tea, Tracy surprised herself by bouncing up and saying, 'I'll get it.'

Sally, who was the voice of the ward, said, 'What's with *you* today? You in love or something?'

Yes, thought Tracy with a thrill at the realization. Somehow, somewhere, she had fallen in love with Mr Deal, and in the blink of an eye, everything had changed.

She had changed – and it felt wonderful.

39

It had taken Sarah an hour to find the matches. She didn't smoke and she didn't have a gas cooker and she didn't even know why she *had* matches, but she knew they were here *somewhere*, and got through most of the second bottle of Vladivar looking for them.

Now here she was, under the gibbous moon as frost formed on the roof of the Fiesta, trying to burn down the shed.

It was a lot harder than she'd expected it to be.

When she'd stumbled out into the frigid night air, she'd thought that a single match held close to the rotting timber would be enough to see the whole thing burst into flames.

Not so.

She'd gone through half the box, squatting beside the corner of the shed in her nightdress and wellingtons, turning slivers of pale wood into scorched twiglets. Once she'd dozed off, mid-arson, and burned her fingers.

She wove back to the house and got the letter, then came out and tried again, but striking the matches *and* holding the letter was close to impossible. Three things and only two hands. She swayed and cursed softly and dropped the box, then the letter, then the box again – before finally finding herself with the letter in one hand and a lighted match in the other, and bringing the two together.

The corner of the paper caught and for a moment Sarah could re-read it by an orange glow.

Dear Mrs Fort, I very much regret to inform you that I have had to ask Patrick to leave the School of Biosciences . . .

She squatted again and fed the paper under a splintered edge. The flame curled languidly around the wood, warming it slowly, as Professor Madoc's words turned into black flakes that floated upwards as if by magic.

'Come on. Come *on*,' she muttered and rested the side of her face against the rough planking. 'Come on, shed, you can do it.' She giggled and opened her eyes. '*Yes!*'

The orange tendrils were feeling their tentative way up first one panel, then the next.

She stood up and backed away. She shivered. She wasn't even wearing a coat. Or socks. Inside the rubber boots, her feet were numb.

The fire had a grip now. It found the vulnerable corner and clawed its way upwards.

Sarah released a long, emptying sigh. Why hadn't she done this years ago? All she'd needed was Dutch courage and half a box of matches.

The corner of the shed was properly alight. Crackling. It would not go out now. It started to throw out heat, and she enjoyed that until sparks spat at her and she took a wavering step backwards.

I very much regret . . .

Patrick would be coming home soon and they would have to start again. Almost from the beginning. All the progress halted. Maybe reversed. She was exhausted by it. Exhausted by *him*. She didn't want it. She wasn't sure what she *did* want, but she knew that forwards was better than backwards, even if the destination was unknown.

'Out of the way!'

Something pushed her aside and she stumbled to one knee, her palms in the gravel; the gravel in her palms.

An animal hiss made her look up to see that the dancing flames had been transformed into ugly grey smoke and cinders, which billowed across the gravel and made her cough.

Weird Nick turned towards her, water still spurting from the garden hose in his hand. 'I got here just in time,' he said, and stood, flushed and panting, waiting for his plaudits.

'Yes,' she said dully, and wobbled to her feet.

'What happened?' he asked.

'I don't know.'

'Oh,' he said.

He was Patrick's age but looked older, slightly chubby, and wearing the kind of tinted spectacles she always imagined perverts did.

Sarah brushed the grit from her hands and was suddenly very cold. She noticed his gaze drop briefly to her breasts and folded her arms across them.

'Well then,' said Weird Nick, gesturing with the hose so that it made an arc of broken silver droplets in the air. 'I'd better go and turn this off. We're on a meter.'

'Sorry,' she said. 'Thank you.'

'No problem,' he said. 'Any time.'

Any time my shed burns down. She only had two neighbours – Weird Nick and his mother; why did both of them have to be so bloody helpful?

'Night, Mrs Fort.'

She waved a vague hand and watched him follow the hose back towards his mother's house like a slim green umbilical cord.

She thought she might be sick. The smoke and the vodka and the disappointment.

Ollie was on the back step, barring her way so she couldn't fail to pet him. She stepped over him into the kitchen, and retched over the sink. Nothing came up. She laid her forehead on the cold steel of the draining board and cried a little, then went to bed.

When she got up the next morning, she left behind a ghost of grey ashes on the sheets.

40

From the corner of her eye, Meg watched Mrs Deal's finger drub mechanically on the bedspread.

'Can you *stop* that!' Meg said sharply, then added, '*Please*. It's driving me mad.'

Immediately she felt a rush of guilt. Mrs Deal's lashes did not flicker over her white crescent eyes. There was no forgiveness and no reproach. The finger paused – and then started again. Tap and stop, tap and stop.

Shit.

Meg closed the book.

'We'll go on next time, Mrs Deal. We're almost at the end. After that my friend Patrick's going to come and read a new book to you. I bet it will be nice for you to hear another voice. I don't know what he'll be reading, but I've told him no war and no sci-fi.'

She stood up and wound her scarf around her neck.

'Anyway, I'll bring him in and introduce you. And check on the book he's chosen in case it's crap. You know what men are like.'

She put the book back on the table and looked down at the thing that used to be Mrs Deal. She was only marginally better than dead. It was easy to imagine her as a cadaver in the dissection room. She would be more swollen, more orange, but essentially the same.

Apart from that finger.

Angie came in and smiled at Meg, then checked the drip on the young man in the next bed. His name was Robert and he was only twenty-five, but his hands were becoming claws, the wrists turning at weird angles and his short brown fingers pulling inwards, despite the efforts of the physiotherapist Meg had seen working on him. She never saw anyone else at his bedside, although there was a huge dusty leopard lying under it, so someone must have cared once.

'You're doing a great job,' said Angie, and came over.

'Am I?' said Meg. 'Sometimes it feels pointless.'

'Never,' said Angie firmly. 'It's never pointless. And Mrs Deal deserves it; she's such a good patient.' She leaned down and stroked the woman's brow.

'I imagine they all are,' said Meg, looking around.

'Oh, you'd be surprised!' said Angie, with a quick roll of her eyes. 'Some of them emerge stark staring crazy.' She held out her left hand to show a crooked finger. 'One of them broke that. It's still swollen.'

'Really?' said Meg in surprise, and looked around. 'Which one?'

'He died,' said Angie. Then she lowered her voice. 'I wasn't sorry.'

Meg said nothing. It seemed like a terrible thing for a nurse to say.

Angie read her face. 'I know it sounds awful, but Mr Attridge was in a shocking state. Really distressed. And he wasn't going to get much better. Sometimes dying is the easiest thing.'

Meg nodded slowly. 'I'd never thought of it like that.'

'Not Mrs Deal though,' said Angie brightly – and for her patient's ears. 'We love Mrs Deal and hope for the best, don't we, Mrs Deal?'

Mrs Deal's finger tapped mechanically.

Angie touched Meg's shoulder. 'Thanks for coming.'

When she'd gone, Meg sat down again, all bundled up. She took Mrs Deal's hand and stroked it. It was cold and so she sandwiched it between her own to warm it up a little.

'I'm so sorry I snapped at you,' she said. She sighed and then went on, almost to herself, 'I'm a bit stressed out at the moment. It's all Patrick's fault. He wants me to take pictures of something important. But I only got my camera for Christmas and I'm totally *shit* at photos.'

It was true. For every in-focus, in-frame photograph she'd lucked into over Christmas, there were two dozen that required immediate deletion. Two dozen shots of huge white faces, giant thumbs, the backs of heads and her own feet. How she was supposed to take clinically reliable close-ups of mucous membranes, precise enough to indicate whether the wounds might have been made post- or ante-mortem, she had no idea.

'And I have to take them in secret too,' she sighed. 'In a place where cameras aren't allowed. If I get caught, I could be expelled and my dad would go effing *bonkers*. So I'm sorry I was rude.'

Mrs Deal just lay there, and Meg blushed at the thought of telling the woman her puny problems, before leaving her here in her bed and rushing off to live her life.

She placed the hand gently back on the cover. Immediately the finger started twitching.

'I'll see you next week,' Meg said, and hurried away.

41

Patrick wasn't sure what to do with his time now that he had been expelled, so spent much of the following week pedalling slowly around the city. The glasshouse at Roath Park was a warm haven – dripping with tropical fronds – while outside the sunshine tried to break through the cloud cover of a Welsh spring. At the lake, he loaded his bike into a rowing boat and drifted slowly around the islands that were home to swans and ducks and old crisp packets. There were even hardy little red-eared terrapins that had survived being dumped after the Mutant Ninja craze, and which now basked on logs, surprising natives.

When it rained, Patrick went to the bookies. The third time he went, two horses died, but it happened away from the cameras. Patrick wrote them in his book anyway – Starbright and Mighty Acorn – and made the little marks next to their names which denoted that they had not helped his cause. Afterwards he went to the museum and bought a Coke for supper.

When he got home, Lexi was sitting on the couch between Kim and Jackson, even though it was really only big enough for two people. They were watching *Deal or No Deal* and Lexi was holding the remote control.

Patrick hovered in the doorway.

'Hi,' said Lexi. 'What happened to you the other day?'

'Which day?'

'At the house. With Jackie.'

'I left,' he said.

'I know *that*,' she said, rolling her eyes at him – something he was used to. 'But *why*?'

'My ears were hurting.'

Lexi made a screwed-up face and Kim explained, 'He doesn't like loud noises, do you, Patrick?'

'No.'

'You missed a hell of a fight,' said Lexi.

'Oh,' said Patrick. 'Good.'

She stood up and dropped the remote in Jackson's lap. He and Kim leaned gently into the gap where she'd been.

Patrick went upstairs and Lexi followed him.

'Any luck?' she said.

'With what?'

'Finding out who killed my dad.'

'No. But Meg's taking some photos of the throat,

where there are wounds that could be ante-mortem.'

'What's ante-mortem?'

'Before death.'

'Oh,' she said. 'Like post-mortem.'

'Yes. But not.'

She nodded and followed him to the bathroom while he filled his bucket with water, then back to his bedroom. He shifted the bed away from the wall and started to scrub the carpet where it had been.

Lexi sat cross-legged on his bed for a while – then wriggled down inside his sleeping bag and stared at the ceiling, which was a-swirl with Artex.

'What did you find in my dad? Apart from the peanut, I mean.'

'Nothing.'

'There can't have been *nothing*.'

'Nothing you wouldn't expect to find.'

The carpet that had been under the bed was dusty as well as dark brown, and the water in the bucket was soon black and hairy.

'It's weird to think about you poking around inside his head when he's dead. I wish I could have done that when he was alive.'

Patrick sat back on his heels. 'Dissected his *brain*?'

'Just to find out why he did some of the shit he did after my mum died. I mean, *God knows* what he was thinking half the time.'

'I understand what you mean,' he said, with an unexpected chink of empathy.

'Was your dad an arse too?' she said.

'No,' he said. 'He wasn't.'

'Oh,' said Lexi. 'That's nice for you.' She played absently with the zip of the bag. It was a heavy-duty YKK that Patrick kept running smooth with WD40. He wondered if she might say something about it, but she didn't.

'Mine wasn't *always* an arse,' she said instead. 'This one Christmas Eve when I was, like, three or four, I was asleep and he and my mum were downstairs with friends.'

'How do you know?' said Patrick.

'How do I know what?'

'How do you know they were downstairs with friends if you were asleep?'

Lexi frowned at him and said, 'They just *were*, OK? You're so fucking weird.'

She looked at the ceiling and Patrick pursed his lips. He didn't like stories where he didn't understand all the reasons why things in them happened.

'So I'm asleep in bed and all of a sudden he grabs me out of bed, so fast I didn't know what was going on, and he *runs* downstairs with me in his arms, and he's so excited he's kind of *shaking*, you know?'

Patrick nodded, even though Lexi wasn't looking at him. Something about this story made him put his brush in the bucket and give her his full attention.

'And he takes me through to the front room and all the lights are off, apart from the fairy lights on the

Christmas tree, and all the presents are under the tree and my mum and their friends are by the window and the curtains are open—'

'That's how you knew,' said Patrick. 'Because the friends were there when you went downstairs.'

Lexi stared at him blankly, then smiled. 'Yes, that's how I knew.'

'Go on,' said Patrick.

She looked at the ceiling again and went on. 'So, my dad ran to the window with me.'

She was quiet for a long moment, and Patrick watched her swallow, even though she wasn't eating.

She went on, 'I remember everyone was looking at me, sort of excited, and I didn't know whether to be scared or excited or *what* was going on. And he holds me in his arms and points outside and whispers, 'Look! Look!'

'What was outside?' said Patrick. He couldn't help himself.

'Outside was dark, but sort of light, too, because it had been snowing all day and it was *still* snowing, and the streetlights made everything orange.'

'And what was *outside*?' said Patrick impatiently.

'And Father Christmas was going past.'

Patrick frowned. 'But Father Christmas doesn't exist.'

'Yes, he does,' said Lexi dreamily to the ceiling, ''cos I saw him. And it was wonderful. He was in a sleigh being pulled by a little white pony you couldn't even *hear* because of the snow, so it was totally silent. And he wasn't stopping or handing out presents; he wasn't waving and showing off or *ho-ho-ho*-ing; he wasn't somebody's dad or uncle dressed up. It was too real and too quiet and too beautiful.'

Patrick sat on his heels and watched while a little silver river swelled out of the corner of her eye and trickled across the plain of her cheek.

She turned and looked at him and he didn't look away.

'It was like magic,' she half whispered. 'And he woke me up so I could see it.' Then she looked back at the ceiling and wiped her eyes.

Patrick didn't believe in Father Christmas. It didn't make sense. And he thought that the Father Christmas that Lexi had seen had probably been somebody's neighbour on his way to hand out presents and to *ho-ho-ho* at a house further along the street.

But, for some strange reason, he didn't say any of that. For some strange reason that didn't make sense either, Patrick said nothing and did nothing, and the silence filled the cramped, chemical-smelling little bedroom with something warm and quite wonderful.

Lexi sighed. 'I like your room,' she told the Artex. 'It's very calm.'

Patrick was not surprised; the ceiling was definitely the best part of his room.

He went to empty the bucket. A cushion of hair and fibres clogged the plughole and he plucked it out like a small, drowned animal and dropped it into the pedal bin. Then he peeled off his bleach-spattered clothes and showered until the hot water ran out.

When he returned to his room, Lexi was asleep. He carefully slid the bed back into place against the wall.

She did not wake up.

42

Meg stopped dead just inside the door of the dissection room, so that Scott almost knocked her over. She had to grasp the edge of Table 4 to keep from falling.

The bodies were gone.

Table 4, which had once been home to Rufus, with his curly red chest hair, was now just a clean and shiny stainless-steel surface under her hand, and Rufus's limbs and entrails had disappeared from the shelf below it.

The room looked completely different. It had changed from white with fleshy orange outcrops, to white – with yet more white reflected in the steel table-tops. Without the cadavers, Meg wasn't even sure at first which was Table 19. She walked over and touched it, as if she could only then be certain of the absence of a corpse.

The other students seemed to feel the same, and they milled about, apparently disorientated.

'Where is he?' Meg asked Dr Spicer.

'Who?'

'Bill.'

Dr Spicer turned and waved a vague arm and, for the first time, Meg realized that there was a row of trolleys lined up against the far wall of the room. On each was a white body bag.

'The final week will just be a recap using prosections, if anyone needs a reminder.'

'When will they be taken away?'

'What?'

'The cadavers.'

'As and when funerals are arranged.'

Meg did a quick count. Already there were only twenty-seven.

'You OK?' said Rob.

She nodded slowly. 'One day he's here, the next he's gone. It just feels weird.'

'And *that*,' said Spicer with a sympathetic smile, 'is why we don't like students to know too much about their cadavers.'

'Now I get it,' she said, wishing fervently that she didn't.

'Anyway,' Spicer added, 'it's not all doom and gloom. On Friday night we'll all have a bit of a get-together at my place to mark the end of dissection. Sort of a wake.'

'I'm up for that,' said Rob, and Dilip nodded vigorously.

'Part*ay*,' said Scott in the fake American accent he thought made him cooler.

Meg nodded but she didn't feel like a part*ay*. Half of her was relieved that taking photos of Bill's throat was now out of the question – she had no idea which bag held his body, or even whether his body was still there. But the other half of her knew it meant that she could no longer hold Patrick to his part of the bargain.

And the thought of reading *Ulysses* or *Moby Dick* while Mrs Deal's restless finger marked erratic time made her feel queasy.

43

Patrick's day started badly when he received a Valentine's card. On the front was a photo of a heart made of seashells pressed into damp sand. Inside was nothing but a question mark. It confused him to the point where he had to seek clarification from Kim, who seemed disproportionately excited.

'Jackson!' she yelled up the stairs, 'Patrick's got a Valentine's card!'

Once he knew what it was, Patrick hated everything about it – the anonymity, the concept and, most of all, the surprise. Patrick liked to be able to prepare; the unexpected was a threat and changes were bad. If he survived them, it was only because he'd taken the precaution of surrounding himself with enough that was *un*changed to see him through the transition. His bicycle. His sleeping bag. His book of names. These were some of the constants that allowed him – with enough preparation and planning – to pick his way through the minefield of life. His mother's drinking, the death of his father, the move to university. These had been survivable only because of his photos of death and his alphabet plate.

So the unexpected appearance of the card filled Patrick with foreboding about the day ahead.

The doorbell rang. It was Meg.

'What's wrong?' said Patrick.

'Nothing!' she said. 'Well, something, but not . . . y'know. Nothing terrible. Can I come in?'

While Patrick was thinking about it, Jackson shouldered his way past them both, winding his scarf around his neck and glaring at Patrick.

'Fucking Valentine's cards,' he hissed.

'What's wrong with Valentine's cards?' said Meg cautiously.

'Everything,' said Patrick, and allowed Meg to follow him into the kitchen, where she told him the bodies had gone.

Patrick reeled. Despite all his precautions, life had blown up in his face.

'Dissection is a twenty-two-week course!' he shouted.

'I know,' said Meg.

'But we've only had twenty-one!'

'Sssh,' she said soothingly. 'I suppose that they consider a recap week using prosections to be a valid part of the course.'

'But it's *not*,' said Patrick vehemently. Prosections were the chunks of abdomen, the slivers of brain, the disembodied hands. Reeking and grey with age, they were lifted, dripping with preservative, from the big white buckets in the second of the refrigerated rooms, to demonstrate what students should be looking for in the less obvious cadavers. Kidneys with renal vessels trailing like shoelaces, faces sliced like toast on a rack.

'You have to find Number 19,' said Patrick firmly. 'We made a deal.'

'Patrick, how can I? I can't march over to the body bags in the middle of class and unzip them all until I find him. And then take *photos*.'

'But we made a deal.'

'The deal's off. I'm sorry. Really sorry.'

Patrick looked lost. 'How will we get the proof now?'

'I'm not sure we can,' sighed Meg.

Patrick turned away from her and stared broodingly at the kitchen tap. He could see Meg reflected in the stainless steel, looking at the back of his head. He realized that it was easier to look at her this way – without having to face her. For the first time he studied her without having to avoid catching her eye. The reflection was slightly distorted, but it made him remember his mother's question at Christmas.

Is she pretty?

Meg had dark eyebrows over brown eyes, pale skin and a curved mouth. He didn't know if she was *pretty*

293

because that was not something he'd ever registered in anyone in the fleeting glances that were all he could manage. But her face was even, and calming to look at, even in a tap.

For the first time in his life he wondered what *she* saw when she looked at *him*. The curved steel tap stretched his face to a narrow strip, his eyes bugging out at the top like an alien stick insect. He closed them and refocused on the struggle to connect the dots of events and motivations.

The body was no longer available. But the peanut hadn't been with the body. Therefore the peanut was still there to be found. Somewhere. It wasn't much, but it would be better than nothing, which was what they had now.

He opened his eyes and glanced at Meg's shoulder. 'Where does Scott live?' he demanded.

'I have no idea,' she said. 'Why?'

'He could have taken the peanut.'

'Why would *he* have taken it?'

Patrick didn't know the answer to that. He was desperate – that was all. At least Scott had threatened to kill him, and had tried to uncover the eyes of the corpse. If it wasn't Scott, he was lost again.

'I think you're clutching at straws,' said Meg.

'I want to speak to him,' he said stubbornly.

'Really?' She sighed.

'Yes,' said Patrick. 'Really.'

'In that case,' said Meg with a wry little smile, 'tomorrow night we par-*tay*.'

It was the second Thursday. Sarah hadn't even noticed the first one after she'd received Professor Madoc's letter; that week had passed in a liquid blur of calling in sick to the card shop, and the smell of her own unwashed sheets.

But this was the second Thursday, and now she sat by the phone all evening, with the cat on her lap, watching the local news. Every bulletin that passed without word of a young man hanged or drowned or found on the railway tracks allowed her to uncap the Vladivar and drink to the fact that Patrick was probably still alive.

Or that he hadn't come home yet; she wasn't sure which.

The thought of his return filled her with a slow panic. So much so that she had not called Professor Madoc or the Cardiff police to enquire as to where Patrick might be now that he'd been expelled. Nor had she driven the forty-odd miles to Cardiff and knocked on the door of the little terraced house where she had left him last September.

Not even when she was sober.

There was no reason for her to worry. She had paid Patrick's rent until the end of the spring term, and he had twenty pounds a week to live on. It wasn't much, but it was all she'd been able to afford without making applications and supplications, and coming to the attention of who knew what authorities? Easier just to tighten their belts. Luckily Patrick didn't really care about clothing or food – or how little there was of either.

Sarah Fort eyed the phone warily. It was already gone eleven. It was unlikely to ring now.

The relief was immense and she celebrated by finishing the bottle.

If Patrick came back, he came back, and she would deal with it then. If he did not – then it would release her in more ways than one.

44

Tracy Evans was fat.

Fat, fat, *fat*.

She glared at herself in the mirror at the top of the stairs. It wasn't just her tummy; fat seemed to be laying itself down in rude slabs on her cheeks, her neck, her upper arms.

She'd looked forward to pregnancy. Gone were the days when a pregnant woman had to waddle around wearing a pup tent to cover her bulge. Nowadays young women flaunted their bumps in little black dresses and posed naked in magazines cradling their perfect, smooth bellies.

Nowhere in the celebrity gossip columns did she remember seeing anyone who looked the way *she* did after a mere five months – like a pumped-up version of herself, with trucker's arms and increasingly piggy eyes. She'd *bought* a little black maternity dress, but she'd blown up so fast that she'd never had a chance to show it off, and now it mocked her every time she opened the wardrobe, where Mr Deal – *Raymond* – had cleared a space at the end of his rail for her. The dress was so narrow she couldn't imagine getting a *leg* into it, let alone her entire bulk.

Mr Deal said she looked fine, but he'd stopped touching her in bed. She had failed to interest him even by expanding her range of sexual positions – like unlocking another level in Mario Kart. She still stayed over three nights a week, but now he only kissed her goodnight on the cheek, with his hand on her beefy shoulder.

Tracy watched the corners of her mouth suddenly tug downwards, as if operated by strings. She loved him. She *loved* him! Shouldn't that have made it easier to eat for one and a tiny weeny foetus, instead of for six men and a boy?

Apparently not.

She pressed the heels of her hands to her eyes and looked at the ceiling, to avoid smudging her mascara. She didn't have time to fix it; they were going for a Valentine's Day dinner at the Thai House. Just the name of the restaurant made Tracy's burgeoning tummy rumble and she was seized by a sudden hostility for the child within her. She imagined a troll: a rubber-faced, sharp-toothed predator, selfish and demanding and always ravenous. Of course, she knew that everything would be different four months from now when she held her in her arms and fell in love for the second time, but until then, her daughter (Jordan or Jamelia, she couldn't decide) felt like an enemy to be routed from her body at the first possible opportunity.

In the meantime, outside the bedroom Mr Deal was displaying surprising enthusiasm. He had painted the fifth bedroom a happy yellow and she'd come round one day to find all kinds of baby stuff – clothes and toys, and a new crib. Not just new to *them*, but new to *anyone*. It wasn't the crib with the white fairy-tale canopy that *she* would have chosen, but, whatever, the ticket said it had cost £895 from Mothercare, and Tracy had never spent that much on a *car*!

Raymond's choice of baby clothes left a lot to be desired, too – all neutrals and whites and yellows, when everyone knew a little girl needed to be smothered in pink.

She thought it a bit strange that they hadn't gone shopping together but she hid her disappointment. At least he was *involved*, which was more than she could have expected from most men of her own age, and she told him it was *all wonderful*.

And Tracy was sure it would be.

Sure because the nursery was her insurance. Where else would the baby live but that bright, sunshiny room? And where else would *she* live, if not with her baby? Raymond just did things *differently* from other men, that was all – and it was part of the reason she loved him.

She smiled bravely at herself in the mirror and poked her hair into perfect place.

Not long now. And once Jordan or Jamelia (or possibly Jaden?) came along, she'd lose the weight, and she'd start going to clubs again, and they would take long, exotic foreign holidays – the kind spent on a fancy lilo, while cute, tanned waiters swam out to serve them cocktails stuffed with pineapple slices and umbrellas.

Her mother had already agreed to have the baby.

45

Patrick hadn't been to a party since he was five years old, when the clamour of twenty over-sugared children in such disorganized proximity had led to a meltdown on a scale rarely witnessed during musical chairs. The very word 'party' had the power to trigger in him flash-backs of wailing classmates, overturned furniture, and a big brown dog gulping down spilled jelly.

It all hit him with fresh clarity when Dr Spicer opened the door of his flat. The music alone made him take a nervous step backwards across the corridor.

'Hi,' said Spicer. 'Come in!'

Meg did just that, but Patrick stayed where he was. Meg turned and pointed at the bottle of wine she'd insisted that they buy at the corner shop. Apparently it was their entrance ticket. He'd bought a bottle of Coke for himself. It was plastic, not glass, but it was better than nothing.

Patrick handed the wine to Spicer and said, 'Where's Scott?'

Spicer laughed and said thank you, and Meg smiled and let their tutor kiss her cheek.

Spicer looked at him. 'Come on in, Patrick. It's nice to see you.'

He looked very different without his white coat and blue gloves, and Patrick didn't like it. He hadn't been prepared for Spicer in jeans and a Cardiff rugby shirt. It made him feel as if he had already lost control of the situation.

'Is Scott here?' he said, without moving.

'Yeah, he found out about it somehow,' said Spicer with a wink that made Meg giggle.

Still Patrick stood rooted to the deep-green carpet of the hallway. 'Can you get him for me?'

Spicer smiled and beckoned with the wine. 'Why don't you come in and find him?'

Patrick folded his arms across his chest and took a step backwards. 'I'll stay here,' he said to Meg. 'You go and get him.'

'Don't be daft, Patrick,' she said. 'No one's going to bite you.'

Patrick looked past her to the people and the lights and the bass that made his stomach vibrate unpleasantly, even from here. He licked his lips, which were suddenly dry.

'C'*mon*,' said Meg, and took a step towards him. For an awful moment Patrick thought she was going to take his hand. Instead she said quietly, 'If you don't, you might never know.'

Then she turned and walked inside as if she expected him to follow.

Not knowing was not an option. So – after a long, long hesitation – he did.

Everyone was there. What seemed to be dozens of students, all looking impossibly sophisticated, with wine glasses and bottled beer in their hands, without their grubby paper coats. There were also several of the younger tutors – Dr Clarke, Dr Spiller and Dr Tsu – laughing and talking with two women Patrick didn't recognize, and fitting in with everyone seamlessly. They all seemed to know why they were here. They all looked as if they *belonged*.

Meg said 'Hi' and waved to a slim, dark-haired woman whom Patrick didn't recognize.

'Hi, Patrick,' said Rob, and Patrick nodded.

'Nice party,' Rob added.

'Is it?' said Patrick.

Rob stared at him for a moment, then shrugged and laughed. 'I don't know.'

'Oh,' said Patrick. 'OK.'

'Want a beer?' said Rob, and picked one out of a barrel filled to the brim with ice and bottles.

'No,' he said, and hurried on.

Meg led him through to the kitchen, which was empty, and furthest from the stereo. Even so, by the time they got there, Patrick wanted to sob or scream with itchy repulsion and the pain in his ears. He sat with his back to the wall, then pulled the kitchen table towards him across the fancy quarry tiles so that no one could pass behind him. There was some small relief in having his back covered, even if his face and chest and hands and legs felt hopelessly vulnerable. There were a dozen bottles on the table and Patrick rearranged them into a glass barrier.

Meg found a tumbler in a cupboard. 'Do you want a drink?' she said.

He shook his head. The Coke was cold and tempting in his hands but he didn't dare open it, because it had become his guardian for the night. Full, it protected him; empty, it lost its power. Opening it would seem like the action of a man who had dropped his guard.

Meg put the tumbler on the table and went over to the counter nearest the sink, where more bottles were waiting for customers.

Patrick noticed that the glass Meg had chosen had a faint smear near the rim. He got up and washed it.

'Thanks,' she said, sitting down and pouring herself some wine. She took a long gulp and smiled at him. 'So, Patrick, how many Valentine's cards did you get?'

'One.'

'Only one? Who was it from?'

'I don't know,' he said. 'You said you were going to find Scott.'

Meg stared silently into her wine glass for a while, then said, 'OK then.'

When she'd gone, Patrick opened the cupboard and examined all the glasses. He ran a bowlful of soapy water and washed them and put them on the rack to dry. Then he opened the cutlery drawer. He emptied the whole lot into the hot water.

He flinched as Spicer came in on a wave of noise.

'I didn't realize the kitchen was contaminated,' he said with a wink.

'That's OK,' said Patrick. 'I'm cleaning it now.'

Spicer laughed, and started to transfer pizzas from the freezer to the eye-level oven. 'I'm sorry you were asked to leave the course, Patrick.'

'Yes,' said Patrick. 'It was inconsistent.'

'I hear you took it out on the porter.'

Patrick shrugged. Removing all the knives and forks and spoons and bits like tin-openers and broken candles meant he could now see that the tray needed washing too. And the drawer underneath that.

Dr Clarke came in and said, 'Hello, Slugger.'

Patrick thought he must have confused him with someone else.

Dr Clarke sat on the corner of the table and drank beer from a bottle and made small talk with Spicer that Patrick didn't listen to. Up to his elbows in warm suds, he felt suddenly more at home. By the time Meg came back with Scott, he was sitting at the table once more, rubbing the clean cutlery to a shine and placing it neatly back in its freshly washed tray.

Scott dragged a chair out with a clatter and flopped down into it. His Mohawk was half up and half down, and his face was shiny.

'All right, Paddy!'

'Patrick,' said Patrick.

'You're such a tight-arse, you know?'

'I know. Did you take the peanut?'

'What peanut?'

'The one I found in Number 19.'

'Hey, I didn't take your stupid peanut, so just get over it.'

Patrick didn't stop polishing the knife in his hand, but he did stop *thinking* about polishing it. His heart sank. Scott had not taken the peanut. He believed that, not because Scott was inherently trustworthy, but because Scott was drunk, and drunks told the truth, in his experience. His drunken mother had once told him that she'd almost killed herself because of him – that on the day his father had died, she'd gone up Penyfan and come *this close* to throwing herself off. *Because of you!* she'd shouted. *Because of you!*

Scott put his head on the table so he could look up at Patrick's face. 'Did you hear me?'

'Yes,' said Patrick. 'I heard you.'

'Nut,' said Scott. Then he laughed and said, 'Get it?'

'No,' said Patrick, which made Scott laugh even harder.

'Don't be an arsehole, Scott,' said Meg. 'Just this once.'

'OK,' said Scott. 'Just for you. You want to dance?'

'All right,' said Meg, and Patrick watched her leave. For some reason, he wished she hadn't. Scott went after her, letting in another blast of gut-churning beat before the door swung shut behind him.

Patrick sighed deeply. At least the knives and forks were clean.

The dark-haired woman Meg knew came in and whispered something in Spicer's ear and he smiled. She stretched her hand out for them both to admire. It glittered with a diamond ring that made Patrick blink. His mother had a diamond ring but it was dull and puny compared to this one. Patrick had taken it off her bedside table once and gone to the greenhouse to see if diamond really could cut glass, and then had left it in the garden. The memory of her fury still sent a little shiver through him.

The woman kissed Spicer's cheek and he squeezed her waist and she left.

Spicer slid another pizza into the oven, then sat down. 'You still on about that peanut?'

Patrick nodded.

'What's the significance again?' Spicer opened a bottle of beer with an expert twist.

Patrick told him the significance, and Spicer nodded between slugs.

Dr Clarke got up and opened the oven to check on

the pizzas, and Patrick felt the hot air drift across the kitchen to warm his face. He curled his hands around his Coke. He longed to twist it open and take a long bubbling swig. The curved coldness felt curiously close to his skin and he realized it felt strange to be in a room with Dr Clarke and Dr Spicer without his blue gloves on. His hands felt as exposed as theirs looked.

'These are almost ready,' said Dr Clarke, peering between his naked hands and through the glass. He had long, bony fingers, and the nails were bitten to the quick.

The smell of hot cheese came to Patrick, and he thought of Number 19's salivary glands, which made him think again of the gouges and the black blood.

'So what are you going to do about it now?' said Spicer, slowly peeling the label off his beer bottle.

'I don't know,' said Patrick. The warmth and the disappointment were making him tired and he couldn't think too well. 'Maybe go to the police again.'

'You went to the *police*?' said Spicer. 'To report the theft of a *peanut*?'

Dr Clarke snorted and looked at him.

'Yes, but there was blood on my hand, so I left before telling them about it.'

Spicer widened his eyes, then laughed. 'I'm not even going to ask,' he said, and put his hands up like a baddie in a cowboy film. He had large, fleshy hands – although he was not a big man – and the right forefinger was ringed with short pink scars.

'What happened to your finger?' Patrick asked, and Spicer looked at him as if he'd forgotten he was there.

'My finger?' he said, then looked at his finger as if he'd forgotten *that* was there, too.

'Oh,' he said. 'I cut it on the tin-opener. Blood everywhere. I nearly fainted!'

Dr Clarke laughed, but Patrick felt a little electrical spark in his chest.

That was a *lie*!

He'd just seen the tin-opener in the cutlery drawer. It was a cheap, old-fashioned one – the kind his mother had at home – and it was rubbish. It worked more by pressure than sharpness, and would be almost impossible to puncture the skin with, let alone cause the two or three deep scars on Spicer's finger.

Liar!

The knowledge made him tingle all over.

Spicer was lying. But why?

Patrick stared at his tutor's hands, while bits of puzzle started a slow new circuit in his head. The scarred finger, the fragment of blue latex, the padlocked door – he wasn't even sure they were bits of the *same* puzzle. There was so much confusion in Patrick's life that he couldn't assume anything. He tried to calm down; tried to think clearly.

Spicer's hands curled slowly into loose fists and Patrick watched him put them down carefully on the wooden table, and from there to his lap. When he looked up, Spicer was staring at him.

The timer on the oven shrieked and Patrick clamped his hands to his ears. One hand was hard and cold; he was still holding the Coke.

'Pizza!' said Dr Clarke.

Patrick stood up, banging the table with his knees. The gleaming cutlery rattled in its tray.

'Where are you going?' said Spicer.

'Home.'

'Don't you want pizza?'

'No.' Patrick opened the door and felt the harsh music hit him like a wall. He had to get out. He took a deep breath and headed straight for the front door. He looked for Meg; if he saw her, he would say goodbye. But he didn't and he couldn't go and find her in the flat that was too hot, too crowded, too loud.

Too much.

He ran down four flights. Outside the damp air was already starting to wrap itself around cars and lamp-posts. He stood on the pavement and sucked down the cold in grateful draughts. Dr Spicer's flat was in what used to be Tiger Bay – where all the new buildings seemed to look a little like ships. They had round windows, and roofs that curved like bows or jutted like sails.

He unlocked his bike from the railings. The metal of both was frigid, and his fingers quickly became clumsy, but he felt his brain starting to recover as he swung his leg over the crossbar and headed towards the city centre, which lay between him and the house.

Dumballs Road was long and lined with industrial units. Garages and workshops that had once been on the fringes of the city, but which now found themselves squeezed by the townhouses and flats sailing up from the redeveloped Bay towards even more prestigious moorings.

But for now it was still deserted at night, and dark, with only the occasional car headlights making his shadow swing around him.

Calm.

The further he went from the party, the better Patrick felt. He stood harder on the pedals, and was rewarded with more speed – and more cold. His breath puffed in short visible bursts in the air, and on every inward breath he caught the exhalations of the nearby brewery that gave the city its malt flavour.

The road in front of Patrick grew suddenly bright – and something hit him like a steel tsunami.

His bike was washed from under him and he landed on the windscreen of a car with a glassy crunch. For a split second he was inches away from two white-knuckled hands clutching the wheel.

The car slewed, screeched, then jerked to a stop.

Patrick travelled fast through the silent air. Then something hit him hard in the back and he dropped to the ground and lay still.

The world was a cold black cube for a long, long time before a door cracked open in the ceiling. Or the floor. A bright white light strobed through his slitted eyelids.

'Patrick?'

It was Spicer.

Patrick didn't move. He couldn't. The pain of no air sat on his chest.

Spicer's shoes met the tarmac with a small grating sound. 'Are you OK?'

ARE you ok?

Are YOU ok?

Are you OK?

The shoes crunched towards him.

Patrick's breath came back to him suddenly and made him wheeze and then cough. With oxygen came motion and he rolled from his side on to his stomach and, from there, levered himself on to his knees, and then to his unsteady feet.

'Patrick! Wait!'

Patrick obeyed, but then he saw his bicycle, blue and twisted, in the road and instead of waiting he started to walk away. His right knee gave out and he stumbled and fell.

Spicer grabbed his hoodie and helped him up. Patrick bent at the waist and wriggled out of it, then started to run.

'Patrick! Hold on! I have to talk to you!'

But he kept going. Kept going, kept going. He didn't know why; it made no sense. But he just kept going.

Behind him someone shouted *Fuck!* and Patrick heard the car door slam and the engine roar.

Spicer was coming to get him.

The thought was even more shocking than the crash had been.

Why? What were the *implications?* Patrick didn't know. He looked ahead – a hundred yards away were the orange lights at the back of the central station. It was too far. He wasn't going to reach it. He had to get off the road.

There was a multi-storey car park. Patrick ducked left and ran into it. Spicer's car over-shot the entrance and nose-dived to a halt, then whined into reverse.

The sound of it coming up the ramp and after him filled the deserted concrete cavern like thunder, and Patrick knew he'd made a mistake. There were no people, just a few late-night cars within layers of grey concrete, bound by low walls. He was a rat in a Guggenheim maze.

Patrick looked for an exit and couldn't see one. He reached the end of the first level and ran on to the second.

He could hear the car squealing up the ramp behind him. Before it could turn the sharp corner at the top, Patrick dropped and rolled under a Land Rover. He lay there on the cold concrete, looking up at the exhaust system, while Spicer's silver car sped past him.

Exhaust, he thought. *Exhausted*.

The wailing of tyres told him Spicer had taken the

ramp to the third level, and he began to roll awkwardly from under the car.

Then – somewhere above his head – he heard Spicer's car stop, turn, and head back down towards him.

Patrick stayed where he was.

The silver car came down the ramp and ground to a ticking halt. Now that it wasn't mowing him down or chasing him, he had the time to see that it was a Citroën. Patrick heard the door open and watched the suspension lift a little as Spicer got out.

He should have run while he could.

'Patrick? It's not what you think.' Spicer didn't shout; he didn't have to – the half-empty car park was like an echo chamber.

What *did* he think? Patrick wasn't even sure, so how could Spicer know it *wasn't* what he thought?

Spicer's feet stopped at the first car at the other end of the short row, and his legs folded as he crouched to look underneath it.

'Patrick?'

Spicer's head appeared and turned his way, and Patrick's breath froze in his lungs.

Then Spicer straightened up and crept a few cars closer.

He hadn't seen him! Patrick felt a huge wave of relief. The shadows had saved him – and the cover of tyres on the ten or so cars between them. But those things wouldn't save him for long.

Patrick shuffled backwards on his elbows and knees, scraping his back on the chassis and number plate, until he emerged between the headlights of the Land Rover, tight up against yet another slab of dark-grey concrete. He straightened up slowly. Keeping the wheels between himself and Spicer so that the man wouldn't see his feet, he waited until he saw the top of Spicer's head bob into view, then quickly lowered himself back down, while Spicer took a few steps to his left. Patrick shuffled carefully to *his* left, between the cars and the wall, then stood up once more as Spicer knelt again.

Spicer rose and moved, Patrick crouched and moved the other way in perfect counterbalance. They pivoted silently past each other. The next time he stood up, Patrick spotted a pedestrian exit. A yellow door with a big 2 on it at the far side of the level, a good hundred yards away across the concrete.

Did he dare make a run for it? The thought of committing to it was terrifying, but if he stayed, Spicer would find him eventually. And what would he do then? Patrick tested his knee and grimaced; it would have to do. He edged between two cars, watching Spicer's head disappear one last time. He was at the Land Rover; the end of the line.

It had to be now.

Patrick lurched from between the cars and ran towards escape.

The noise of his feet was like uneven gunfire.

'*Shit!*' Spicer shouted. Patrick didn't look back. Behind him a door slammed, an engine roared, tyres squealed. He threw a desperate look over his shoulder. The car was coming at him fast. The yellow door was miles away.

I'm not going to make it. The thought was dull and dreadful. He had made a terrible miscalculation. His legs worked, his arms pumped, his breath burned, and he dawdled before the speeding car.

The headlights threw his long shape on to the low grey wall alongside him. Beyond that – through the uppermost branches of a tree – he could see the station, illuminated, and with people standing on platforms. A woman with a pink suitcase; two girls hugging their knees on a bench.

Unaware.

Patrick turned and ran towards them anyway, as if for help. The car was almost on him. Spicer wasn't going to stop – he was going to spread him like jam along the wall. All his arms and his legs would be in the wrong places and his eyes would look nowhere.

And he would have all the answers.

Patrick jumped.

Over the wall and into the black night beyond.

46

The car hit the wall with a sound like a bomb.

Even as he hung for an infinite beat in the frigid air, Patrick saw the woman with the pink suitcase and the two girls turn their faces towards the explosion, while shards of concrete spat against his back and legs like shrapnel.

He didn't want the answers!

Too late.

He dropped into the branches of the tree. He squeezed his eyes shut and tried to cover his head, and a million firecrackers went off as twigs snapped and popped in his ears. His unprotected arms were pierced and scraped; a branch smashed into his back and he thought of a hammer and chisel and a breakable spine. He hit another and bounced off in a different direction. The next branch he hit, he snapped his arm around. The rough bark slid down his bare skin and tore at his fingers, and he couldn't hold his weight there for more than a moment, but when he next fell, he only dropped a short distance to the ground and landed almost on his feet.

He rolled, then stood and looked up.

Spicer looked down at him. They said nothing.

Patrick jogged lopsidedly across the road and to the phone boxes at the back of the station.

He dialled feverishly, not caring even to cover his bloodied fingers. The phone rang and rang and rang and then went to voicemail, so he hung up and dialled again, jabbing the numbers without hesitation.

07734113117. It was a simple and beautiful number, filled with a lyrical rhythm of sums and products and patterns. He had often thought of it since the day he'd first heard it and wished that it were his.

'Hello?' Meg answered with the sound of Spicer's flat behind her. Music and laughter. For a moment Patrick was struck dumb by the sheer strangeness of having been *there* so recently, when now he was *here* – light years away. For him the party had ceased to exist so completely that he was stunned that, for others, it could still be going on.

'What's your code?' he said.

'What code? Who is this?'

'It's Patrick. I need your DR code.'

'Patrick? Why?'

'I have to get in.'

There was a long silence. Something tickled the

side of Patrick's face and the back of his hand came back bloody.

'Where are you?'

'At the station,' he said. 'And my money's running out.' It was true – the digital readout on the phone was counting down his last sixty seconds. He fumbled in his pocket and came up empty.

'When did you go? What's happened?' said Meg.

'Dr Spicer tried to kill me.'

'What! What are you talking about? He's here.'

'No, he wrecked my bike and crashed his car. I have to—'

'Hold on,' said Meg.

'No!' said Patrick, but she wasn't listening to him. She was talking to someone else nearby. *Where's Dr Spicer?* And the muffled response. Patrick looked back towards the car park and felt like smashing the phone and the box. But he needed the *code*. He gritted his teeth and held on as the numbers fell in front of him.

20 . . . 19 . . . 18 . . . 17 . . .

'Patrick? Angie says he's not here.'

'I *know* he's not there! He's *here*.'

More muffled noises.

'She says he popped out for beer.'

Another lie. There was lots of beer in the icy barrel.

12 . . . 11 . . . 10 . . . 9 . . .

Patrick dug for more coins. There was nothing there.

A car emerged under the fluorescent exit of the car

park. A silver Citroën with a nose crumpled like a bad boxer's. It swung into the road and turned his way.

'Meg!' he cried desperately, 'Give me the *code*!'

4...3...2...

'Five-five-fou—' she said, and the line went dead.

Patrick dropped the receiver and ran away from the lights of the station and under the railway bridge, where his footsteps rang like bells and pigeons cocked their beady eyes from the steel girders. He ran past the pubs and clubs of St Mary Street, where youths clustered to shout and fight, and girls warmed by drink defied the cold in skimpy tops and sparkly shoes. He ran up Queen Street, with its bright windows wrapped around the homeless in the dark doorways, and then over the road, across the grass, past the circle of standing stones and into Park Place.

The door of the Biosciences building was locked.

Of course it was.

Patrick banged it once with the side of his fist, then leaned his hot face against it to recover his breath. His knee shouted for attention. He ignored it. He had to get in. Maybe there was a back door with glass he could break. He slipped quickly around the side of the building, through a narrow passage between this building and the next, and slithered down a steep muddy slope.

There he skidded to a stop.

Light spilled from a broad doorway at the back of the block. An ambulance was parked outside.

Patrick sneaked closer, hugging the dark wall.

He heard voices coming from inside. One of them was Mick's.

It was the entrance to the embalming room. This was where the bodies were delivered and where Mick prepared them for the students. From here he could get to the dissection room! *Must* be able to! But he had to be fast. He guessed Spicer had the keys to the front door.

Without thinking about it, he stepped through the entrance and into a long, dark corridor. The only light overflowed from the windows in the double doors immediately to his right. Through them he could see Mick and two people he assumed were ambulance drivers. They were lifting a white body bag from a steel table on to a light gurney.

They weren't delivering; they were picking up.

Panic gripped Patrick.

Had Number 19 already gone? Was he even now six feet under, or fallen in fine ashes over the roofs and gardens of Thornhill, where the crematorium lay?

He turned from the windows and hurried to the end of the corridor, where a flight of stairs led him up to a fire door. When he opened it, he wasn't sure which way to go, so chose left and chose well – after two more doors he recognized the dissection room, even though it was from a new direction. And from this end of the corridor – where no students were supposed to be – no entry code was needed.

Patrick switched on the dissection room lights with a sense of déjà vu. Except this time he already guessed he would not be alone for long.

The room looked desolate without its corpses. He saw the white bags lined up along the far wall, where Meg had said they would be, and did a quick count. There were twenty-one left. Twenty-one out of thirty. The odds were still in his favour.

The gurneys holding the cadavers stretched nearly the length of the back wall. He hurried straight to the last one on the right, closest to the refrigerators, without even picking out a pair of gloves. The tab of each black zip was located halfway down the side of its white bag. The first Patrick opened exposed Dolly's eternal nail polish, and the next revealed a woman too. The third was Rufus – the curled red hair down his freckled forearm giving him away even before Patrick registered the '4' stamped on the dutiful tag on his wrist.

Patrick unzipped a gash of less than six inches in the fourth bag, and recognized Number 19's hip as if it were his own. The faint tan-line under the orange hue of embalming, the dark hair that stopped at the top of the thigh in a remarkably straight line. Here was the jagged edge that Scott had made; here was the mark on the ball joint where Dilip had dug too deep. The dull metal tag was redundant. Patrick unzipped the entire side of the body bag and threw it off the cadaver. Mick had packed Number 19 away in roughly the right shape: the legs at the bottom, the head at the top, the torso and arms in between. The organs and skin and fat were in neat bags where Number 19's stomach used to be, and his spine was draped across his chest like an ambassadorial sash.

Patrick pulled the mouth open and peered inside, surprised by how much sharper the teeth felt without the protection of latex gloves—

The realization hit him as hard as the car had, and he almost shouted with the thrill of discovery.

The scars on Spicer's finger were bite marks!

Patrick stared down at the teeth, instinctively knowing it made sense, but trying to understand *why*.

Had Number 19 bitten Spicer? If the fading marks on Spicer's fingertip matched *these* teeth in *this* head, then it meant Spicer had interacted with the living, breathing Samuel Galen.

And not in a good way.

The teeth would be proof. And all Patrick knew for sure was that he needed to keep that proof from Spicer at all costs.

Patrick seized the gurney at one end as if to push it from the room. Then he stopped. Even if he made it out of the building without running into Mick at one exit or Spicer at the other, how far was he going to get pushing a corpse through the city on a trolley?

There was only one solution.

Patrick skidded over to the white trays full of the

odd assortment of tools and cutlery, and picked out what he needed.

Then he started to saw off Samuel Galen's head.

47

It was repulsive. There was none of the clinical finesse Patrick had come to expect. Instead, the head lolled from side to side with every stroke, as if begging him not to continue the outrage; frayed flesh spattered from the metal teeth and settled on the waxy cloth of the body bag; the thick neck muscles and the gristle of the larynx made him sick with the brutality of it all.

And all the time, the single remaining eye looked nowhere, and Patrick did not look at it.

Patrick wiped the sweat from his forehead and tried not to think about anything but the job he needed to do.

Not Samuel Galen smiling in the winter sunshine; not Lexi.

Definitely not his father.

He kept close to the shoulders, to preserve as much of the throat as possible. Luckily the spine was gone, and within five minutes the head was held on by no more than a few minor strands at the back of the neck.

Four small, familiar beeps made Patrick spin to look at the dissection-room door.

Someone was entering the code that would allow them on to the anatomy wing.

Spicer.

His time was up.

Patrick dropped the saw, seized the head and pulled. The gurney slid towards him and he put a foot on it and pulled again, as hard as he could – his fingernails digging into the raw flesh under the stripped chin. He tugged and yanked. Then he staggered a little as the frayed tendons snapped with a twang.

And the head was his.

Footsteps approached down the echoing corridor. Patrick tugged the body bag back over what was left of the cadaver. No time to zip it up. No time to run. The lights were on and he was exposed, his only way out blocked.

He pulled open the white sliding door of the nearest refrigerator – the one filled with large yellow plastic receptacles that Scott called the 'skin bins'.

Patrick slid the refrigerator door almost closed behind him, clambered awkwardly into the nearest bin and let the lid drop over his head.

The stench was unbelievable – even for someone who had spent almost six months in the close company of death. The bins had been emptied of the bulk of their contents, but had not yet been washed out, and the sides were slick and gobby with fatty deposits, while the bottom held a half-inch of stinking bodily juices that seeped through Patrick's trainers and thick socks, and rose coldly between his toes. He retched and then swallowed the vomit, desperate not to add to the contents of the bin.

He lifted the lid a little so he could breathe. The head in his lap squinted upwards, its mouth open as if even *it* were trying to suck cleaner air into its absent lungs.

Patrick could hear Spicer moving about, going down the line of bodies, he presumed.

He heard the moment when Spicer found the headless corpse of Number 19. It was marked by a word he'd never heard before, but which he assumed was an expletive just by the venom with which it was said.

The narrow strip of light that marked the edge of the fridge door darkened suddenly, and Patrick let the lid settle quietly again.

The heavy door slid open.

'Patrick?'

The light went on, making the yellow plastic seem a poor defence. Patrick felt like an embryo in a jar.

He held his breath and looked fearfully up at the lid. He waited for Spicer to lift it, and thought of how he would find both of them – him and Number 19 – staring back at him, mouths agape.

But Spicer didn't lift the lid. He didn't lift any lids.

The light went out and the door closed, and Patrick heard the door of the second fridge open instead.

'Patrick?'

'*Sssh*,' Patrick whispered at the head. Or himself. One of them, anyway.

The head was quiet and Patrick was grateful, and felt an unexpected surge of protectiveness. The head was *his* responsibility now. No longer attached to its body, or cocooned in its waxy white bag, Number 19 was relying on him.

RELYING on me.

Relying ON me.

Relying on ME.

Instead of feeling that pressure, Patrick felt proud and fierce, and curled his arms more tightly around the head.

The sound of the second fridge door closing.

The sound of brisk footsteps receding across the lino.

The sound of the dissecting-room doors swinging together with a creak and a bump.

Patrick strained to hear the beeps of the keypad, but couldn't. Instead he waited until he realized he'd just woken up, freezing cold, still jammed tightly into the fetid yellow bin.

'OK,' he said, 'let's go,' and he struggled out of the bin and made his quiet way to the anatomy-wing door, where Meg's code turned out to be 5544. Typically balanced and memorable.

The outer door was also an emergency exit, which he opened easily from inside by pushing a metal bar. An unexpected break.

Patrick tucked the head under his arm and walked home as fast as his knee would allow. All the way there his chest fizzed with adrenaline.

The dead can't speak to us, Professor Madoc had said.

But that was a lie.

Samuel Galen was dead – but he was still telling Patrick all the truth he needed to know.

48

Patrick heard the scream of a rabbit being taken in the night. Without truly waking, he listened for another but nothing came, and so he drifted back into sleep.

'Wake up,' said his father. It was dawn and they were going to go hiking on the Beacons. Maybe up Penyfan if it wasn't too busy. At the weekends it was one long string of over-equipped hikers, but midweek it was almost deserted – especially if the weather was lousy. Patrick hoped it was hot and too busy because, for some reason, every part of him ached.

'Wake up.'

'My head hurts, Daddy.'

'I said wake *up*!'

Patrick opened his eyes slowly and looked into the hole in the middle of a gun. Not the middle; the *end* of a gun. Where the bullets come from. The deep black holey thing. The—

'Barrel,' he said, relieved that he'd remembered.

'Shut up,' said the policeman at the other end of the gun. 'Shut up and turn over. Hands behind your back.'

He was short and shaven and not alone; there was another, older man in the doorway, and Patrick's landlord – the waspish middle-aged Mr Boardman – hovered in the background.

From somewhere downstairs he could hear Lexi crying.

'What's going on?' asked Patrick.

The shorter policeman made a snorting noise and said, '*You* tell *us*, sunshine. There's a *head* in the *fridge*.'

'Yes,' said Patrick. 'It's mine.' Then he laughed because it wasn't *his* head, of course – it was Number 19's.

'Jesus Christ,' said Shorter. 'He's completely crazy.'

'And look what he's done to my *carpet*!' wailed Mr Boardman.

'It was dirty,' shrugged Patrick.

'It was *brown*!' yelled Mr Boardman.

'I told you to get this man *out* of here!' said the older policeman sharply.

There was a noisy pause while several sets of feet pounded up the stairs and Mr Boardman was led down them, muttering.

Older cleared his throat. 'Patrick Fort,' he said, 'I am arresting you on suspicion of murder.'

Patrick frowned. 'That doesn't make sense.'

The policeman held up a hand, closed his eyes and

spoke over him. 'You do not have to say anything—'

Patrick interrupted him, finishing more quickly. 'But it may harm your defence if you do not mention when questioned something that you later rely on in court. Anything you do say may be given in evidence.'

'Done this before?' said Older.

'No,' said Patrick, 'I watch TV. Aren't you supposed to ask me if I understand it?'

'*Do* you understand it?'

'Of course. I'm not an idiot.'

'Smart-arse,' said Shorter. 'Turn over and put your hands behind your back.'

'Why?' said Patrick.

'Because you're under arrest.'

'But I didn't *do* anything. The head in the fridge is just proof.'

'Of what?' said Older.

Patrick frowned. 'I don't know. There's a lot of *bits* to it. Number 19 had a peanut in his throat, although he was allergic to them. Dr Spicer has bite marks on his finger. But he lied about them and then tried to kill me. So I took the head because of the gouges and because of the teeth. Maybe Number 19 bit Dr Spicer, but I'm not sure.

'It's your job to find out the rest,' he added. 'I've done my bit.'

'What the *fuck* are you talking about?' said Shorter.

'*Patrick!*' yelled Jackson up the stairs. 'Don't say anything without a *lawyer*!'

'I don't need a lawyer,' Patrick told Older. 'I haven't done anything wrong.'

'That's good,' said Older, jotting down notes in a small black book. 'Then you won't mind answering a few more questions down at the station.'

'No,' said Patrick. 'I don't mind.'

Older nodded at Shorter.

'Then turn over and put your hands behind your back!' said Shorter.

'I have to get the head,' said Patrick and stood up. Shorter gripped his shoulder – and everything went from calm to mayhem in the blink of an eye. Patrick punched and flailed against the hated hands on his bare skin, and soon had his face in the pillow, a knee in his back, what felt like hot wire around his wrists – and a left ear that buzzed so hard that the only under-water sound he could hear was Kim shrieking, '*Don't hurt him! Don't hurt him!*' over and over again.

While Patrick Fort was half dragged, half carried out to the car, Detective Sergeant Emrys Williams stared once more into the fridge and thought, *This is how everything changes.*

There was salad and chocolate on the top shelf, old rice and curling bacon on the bottom, and – squeezed on its side on the middle shelf – a severed human head, lips drawn back, veins poking from the frayed flesh and pressed against the frosted glass. One eye socket was empty, the other was hidden by a jar of Tesco Value peanut butter.

Williams stood, bent at the waist, lit by the fridge as if bowing down before a golden calf, and knew that here, finally, was the Big One – the case that would put him on the map.

Emrys Williams had become a policeman straight out of school because the careers master had told him he'd be able to retire at forty on two-thirds of final salary. The careers master had seduced a lot of them that way – early retirement on good pensions or – for teachers – long summer holidays. He'd been more of an *anti*-careers master, really, selling them the spaces between work.

But neither the careers master nor the young Emrys had foreseen that life's rich tapestry would weave him two ex-wives, four gadget-hungry sons, and a girlfriend who only seemed happy to drain *him* at night if she were permitted to drain his wallet for the other twenty-three and a half hours a day.

So, at the age of forty-eight, Williams was still a policeman. And a policeman who was still only a detective sergeant, years after his contemporaries had climbed the promotion ladder. Somewhere along the line, petty crime and paperwork had squeezed all the ambition out of him.

Of course, he'd helped to put away his fair share of burglars and muggers and rapists and wife-beaters.

They'd had murders knocked down to manslaughter on a plea, and murders that had stuck. But never – not once – had DS Williams been involved in a Big One. He had never been part of the kind of high-profile case that captures the public imagination and the newspaper headlines. He'd never been on the telly – not even the local news; never worked a case that anyone else would have heard of or cared about – bar Gary in the canteen, who was some kind of OCD memory freak.

Sometimes Emrys Williams felt as though he had spent the entire thirty years of his working life in an interview room with hard chairs and bitter coffee, and achieved little more than bad breath and piles.

But this was different.

Whatever the outcome, Emrys Williams knew that *this* case would always be about this moment. *This* was what the boys in the station would remember about him; *this* was what they'd joke about every time someone opened the staff-room fridge to get a Coke or a cheese triangle. And even though he would hand the case over to a superior as soon as the day shift arrived, it would be *his* testimony of discovery that the reporters would be crowding the benches to hear when the case went to trial at the city's Crown Court. *The head-in-the-fridge case*, they'd call it. Or something clever and journalisty that he couldn't think of right now.

Something he would be remembered by, even in jest.

Emrys Williams straightened up into a new phase of his policing career, and found he *did* have a tiny sliver of ambition left.

He puffed out his chest.

'This is a crime scene,' he said. 'Everybody out.'

The car swung away from the house, and from Jackson and Kim with Lexi between them, and from the curious, slippered neighbours.

Patrick had calmed down as soon as Shorter pushed him arse-first into the back seat and shut the door. Now he rested his head against the glass and watched the bright, Saturday-morning city pass through his vision, while a great peace settled over him like warm silk.

He had solved the mystery of Number 19.

Soon the police would realize their mistake and let him go, and arrest Dr Spicer instead. Soon Lexi would know what had happened to her father, and for some strange reason, that felt good – even though it didn't benefit *him*. Without knowing how or why, Patrick felt there was something about having given something *back*. It was curious and he didn't understand it, but that didn't make it untrue, even if it had not helped him in his own quest.

In that he had failed, and yet he no longer *felt* like a failure. He had come to the city for answers and he had found them here. They were just different answers – and to different questions.

There were mysteries that could be solved, and others that could not. Maybe what had happened to his father was one of those that could not. The idea had never occurred to Patrick before and it did now with a sudden surge of hot emotion. He had done his best. Maybe that would have to be enough. He didn't think he had any more left inside him.

The idea of his quest slipping away brought heat to his eyes. He wiped them, then stared curiously at the shimmering trail on the back of his hand.

It made him feel strangely normal.

49

DS Williams had only been in charge because he was on night shift. The big guns came in by day.

Williams briefed DCI White as soon as he arrived, then went down the corridor and opened the flap in the cell door to check on the suspect, who was pale and wiry, and still wearing only his boxer shorts.

He didn't look much like a killer, but then, killers rarely did.

'All right?' he asked.

'No,' said the boy. 'My head hurts.'

'Drink much last night?'

'I don't drink,' said the boy, with an edge that surprised him. 'I went to Dr Spicer's party but I only did the washing up. Then I saw the bite marks on his finger and left. That's when he ran over my bike and tried to run *me* over. I had to jump out of the car park and into a tree.'

Williams wondered what he could say in the face of such craziness. 'First time in a police station?' he asked cautiously.

'No,' said the boy. 'I went to a police station after my father died.'

Emrys Williams bit his lip. He always tried to keep an open mind about suspects – even when they were found covered in blood and with a severed head in their fridge – but Patrick Fort wasn't doing himself any favours. The skinny goth at the crime scene had said something about him having some mental health issues. They had to do this properly; they didn't want a killer wriggling off the hook on a technicality.

So he just said, 'The doctor will be here soon. And the duty solicitor.'

'I don't *need* a solicitor. I haven't done anything wrong. I just want to tell you what happened. But nobody wants to *listen*.'

'All in good time,' said Williams. 'We're trying to get hold of your mother now.'

'My *mother*? Why?'

'She needs to be with you.'

'She won't come,' said the boy.

'Why not?'

'She doesn't like me that much.'

'I'm sure that's not true,' said Williams, even though he thought it might be.

The suspect shrugged and then shivered. Williams could see the gooseflesh on his chest from here. It reminded him of drying the boys after swimming when they were younger. Rubbing warmth back into them while their teeth chattered.

He fetched an old blue sweatshirt from Lost Property.

'Here, put this on.'

Patrick Fort took it from him warily and held it up, wrinkling his nose. The slogan on the front said LITERACY AINT EVERYTHING.

'It has sick on the sleeve,' he said, pushing it to the other end of the slatted bench. 'And no apostrophe.' Then he looked around the cell and said, 'Do you have a dustpan and brush?'

Williams sighed and withdrew, shaking his head.

Sergeant Wendy Price passed on her way from the machine with a cup of grey coffee. 'What's up?'

Williams jerked a thumb at the cell door. 'Kid's got a severed head in his fridge but he wants a bloody feather duster to do a bit of housework.'

She grinned and leaned up to peer through the flap. 'Oh, *him*,' she said.

'You know him?'

'He came in a few days ago with blood on his hands and said he wanted to report a murder. When he saw I'd clocked the blood, he legged it. I chased him halfway to Splott!'

'You gave up before the war memorial,' Patrick corrected her.

Sergeant Price blushed and snapped the flap shut.

She lowered her voice and added, 'I think he knew Darren Owens.'

Williams looked at her sharply. Darren Owens who had been found in the park, up to his elbows in a disembowelled jogger? 'What makes you think that?' he asked.

Sergeant Price shrugged. 'They said something to each other in Reception. I don't know what, but I'd definitely say they'd met before.' She lifted her cardboard cup in a toast of 'You're welcome,' and disappeared through a doorway.

Emrys Williams watched her go, and – with a growing sense of foreboding – wondered just how much he'd really discovered when he opened that fridge door this morning.

If the boy knew Darren Owens, then a severed head might be just the start of it.

He looked through the flap again with new eyes.

This is how things change.

When Sarah Fort finally got the call, it wasn't the one she'd been expecting.

A Sergeant Price told her that Patrick had been arrested.

'For what?' Sarah asked. 'Not wearing his helmet?'

'Resisting arrest, theft and murder,' said the officer, apparently reading off a list.

'*Murder?*' said Sarah.

'Yes,' she answered, as if this was old news.

'Murder of *whom*?'

'I'm afraid I can't tell you that at this stage.'

'Oh,' said Sarah, because she didn't know what else to say. She thought of the picture of the dead girl, and of the countless birds and animals Patrick had dissected over the years, and wondered whether he really did have it in him to kill a person.

Probably.

Didn't *everyone* have it in them, if circumstances were bad enough?

'Has he admitted it?' she asked.

'We haven't questioned him yet. Is it true that he's handicapped?'

Sarah had long since stopped getting angry about *handicapped*. Everything was a matter of degree. Patrick *was* handicapped, in the most literal way, by his condition – just as *she* was handicapped by *him*.

She said, 'He has Asperger's Syndrome.'

'Is that like Alzheimer's?'

'No, it's like autism. He finds it difficult to interact with people.'

'Oh.' Sergeant Price sounded disappointed. 'We thought he was just rude.'

'Yes,' said Sarah, 'he *is* rude. But he can't help it.'

'Hm,' said Sergeant Price. 'That's what my sister says about *her* kids. But they can't *all* be bloody autistic, can they?'

'Probably not,' agreed Sarah.

The officer sighed heavily. 'Well then, in that case, he needs to be interviewed in the company of an appropriate adult. Can you come down to Cardiff?'

Sarah thought about that for so long that the officer said, 'Hello?'

'Hello,' said Sarah back. 'Yes, of course.'

She hung up and stared across the kitchen for an hour or two.

Then she fed Ollie and went to work, feeling better than she had in a long, long time.

Emrys Williams told DCI White to expect Mrs Fort any time now. Then he hung about, reluctant to go home, hoping White would remember him when it came to putting a team together – and when he spoke to the press. He also wanted to tell the head-in-the-fridge story to the day crew in person.

That was worth it. Colleagues laughed and shook their heads and said 'lucky bastard'; WPC Dyer made a little paper nameplate for his desk that read HEAD BOY, and, before the hour was up, some joker had put a doll's head in the vending machine where the Curly-Wurlys ought to be. It all gave him a warm glow.

And then – just after nine a.m. – a well-spoken young man came in, identified himself as Dr David Spicer and said he had come to report the theft of a head from the university medical school.

And just like that, the Big One was over. Emrys Williams could almost *hear* his career farting around the room like a balloon, and dropping into a corner, all sad and shrivelled and a bit of an embarrassment.

Patrick Fort was not a murderer; not a crazed killer; nothing to do with Darren Owens and his empty jogger. The Big One was just a student prank that had gone beyond the bounds of the acceptable because the student in question had a tentative grasp on what was normal human behaviour and what was not.

Williams felt the disappointment like a physical thing – a sharp pang in his belly and a burning neck of shame.

This was what they'd all remember now, every time they opened the staff-room fridge.

Still, he was not the type of man to leave someone else to clean up his mess, so he told Wendy Price he'd sort this one out on his own time, and then ushered Dr Spicer over to his desk and took his statement.

The more Spicer talked, the more it all made sense to Detective Sergeant Emrys Williams. Patrick Fort had been expelled and had apparently taken the head out of some kind of revenge.

'He can't help it,' said Dr Spicer.

'So we've been told,' sighed Williams.

'He's not a bad kid. As long as we get the head back, I doubt the university will want to press charges.'

'That's very generous.'

'What *will* happen to him?' said the young doctor.

'I'm not sure,' said Williams, because that was true. 'Would you mind reading that, Dr Spicer, and then signing your name at the bottom?'

Williams watched Spicer read the statement carefully and then sign his name.

'Thank you.'

'Not at all,' said Spicer, standing up. 'Where's the head?'

'It's with our forensics team.'

'Good,' he said. 'I would very much like to get it back to the university as soon as possible.'

'Of course,' said Williams. 'But until we decide whether to charge Patrick Fort with a crime, the head is evidence.'

Spicer nodded slowly and chewed the inside of his cheek. 'Hmm,' he said. 'The trouble is that the body is supposed to be released to the family on Monday for cremation. Obviously that can't happen if it's incomplete.'

'Oh dear,' said Williams. 'I can assure you we'll get it back to you as soon as we can.'

'By Monday?'

'As soon as we can.'

Still Spicer didn't let it go. He stood there, drumming his fingers on the corner of Williams's desk. 'What if I personally guarantee that we will not press charges against Patrick?' he said.

'I'm sorry, sir,' said Williams. 'We have made an arrest and I cannot pre-judge the outcome of our own independent inquiries.'

'What inquiries?' said Spicer. 'Surely it's quite clear what has happened? It seems like a waste of police time to do more.'

'It seems that way, sir, I agree. But we have our procedures. Believe me, when we are able to release the head, the university will be the first to know. Now, I'm on my way home, let me walk out with you.'

Williams pulled on his jacket and let them both out through the double doors. Spicer thanked him and left, but DS Williams stood and stared through the glass after him for so long that Wendy Price said, 'You all right, Em?'

'Yes,' said Williams. 'Just thinking.'

He was just thinking about Dr Spicer's reluctance to leave the head in police custody.

And about the jagged scars around the tip of his index finger.

They *did* look like bite marks.

50

It had been a long night, but Emrys Williams still didn't go home. Instead he copied Dr Spicer's address off the statement, then drove his ten-year-old Toyota down to the Bay, against a tide of red-shirted rugby fans walking into town for the international.

It was only ten a.m. This wouldn't take long and it was on his way.

Sort of.

He swung the car around outside Dr Spicer's flat, and started to drive slowly back along Dumballs Road. It was Saturday, and most of the industrial units on the broad, grubby street were closed by steel shutters.

Williams stopped twice, once to look at broken glass that turned out to be a Heineken bottle, and again towards the station end of the road for a pigeon that refused to take off as he approached. It strolled defiantly across the road while he sat like a lemon, instead of like a vastly superior being on vital police business. Rats with wings, his father called pigeons, but Emrys Williams had always rather liked them – especially these city pigeons with the iridescent throats and all the attitude. So he watched in vague amusement as it strutted between two parked cars and hopped on to the pavement. If he hadn't, he would never have seen the short skid mark that had left rubber on the kerb.

He double-parked and got out. Only one tyre mark was visible from the road; the other was under one of the newly parked cars. He got down on his knees to look. There were fragments of red plastic in the gutter under the car. He picked up the largest of them, which was about the size of his thumb. It looked like part of a lens cover. A brake light, maybe?

He checked the lights of the parked car, then stood up and stared around. He was standing near the corner of a brick-built unit. SPEEDY REPAIRS AND MOT. Williams walked to the end of the building, which was the last in the row before the multi-storey car park. Between the two was an alleyway, a patch of littered grass, a steel fence.

And, behind the fence, a bicycle.

It was years since Emrys Williams had climbed any-thing, and he'd got heavy or his arms had got weak – one or the other. Maybe both. He got halfway up and then just hung there, and three men in Wales shirts stopped and shoved him the rest of the way with encouraging grunts and a general-purpose 'Oooooooh' as he hit the ground on the other side.

He brushed himself down from the ungainly drop and thanked them, and they waved and went on walking.

Williams gazed down at the bike. It was an old Peugeot ten-speed racer, but it had been in good condition until whatever had happened had happened to it. Now it was just a Chinese puzzle of blue and chrome, the chain drooping and the wheels twisted rubber loops.

The lens of the rear light had been smashed. Williams put the thumb of red beside it.

It matched.

He hauled himself back over the fence with new gusto and twisted his ankle as he dropped on to the pavement. He cursed out loud and vowed to start jogging again. He walked feelingly back to the car and drove the short distance to the car park.

He found one of the few spare bays on the second level and got out. From here he could see the back of the station, through the bare branches of a tree.

I had to jump out of the car park and into a tree.

With curiosity bubbling in his belly, Emrys Williams walked as briskly as his ankle allowed to the concrete wall that hemmed the second level. It was chest high. You'd have to be mad to jump it. Mad or desperate.

Cars were parked all along the wall and he squeezed behind them.

Directly opposite the tree, the concrete wall was cracked and missing several large chunks, which lay on the ground, along with more broken glass – clear and orange this time. Headlight and indicators.

Williams leaned against the wall and looked over the parapet. It was a good twenty-five feet to the grass below. The dark branches of the tree were flecked with raw cream, where boughs and twigs had snapped and splintered as something large had fallen through them.

Something as large as Patrick Fort.

It was eleven forty-four.

Emrys Williams thought the dissecting-room technician looked like a cadaver himself. He was gaunt and pale and had a funereal air about him. He also smelled of rotting flowers.

Williams did his best to hold his breath while he spoke, which was less than successful.

'I understand you are missing one of your heads,' he opened.

Mick Jarvis looked at him in almost comic astonishment.

'*What?*' he said. 'First I've heard of it.'

'Really?' said Williams. 'That does surprise me. Would you mind checking?'

The technician immediately strode to the back wall of the hangar-like room and started unzipping what Williams now realized were body bags. He kept his distance.

'Head,' said Jarvis impatiently as he went down the row. 'Head. Head. Head. Shit.'

'No head?' enquired Williams, and Jarvis nodded.

Jarvis called the chair of the medical school to report the theft, and then made them both a cup of strong tea.

'I'm not surprised,' said Jarvis. 'That kid was always weird. He broke in twice before, you know?'

'Really?'

'Yes. Found him in *here* once, going through confidential files. Then one night he threw a shoe at me in the dissecting room. Biscuit?'

Williams took a HobNob. 'How does one break into a place like this?'

'Well, the first time he used his own entry code, but at a time when he was not allowed to be here. But that code was suspended once he was expelled.'

'So how did he get in last night?'

'Let's see,' said Jarvis, and fired up the computer. He stared at the screen, while making annoying little half-sounds that he seemed to imagine were keeping Williams informed.

'That's there. Here we . . . There. Now we'll see . . . OK, I get it . . . Cheeky little bastard!'

'What?'

'He must have used another student's code. Belongs to a girl called Megan Jones. Here, you see? At 11:22 and a quarter past midnight.'

Williams nodded slowly. He had a thousand questions, but as he dunked, he asked the one he felt was most pertinent. 'This sounds like a silly question, Mr Jarvis, but I'll ask it anyway. Is it at all possible that Number 19 was a murder victim?'

Jarvis laughed. It was a strange sound in a strange place and from a strange-looking man. 'Absolutely not. Our donors have generally died from age-related heart conditions or cancers, or complications like pneumonia. Every death is properly certified by an attending doctor. Even then, we can only accept donations if the body has not been too badly damaged by an illness or injury. We need them to be in reasonable shape so that students know what a standard body looks like. There's no point training students on bodies with broken limbs or with severe internal degradations.

'For the same reason we can't accept autopsied bodies, so the donors will have been expected to die from their disease or injuries. Autopsies are *always* performed on murder victims.'

'If you know they've been murdered,' mused Williams.

'True,' nodded Jarvis and took another biscuit, so Williams did the same. He'd missed breakfast because of all this.

'Would it be possible to see the paperwork relating to Number 19?'

'Of course.' Using a key that was poorly hidden

under a saucer, Jarvis opened one of the two filing cabinets and withdrew a slim folder.

Emrys Williams studied the records. The first form was a donor application in the name of Samuel Galen.

'This is dated almost ten years ago!' he said.

'Yes,' said Jarvis. 'People can make a donor application at any time. If they change their minds, they only have to let us know and we destroy the documentation.'

Williams ran his eye down the form. He noticed that Samuel Galen and he shared a birthday. Same day, same year. Emrys and Sam. He wondered whether Sam had celebrated his birthdays the same way he did – with a few pints down the Three Tuns and a phone call from his aged mother, who never forgot.

It gave him an uncomfortable sense of his own existence being on temporary loan, and he had to brush the idea aside to concentrate on the matter at hand.

The donation form was short and contained questions that left no room for sentiment.

I consent to my body parts being retained by the nominated establishment.

I consent to unidentifiable photographs of my body parts being taken and retained for training, education and research.

Burial/cremation

All the donor had to do was tick boxes. Mr Galen had ticked burial, then apparently changed his mind and gone for cremation.

In a different pen.

Williams pointed it out to Jarvis, who frowned.

'I don't know how I missed that. Any changes should be signed at the point of the change, or a new form must be filled in. They can't just cross things out!'

Williams flicked to the back of the thin sheaf. Attached to the rear of the form was a largely blank page headed PERSONAL DECLARATION (OPTIONAL).

Samuel Galen had exercised the option.

My daughter, Alexandra, is an alcoholic. I am donating my body to help to train doctors who may one day find a solution to this heartbreaking disease.

Emrys Williams was caught off-guard. The declaration was an oddly moving thing to hold in his hands when just this morning he had found the man's head in a fridge, crammed between the best and the worst of student cuisine.

'Most applicants attach a personal statement,' said Jarvis. '*Why* they choose to donate is important to them.'

Williams went through the rest of the file more quickly. There were next-of-kin consent forms, signed by a Mrs Jackie Galen one day after the date of death, transfer documentation from the local hospital to the university, undertakers' permissions, and a copy of the death certificate, which gave the cause of death as 'heart failure due to complications of coma'.

'Another HobNob?' said Jarvis, shaking the packet at him.

Williams didn't hear him.

The death certificate had been signed by a Dr D. Spicer.

51

Just before three p.m., Emrys Williams opened the double doors and said, 'Thank you for coming back down so quickly, Dr Spicer.'

'No problem.'

Williams stood aside for Dr Spicer to pass him, then lingered for a moment to listen to the national anthem swell out of the stadium and float across the city – a sound that never failed to take hold of his heart and give it a patriotic squeeze. The city would be loud tonight and filled with Welshmen dressed as daffodils with their arms around the shoulders of Frenchmen in berets, all celebrating the result in the common language of not being English.

Williams sighed and closed the door.

They talked while they walked. 'There are just a few things we hope you can help us with. About Patrick Fort, mostly.'

'Of course,' said Spicer. 'Is he OK?'

'Oh yes.'

'Good,' said Spicer. 'Because he's quite vulnerable, I think.'

'Really?'

'Yes. You know he was at the university on a disability quota?'

'I didn't know that.'

'Yes. He's autistic.'

'I thought he had Asperger's?'

'Well, it's all on the spectrum. He can be quite detached from reality at times. Paranoid. Confused. That kind of thing.'

'Sounds like my ex-wife.'

Spicer laughed.

Williams opened the door to Interview Room Three and ushered him inside.

'Dr Spicer, this is DCI White, who is in charge of the case,' he said. 'And you already know Mr Galen.'

The head was on the table in a clear plastic evidence bag.

There was a long silence.

Spicer finally looked at White and said, 'Hi.'

'Thanks for coming, Dr Spicer.'

'No problem.'

'We'll try not to keep you long,' said White. 'DS Williams is a long way past the end of his shift, and I'm supposed to be at the match.' He smiled ruefully. Spicer only nodded.

They all sat down, the head between them. Williams and White never glanced at it; Spicer could look at little else. The head was a magnet for his eyes, dragging his gaze back to it whenever it strayed. A fold in the plastic touched the remaining eyeball, making it stand out as if peering directly at Spicer through a peephole to another dimension.

DCI White opened a folder. 'Patrick Fort has told us *some* story, Dr Spicer.'

'I'm not surprised. World of his own. He needs help really.'

'I agree. But maybe together we can separate fact from fiction.'

'Yes.'

'Good,' said White. 'Patrick says that you tried to kill him last night.'

'Does he? That's ridiculous.'

DCI White flicked through the folder in a show of not knowing what it contained. 'He says you knocked him off his bicycle on Dumballs Road and then tried to run him down in a car park.'

'That's not true.'

'But he *was* injured.'

'How would I know?' said Spicer. 'Look, Patrick came to a party at my flat last night. He got very drunk. He left early. If he fell off his bike or got knocked off it, I wouldn't be surprised.'

DCI White nodded and flicked through the

paperwork again. 'This morning he had a blood alcohol level of zero.'

'I'm surprised,' said Spicer, and folded his arms across his chest.

'Did you leave the party at all?'

'Yes,' said Spicer. 'I went out to get more beer.'

'Bad planning?' said White.

'Students. Free booze. You know?'

'But not Patrick Fort.'

'Not if you say so.' Spicer shrugged. 'He appeared a little irrational. I assumed he was drunk.'

'What time did you go out?'

'I'm not sure.'

'Guess.'

'About eleven.'

'And what time did you get back?'

'About half past, I should think.'

'Get a receipt for the beer?'

'I'd have to check.'

'Which shop did you go to?'

'Asda. In the Bay. What has this got to do with Patrick Fort?'

'I'm getting there. You didn't go out again?'

'No.'

'You have witnesses?'

'Yes! Everyone. My fiancée, other students. Anyone can tell you where I was.'

'Patrick tells us you were trying to run him over at the time.'

'Well, he's wrong.'

'We found his bicycle. Someone threw it over a fence. Certainly *looks* mangled. Forensics are taking prints from it now.'

'Good. I hope you catch whoever did it. *If* someone did it.'

'DS Williams here also found paint and headlight debris from a car that hit a nearby car park wall at speed. What kind of car do you have, Dr Spicer?'

Spicer paused. 'A Citroën.'

'Colour?'

'Grey.'

'Silver grey?'

'Sort of.'

'In good nick, is it?'

'I've had a few bumps. Nothing major. My fiancée drives it too.'

'That's nice.'

Spicer shrugged and looked at his watch. 'Is this going to take much longer?'

'I'm sorry,' said DCI White. 'But you appreciate we have to check out Patrick's story, Dr Spicer. We wouldn't be doing our jobs otherwise.'

'Of course,' said Spicer.

'Thanks for your forbearance,' smiled DCI White.

'No problem.'

'Can we get you a cup of coffee or anything?'

'No. I'm fine.'

'Good. Patrick admits that after he escaped from you, he went—'

'He didn't *escape from me*,' said Spicer with air-quotes. 'I wasn't there.'

'After he was knocked off his bike,' amended White, 'he went to the dissecting room, where he removed the head of poor Mr Galen here.'

'That's appalling.'

'Indeed. Although *he* says he removed the head to preserve the evidence that shows that Mr Galen was in fact a murder victim. And that you followed him there to try to stop him doing just that.'

White raised his eyebrows at Spicer, who gave an expansive shrug.

'I'm sorry, Inspector, but you can't expect me to comment on paranoid delusions.'

'I don't,' said White. 'And it's Detective *Chief* Inspector.'

'Sorry,' said Spicer. 'I'm just getting a little bit fed up with you seeming to believe everything this clearly delusional student has told you, however bizarre.'

'Oh, we didn't believe it!' said White. 'Not one little bit!'

Spicer looked surprised for the second time and White went on, 'That's why DS Williams here took it upon himself to see if his story was supported by any physical evidence.'

DCI White waited for Spicer, but when the young doctor said nothing, he continued. 'And it was. Apart from the bicycle and the evidence in the car park, DS Williams discovered that you used your dissecting-room code twice last night – once at 11.45 and again at 11.57.'

Spicer stared at White for a long moment. 'That's not true. Someone else must have stolen it. Patrick no longer had a code; it was suspended when he was expelled. He had to get in somehow. Why don't we ask him? Why don't we get *him* in here and ask *him* a few questions? I don't see why I should have to sit here and listen to all these accusations and insinuations without my accuser being present.'

'Patrick Fort is no longer in our custody,' said DCI White.

'Well, whose custody *is* he in?'

'Nobody's.'

Spicer looked stunned.

'*What?* He cut off a man's *head* and you let him go?'

'Wasn't that what you wanted?' said Williams.

'No! I mean, not now I hear all this other stuff. Now it seems he's more crazy than I thought.'

'Well, you're the doctor, of course,' said White. 'But, all things considered, we felt there was no need for anything stronger than a caution.'

'That strikes me as very odd.'

'Well, we're all capable of odd things at times, Dr Spicer, wouldn't you agree?'

Spicer frowned. 'I'm not sure I would.'

'Anyway,' continued White, 'before he left, Patrick

told us that he thought it was possible that Mr Galen here died after being force-fed a peanut, to which he was dangerously allergic.'

Spicer made a sound that was a cross between a bark and a laugh. 'That's ridiculous! Look, Detective Chief Inspector, this is a mentally disturbed student who spent two days a week for six months doing a pretty poor job of learning anatomy. He wasn't even doing medicine! *And* he was expelled for discreditable behaviour. Now you're relying on his diagnostic expertise?'

'Mr Galen's allergy was clearly stated on his hospital notes. To which you had access.'

'Along with many other people,' said Spicer.

'I'm told – and I'm sure you'll correct me if I'm wrong – that anaphylactic shock can cause death by the swelling shut of the airways. And that such swelling would subside to the point of being almost undetectable after death.'

Spicer shrugged.

'Is that possible?' asked White.

'Many things are *possible.*'

White went on, 'Forensics haven't yet found any evidence of a peanut, but they say that gouges in the palate and throat of Mr Galen were likely to have been made very shortly before his death. If there *were* a peanut in Mr Galen's throat – and I'm sure other students will remember if that was the case – then it's possible that somebody tried to retrieve it as he was dying. And that that alone could have led to something called . . .' He looked down at his notes in a show of getting it right. 'Vagal inhibition. Have you heard of it?'

'Of course,' snapped Spicer.

'Oh,' said White. 'I hadn't. Apparently pressure on certain parts of the body, or extreme shock, can cause such a sudden drop in blood pressure that the heart simply stops beating. It fails.' He made a helpless gesture with his hands. 'Heart failure, Dr Spicer.'

'Yes?' said Spicer.

'Which is what you wrote on Mr Galen's death certificate.'

Spicer stared at him for a long, long time.

'I don't remember,' he said tightly. 'I've signed a lot of death certificates.'

'I'm sure you have,' said White. 'We'll take a look at those, too.'

'What are you saying?' Spicer stood up, angry at last. 'If I'm being accused of something, then say so. And if I'm not, then I'm going home.'

White and Williams remained seated and looked up at him calmly.

'Sit down please, Mr Spicer,' said White. 'We're nearly finished.'

Spicer stood for a moment longer, then sat.

White continued, 'Have you ever been bitten by a patient?'

'Bitten?'

'Yes. Teeth. You know?'

'I *have* been bitten by patients.'

'But not by *this* patient?'

'I have no idea.'

'I see you have scars on your fingertip.'

Spicer looked down at his own hand. 'Yes,' he said. 'I cut it on the tin-opener.'

'Really?' White raised his eyebrows. 'Because Patrick Fort seems to think that you may have been bitten by Mr Galen while he was alive – or in the process of dying.'

'Patrick Fort is mistaken. Yet again.'

White leaned back in his chair and glanced at Williams. 'That's possible, I suppose.'

'Many things are possible,' agreed Emrys Williams.

'Well, there's an easy way to find out,' said White cheerfully and nodded at Williams, who pulled on blue latex gloves with some difficulty, and then started to remove the head from the evidence bag.

Spicer tucked his hands into his armpits. 'What are you doing?' he said.

'You just pop your finger in the mouth, would you?' said White.

'What? Why?'

'Because if the marks don't match the teeth then we'll all agree that Patrick Fort is completely deluded.'

Spicer licked his lips.

'Don't worry,' said White. 'I have hand sanitizer.'

To prove it, he put the little bottle of gel on the table between them and smiled reassuringly while they waited for Williams to complete the unveiling.

Finally the head was exposed on the table, the teeth showing between the strange, stretched lips, the single eye glaring from the sunken socket.

'This isn't scientific,' said Spicer.

'No, but it's a start,' said White. 'It seems like a simple way of discrediting Patrick Fort's story, and I don't want to waste your time, Mr Spicer.'

'*Doctor* Spicer.'

'We'll see,' said White. 'Now, would you mind?'

He gestured towards the head. Spicer didn't move.

'Would you mind?' said White again.

Emrys Williams noticed that Spicer's fingertips were pressed so hard into his own sides that they had gone white. It made the pale-pink scars on the right index finger stand out even more starkly.

The silence was so deep that the loudest sound was the electric flicker of the fluorescent lights.

'Would you mind?' said White again, more softly.

Still Spicer did not move.

Williams realized that the clock on the wall was starting to tick. Or maybe it had always been ticking. He'd never noticed it before.

'You don't understand,' said Spicer tightly. 'People like you – *ordinary* people – don't understand.'

'What don't we understand?'

Spicer hugged himself and shook his head slowly.

'What it's like on those wards. People like you think people are *in* a coma or *out* of it. That's what you see in films. Someone dies and everyone's sad, or someone opens his eyes and everyone's happy. That's just Hollywood *bullshit*.'

Williams was surprised to see a sudden crescent of bright tears in Spicer's eyes. They tipped over his lower lids and he brushed them angrily away, then stuck his hands back under his armpits once more, as if to protect them as he went on.

'But some of them only emerge halfway. Halfway between life and death. Like zombies. Sometimes they can only blink. For the next forty, fifty, sixty years, they only blink and look at the ceiling. Sometimes they sing the same song until they die. Ask the same question. Sometimes they scream until their throats bleed. Sometimes they tear their hair out, or their eyes – or try to bite *you* or strangle *you*. Sometimes they cry and beg you to let them go. *Beg you*.' He punched the table with the side of his fist, making the head wobble. Emrys Williams briefly put out a hand to steady it; and thought of doing the same thing to the boys when they were younger. A touch of acknowledgement and of reassurance.

'Killing them is not the sin; keeping them *alive* is the sin.'

Spicer jutted a challenging chin at Williams and White, but when they said nothing, he wiped his eyes again and sighed deeply.

'One of them was always ranting and raving. Crying. Violent. Always lashing out. He broke my fiancée's finger. They had to cut her engagement ring off. I only gave it to her the night before, and she was so happy. Then she came home the next day and her finger was black and twisted and her ring was in pieces and she cried and cried.

'I had the ring repaired but she's only recently been able to wear it again.'

'So you killed Mr Galen for breaking your fiancée's finger,' said White carefully.

'No!' Spicer shook his head. 'His name was Attridge. Charles Attridge.'

Williams glanced at DCI White. Who the hell was Charles Attridge?

But Spicer went on, 'His family were *relieved* when he died. They *thanked* me for everything I'd done. They understood. Nobody understands. Until they have to go through it themselves.'

There was a silence that somehow made the Spartan interview room seem just a little bit sacred.

'And what about Mr Galen here?' asked White quietly.

There was a long hesitation before Spicer said, 'He saw me do it.'

Emrys Williams's gut twisted.

Spicer went on in a dull monotone. 'And then . . . and then he started to emerge.' He blew his nose between his finger and thumb. He looked around, then wiped the resulting clear mucus across the front of his own sweater with a resigned shrug, and added, 'Started to talk.'

Williams felt his throat tighten with tears, and was

grateful he was not leading this interview. Samuel Galen had not been put out of his misery – Sam Galen had been murdered in cold blood just as recovery was within his grasp. Emrys Williams was not a wildly imaginative man, but even he felt sick at the idea of the fear, the sheer terror Galen must have felt, when he realized that he was about to be murdered – and couldn't lift a finger to stop it.

'So you killed him?' said White quietly.

'Yes,' said Spicer.

'With a peanut?'

Spicer nodded.

'Answer verbally, please. For the tape.'

'Yes,' said Spicer. 'With a peanut.'

'And what about the dissection?' asked White. 'How did that come about?'

Spicer sighed. 'That was just bad luck. I didn't even know until we uncovered the head. It was a shock. A terrible shock. I could barely even touch him after that.'

He folded his arms on the table and rested his forehead on them like a man exhausted. He spoke but his words were muffled, and White and Williams both leaned in a little to hear him.

'I did feel bad. I told him I was very sorry.'

Then he raised pleading eyes to the two detectives. 'But what was I supposed to do?'

Spicer dropped his head on to his hands again, and wept.

52

Emrys Williams stood under a streetlight on the glistening pink avenue outside the police station, and checked his watch. He only had an hour before his next shift started.

He didn't mind. He was on an adrenaline high, and felt happier than he had in many years.

What a night and day and night again! Every part of it seemed bright and vibrant in his memory, filled with shining images of discovery and justice. Williams wished he smoked. Now would be the perfect time to light up and savour.

Across the Boulevard de Nantes, he could hear the sounds of liquid celebration, and he smiled, even though he didn't know who'd won.

A white cockerel with a small French flag knotted jauntily around its neck strutted towards him from the direction of the stadium. He leaned down in a wide-armed but half-hearted effort to catch it. It eluded him with ease and a squawk, then resumed its journey to who knew where.

His phone shook in his pocket and he checked the messages. Shelli (with an i) had left several about a cruise to Mexico she'd seen online.

He didn't call her back. He didn't want to share this with her. She wouldn't understand.

Because she didn't care.

The realization didn't hurt him, so he obviously didn't care either. He would go home soon and tell her it was over. No hard feelings.

He was moving on.

Just the thought gave him a thrill inside.

DCI White had shaken his hand for far longer than was merely formal, and if he'd been clapped once on the shoulder by passing colleagues, it had happened twenty times. Even the forensics lads had been uncommonly chatty when they'd come to reclaim the head of Samuel Galen.

Only Patrick Fort had been unimpressed by Emrys Williams's extraordinary accomplishment. When Williams had opened the cell door and told the boy that his story had been checked out and that he was free to go, Patrick Fort had simply shrugged and said, 'I told you so.'

Williams had laughed then, and now laughed again softly at the memory, as the golden moon rose slowly over the city.

Soon he would start his shift, and work and life would go on, but nothing would be the same. For the first time in years, he had a sense that life was still his to be lived.

He was too young to be a fat old man.

This is how things change, he thought.

THIS is how things change.

53

The funeral was only delayed by two weeks, because David Spicer had pleaded guilty at his very first court hearing, and the head of Samuel Galen was released to the family.

By then, Patrick had run out of rent money, but not out of goodwill, and Kim, Jackson and Lexi let him stay on the couch for free so that he would be able to attend the service.

It took place on the first weekend in April, when the verges were still sunny with daffodils and the sky was seaside blue.

It was also Grand National day, but – by his standards – Patrick barely made a fuss about missing the world's most famous steeplechase for the first time he could recall. *And the last*, he vowed silently, as he watched post-time roll around, right in the middle of 'The Lord Is My Shepherd'.

Despite the fact that Sam Galen had died almost nine months before, the church was full, and heady with the scent of spring flowers, with no accompanying smell of shit.

As he didn't sing and didn't pray, Patrick remembered fleeting snatches of his own father's funeral. The day had been bitterly cold, and the church had seemed even colder, and throughout he could smell the black polish his mother had made him apply and re-apply to his school shoes in an attempt to cover the scuffs.

His father had been in a box just a few feet away, and while the vicar talked about tragedy and God, Patrick had been overwhelmed by a desire to open the box and see if he was really in there. He had fidgeted and fretted until finally his mother had held his hand so tight that he'd cried.

This was very different. He had seen Number 19 with his own eyes – opened his heart, cradled his brain, sawn off his head. He knew now exactly why Number 19 was dead, and there was no doubt that he was inside the coffin that floated on a sea of flowers – some of which spelled the words THANK YOU in white and blue. Meg had organized that, and it had cost a fortune, but they had all chipped in.

Lexi sat in the front pew with Jackie and when she cried Jackie put an arm around her shoulders – and Lexi let her.

Mick was there from the dissecting room, and

Professor Madoc too. As they left the church, Patrick saw DS Williams standing at the back.

'Did you want to talk to me about Dr Spicer?' he asked, but DS Williams said no, it wasn't the time or the place. Patrick didn't understand that; they were both in the same place at the same time, weren't they? Surely that was ideal?

Then DS Williams said goodbye and tried to shake his hand, but Patrick saw it coming.

Later, at the graveside, Jackson and Kim stood on either side of Lexi and held her hands. Not to make her squirm, but just *because*.

Afterwards they all went to a pub and Lexi cried some more and drank too much, but Patrick didn't say a thing. Meg sat close to him, but not *too* close, and there were sandwiches and cakes and large bowls of potato salad with chives in it, and Patrick wondered if this was the exception, or whether this was the way a funeral was *supposed* to be.

Much later, back at the house, Jackson – who had become a lot more free and easy with the remote control – let Patrick watch the repeat of the Grand National on BBC2.

Nobody died, and Patrick felt oddly pleased.

54

The Tuesday after the funeral, Meg went back to the coma ward to finish reading *The Da Vinci Code* to Mrs Deal.

The day was unseasonably cold and wet, and it took some willpower to go, but kindness and responsibility were her crosses to bear.

Jean waved brightly at her from down the corridor, and Meg draped her jacket over Mrs Deal's motionless legs and pulled up what she'd learned was the least obnoxious of the vinyl easy chairs.

The book sucked her into its vortex and two hours passed, when she'd only planned one. It seemed to have the same effect on Mrs Deal, who lay motionless the entire time, which Meg interpreted as rapt attention.

'The End,' said Meg at last. She closed the book and put it in her lap, and blew out her cheeks as if she'd just run a mile. 'How bloody brilliant was *that*?'

Mrs Deal was speechless in her appreciation for Dan Brown.

And then she started tapping.

Jeeeesus Christmas, thought Meg. She needed to go home, have a hot bath and then eat a lot of chocolate ice cream in front of the telly.

'Hi,' said Patrick.

'Shit, you made me jump.'

He didn't say sorry or anything else, so Meg went on, 'What are you doing here?'

'I came to say goodbye,' he said. 'I'm going home.'

'*Home* home?'

He frowned in confusion and repeated, 'Home.'

'I mean, to Brecon?'

'Yes.'

'Oh.' Meg wasn't sure how she felt. She would miss him, but she wasn't quite sure how much there was to miss.

'What will you do there?'

'I don't know,' said Patrick.

'Are you going to apply to another university?'

'I don't know.'

'Will you come back to visit us?'

'I don't think so.'

Meg tried not to feel hurt. There was only so much you could expect from someone like Patrick. Still, he *had* come to say goodbye, which was surprisingly socially interactive of him.

'How's Lexi?' she asked.

'She likes my bedroom,' he shrugged, and Meg was confused into silence.

Patrick looked past her. 'Is that her?'

'This is Mrs Deal,' said Meg. 'Come and say hello.'

Patrick stepped forward a few tentative paces until he was at the foot of the bed. 'Hello,' he said to the wall over her head.

'She can't speak. Come closer, so she can see you.'

'*Can* she see me?'

'Of course,' said Meg, even though she realized now that that was an assumption she had made just because Mrs Deal's eyes were open.

Patrick edged closer.

'Mrs Deal, this is Patrick. Remember I told you he was going to read to you? Well, he can't now, but he's come to say hi anyway.'

'Hi,' he said. He waited, then added, 'Does she know I'm here?'

'Don't be rude,' snapped Meg. 'She can hear you!'

'OK,' he said. 'Why is her finger twitching like that?'

Meg was annoyed at his insensitivity. She was about to snap again, then she remembered that she'd asked the same question herself. She reddened at the memory. 'It just does. She can't help it. You don't notice it after a while.'

'Oh,' said Patrick, and seemed to lose interest. He looked around the ward. 'Is the girlfriend here?'

'You mean Angie?'

'Spicer's girlfriend.'

'Yes, that's Angie. She left, apparently.'

'Why?'

'I don't know. Maybe she had to. Or maybe she just *felt* she had to. I feel very sorry for her. I mean, it wasn't *her* fault, was it? She only ever did her best for the patients.'

'Eight and five,' said Patrick.

'What?'

He pointed at Mrs Deal's fingers. 'Eight and five, eight and five, see? Then she starts again. Eight and five.'

Meg counted. Eight taps and then five. Eight and five. She had never noticed.

'You're right! What does that mean?'

Patrick shrugged. 'I don't know.'

'That's helpful.'

'Not really,' said Patrick. Then, after a short pause while they both stared at Mrs Deal's hand, he went on, 'It could mean lots of things. Or nothing. Thirteen. Or eighty-five. Or it could be simple code, like for the alphabet. The eighth letter is H and the fifth is E.'

They both looked down at Mrs Deal's still finger and waited. Meg giggled nervously. 'Watch, I bet she won't do it now!'

But she did.

Eight and then five.

And then sixteen.

'There goes your theory!' laughed Meg.

'P,' said Patrick.

'HEP,' said Meg. 'Help?'

Patrick ignored her. Mrs Deal was tapping again. For a long time without a break.

'U,' said Patrick.

'HEPU?' Meg screwed up her face. 'What does *that* mean?'

'Get a pen,' said Patrick. 'It's starting again.'

Meg took a pen from her bag and wrote on the rear inside cover of *The Da Vinci Code*.

Mrs Deal tapped and Patrick called out the letters and Meg wrote them down in one neat stream of randomness.

Finally Mrs Deal's finger rested. They waited but there was no more.

Patrick looked over Meg's shoulder as they ran their eyes across the letters, looking for natural breaks.

They both saw it at the same time, and Meg felt a weird tingle lift the hairs on the back of her neck, all the way up to her ears.

'HE PUSHED ME,' said Patrick.

Monica didn't like the crib either. She agreed with Tracy that the traditional wooden bars were too masculine, and then agreed with her again about the one with the fairy-tale canopy.

'I mean,' she said, 'you're having a girl, not a *monkey*!'

Tracy giggled, but thought that that was pretty rich, coming from someone who had brought nothing but a pair of home-knitted bootees and a bottle of Asti Spumante to her baby shower. She didn't *say* anything though, because although six friends had said they'd come, Monica had been the only one who'd actually turned up. Also because Monica had been quite adamant that Tracy would have a baby that weighed no more than seven pounds, 'because that's all you look like you've gained'.

'It's scientific,' she'd added, stubbing out her cigarette with authority, and Tracy had had another cupcake.

Monica did too. There were dozens of them, all with pink icing and little silver balls. Raymond had agreed that she could have the shower at his house. She told him it was because it was closer for everyone, but really it was so she could show off.

'Maybe you could swap it,' said Monica.

'What? The baby?'

They shrieked with laughter; Asti was fizzy as hell.

'The *crib*. I bet Mothercare would take it back and he'd never even notice.'

'I'm not sure about *that*,' said Tracy. 'He notices *everything*.'

That was true. Badly squeezed toothpaste and drips on the toilet seat were prime among them.

Monica shook her head, dismissing all men with a wave of a cupcake. 'Oh, they never notice stuff like that. He probably just went in and bought the first one he saw.'

'You think so?'

'I *know* so.'

After Monica left, Tracy vacuumed the rug around where her feet had been, and thought about the crib.

She didn't plan to have another baby, so this was her only chance of a fairy-tale canopy. She'd always regret it if she didn't get exactly what she wanted.

She went through the bathroom bin and found the price ticket. £895. Incredible.

Then she called Mothercare and asked whether she could exchange the crib for the fairy-tale one.

The lady on the phone was as nice as pie. She checked the prices and said that the crib with the canopy was actually only £650, so there would be a refund as well, as long as Tracy had the receipt.

'Oh, I don't,' said Tracy. 'My husband has that. I don't want to ask him for it because I don't want him to know I'm exchanging the crib he bought.'

'I totally understand,' said the nice lady, 'but I'm afraid in that case it would just have to be a straight swap.'

Tracy was a bit cheesed off about that. Bloody Mothercare, making money on the deal! Still, she really wanted the fairy-tale crib, so said that that would be OK.

The lady only needed the code off the price tag, but when Tracy gave it to her there was a long pause, while there were the clicks of a computer keyboard and a few puzzled little sounds.

'I'm not *sure* that's one of our models,' the woman said slowly.

'It's got Mothercare on the ticket.'

'Has it? Hold on.' More clicking and soft, internal noises.

'Ah yes, here it is,' said the woman. 'But it's not current stock. I'm afraid that means we wouldn't be able to exchange it, after all.'

'He only bought it two weeks ago,' said Tracy.

'From which branch?'

'Yours, I suppose. We only live a few miles away.'

More clicking.

'I've just checked, madam, and that particular crib hasn't been stocked in any of our stores for at least two years.'

'That's impossible,' said Tracy crossly. 'He bought it two weeks ago!'

'Are you sure?'

'I think I'd notice a bloody great wooden cage in my house if it had been there any longer!'

That wasn't strictly true; she didn't *live* here, after all. There was a garage she'd never been in, and a hatch to an attic at the top of the stairs.

But it *sounded* true, and that was the main thing.

There was a longish silence at the other end of the line. 'Perhaps he bought it elsewhere? Secondhand?'

'He wouldn't buy it secondhand!' spat Tracy. 'He's *rich*.'

'Well,' said the lady coolly, 'he didn't buy it from us in the past two years, and it is no longer current stock, so I'm afraid I can't help you.'

'Fine!' said Tracy and slammed down the phone.

'Fucking bitch!' she yelled at the vacuum cleaner, then she frowned hard at the ticket on the crib.

Raymond *was* rich. He had a big house and an expensive car, and Tracy had found his bank statements while he was in the shower. He didn't need to buy anything secondhand. The crib still had the tags on it. It *must* be new!

Maybe he'd hidden it from her for a while, as a surprise. Raymond didn't like surprises, but maybe he'd made an exception. Maybe he'd bought it as soon as he'd found out she was pregnant. Maybe there was an Aladdin's cave of gifts for her up in the attic, waiting to be dispensed.

He *was* a dark horse.

She should just ask him, really, but Raymond was not the kind of man you could just *ask*. He didn't get angry, but he did get quiet, which was worse.

Tracy glanced at the mantel clock; he wouldn't be home for an hour. Plenty of time to see what she could find.

She giggled and finished what was left of the Asti, which was only a gulp. Then she went upstairs carefully, holding on to the banister. The stairs were steep, and Jordan/Jamelia/Jaden unbalanced her even at the best of times.

She found the pole that Mr Deal – *Raymond* – kept behind the bathroom door. It was heavy and wooden and the brass hook on the end was tiny and had to go into what seemed to be an even tinier brass ring on the attic hatch. The pole waved and wobbled in her hand. Stupid thing!

She knew she was snooping and that that was a bad thing to do, but if Raymond didn't want her asking questions, he shouldn't be so mysterious! Buying her a crib that was two years out of date. Getting baby clothes without her. And all the wrong colour, when they *knew* they were having a girl. What was *wrong* with him?

She got impatient and off-balance, and the hook banged the wall and tore the paper.

'*Shit*,' she said. Mr Deal's house was very, very neat and tidy, and he would be sure to notice a six-inch gash and peeling paper right there on the landing. He'd be terribly cross. She'd have to stick it back on before he got home.

Suddenly an hour didn't seem like a long time at all.

She took twenty minutes to find glue, then she couldn't reach the tear, and so she got a chair from the second bedroom and placed it on the landing.

That's where Mr Deal found her when he got home, glueing her own stupid fingers to the wallpaper as she teetered like a beach ball on the delicate chair that was far too close to the top of the long, winding staircase.

And he *was* cross.

Terribly.

PART FOUR

55

Patrick called his mother to tell her he was coming home, but she wasn't there. He left a message instead, with the time of the train, so she could come and pick him up from Merthyr.

On the ride home, he sat at a table and unpacked the mobile phone Meg had given him on the station platform.

'For emergencies,' she'd said.

'But I don't *have* any emergencies,' he'd said.

'Patrick! How can you—'

Then she'd realized it was a joke, and laughed.

Still, he didn't want it or like it.

'Will you call me?' she said, as the train squealed in.

'I don't know,' he answered.

'OK,' she said, with a strange look on her face.

Now Patrick read the manual, just for something to do.

Outside, the glittering Taff wound under the tracks, and the city dissolved quickly to green. Castell Coch came and went in the morning sunlight, and then the Valleys started for real – the rows of grey and brown stone cottages, set into the sides of the mountains that were sometimes rock and sometimes coal and all coated in careful grass and dotted with sheep.

'Is it a BlackBerry?' said one of the two twelve-year-olds who'd got on at Taffs Well.

'No, it's a phone,' said Patrick and the boys grinned at each other.

One twisted his head sideways and peered at the picture on the front of the manual. 'It's not even a smartphone,' he said.

'It's fucking shit,' said the other.

Patrick put down the manual and said, 'Three weeks ago, I sawed off a man's head.'

The boys said nothing else, and got off at the next stop.

Patrick was at Quakers Yard before the stupidly complex manual told him how to make a call, and close to Troedyrhiw before he found out how to use the loudspeaker facility so that the phone didn't fry his brain.

He dialled Meg's beautiful number.

'I'm calling you,' he shouted from a safe distance.

'I can hear that,' she laughed. 'Thank you.'

'OK!' he yelled. 'Goodbye!'

* * *

His mother was not at the station to meet him, so he waited on the wooden bench outside for an hour.

Still she didn't come, so he used his new phone to call the house, but there was still no answer, and this time it didn't even switch to the machine, so he couldn't leave another message.

He waited for another hour and went across the road to buy himself a burger, then ate it and waited some more. Not having a bicycle was like not having legs.

Around three p.m. he got a bus to Brecon and then a taxi home.

Not quite home. The meter clocked up the exact amount Patrick had left in his jeans when they were three-quarters of a mile from the house, so he asked the driver to drop him off, then walked the rest of the way. His suitcase was no fuller than when he'd left home, but that was full enough to be awkward, so he left it inside a field gate, up against the hedge, and walked on without it.

The Fiesta was not in the driveway and the back door was locked.

Patrick walked around the house, peering into the windows, and then fetched the spare key from the hook on the apple tree and let himself in.

It was April, but the old stone house still felt cold.

The cat ran into the kitchen to greet him, then stopped when it saw who it was, and sat down to lick its own arse instead.

Patrick noticed that the cat's bowl was full to the brim with food, as was the one next to it – and the one next to *that*, and the water bowl was also full to overflowing.

He went upstairs to check her bedroom. There was no sign of her. No indication of where she was.

Back in the hallway he noticed the answerphone was unplugged from the wall. He plugged it back in. There were no new messages, even though he had left one just this morning. That meant his mother had listened to his message after he'd called from the station. She'd known he'd be arriving at midday. Had he missed her at the station somehow? He didn't see how that could have happened.

He made a fire in the kitchen, and then a sandwich. The bread was stale, so he took the sandwich apart and toasted it instead. That meant he had to eat the cheese and chutney by itself and search through the cupboard for something that started with a late 'T' instead of anything after 'B'. There was a can of tuna, and he forked that between the two slices.

Then he made a cup of tea. When he picked up the kettle to fill it, he realized it was still lukewarm.

It was only when he sat down at the table to eat that Patrick noticed the letter propped between the salt and pepper.

It had his name on the envelope, so he opened it and read it.

Patrick,

Welcome home. I am sorry I am not there but things have been very difficult for me and I cannot go on like this.

My will is at the offices of JMP Legal in Church Street. The house is not paid off but the mortgage is not big because of your father's life insurance, and if you get a job you should be able to stay there if you want.

I hope you can forgive me, as I have forgiven you, but I cannot face the future if it is to be the same as the past.

Whatever you do, please take care of the cat.

Love

Mum.

Patrick sat and thought about the letter while he chewed slowly on his sandwich. He didn't like it. Something bad came off it in waves, like a smell. There was definitely a message in it. He wasn't sure, but it sounded as if she wasn't coming back. And all that stuff about the will made it seem like she was dead, but that couldn't be true because nobody knew when they were going to die.

It irked him that he couldn't quite work it out, but at the same time he felt a strange urgency. So he left the second half of his sandwich, and took the letter round to Weird Nick.

Weird Nick shook his head and said, 'Shit, Patrick! This is a *suicide* note!'

'Is it?' said Patrick doubtfully.

'Yes it *is*,' said Weird Nick. 'I'm sorry to tell you this, mate, but your mother's been behaving like a total *nutter*. A few weeks back she tried to burn down the shed! I had to put the fire out with the garden hose, and we're on a meter.'

'Why would she do that?'

'Who knows?' said Weird Nick, shaking the note like a farewell handkerchief. 'But *this* is *serious*, Patrick. She's going to *kill* herself.'

'She told me she tried to do that once before.'

'When?'

'The day my dad died.'

'Yeah? Well, that proves it. How did she try then?'

'She said she was going to jump off Penyfan,' said Patrick. 'And the Fiesta is gone.'

'We need to get to Penyfan *right now*!' said Weird Nick decisively. Then he said, 'Shit! I'm not allowed to drive my mum's car.'

'I don't understand *why* she wants to kill herself,' said Patrick.

'It doesn't matter *why*, does it?'

Patrick looked Weird Nick in the eye for the first time in his life. 'Why is *all* that matters,' he said.

Patrick's mind started to bubble – battling once more with the implications of everything he knew. How the puzzle pieces fitted together. He turned suddenly and walked briskly back towards his own garden.

'Hold on!' said Weird Nick. 'Patrick! Where are you going? I've only got slippers on.'

Patrick didn't wait for him.

He only knew three things for sure that had changed since he was last home. His mother had written a suicide note. He had told her he was coming home. She had tried to burn down the shed. He could see no correlation between the three things, but he felt that somehow they must be connected.

He could see the scorched wood at the corner of the shed as he crossed the gravel – a dark scar that must tell a story, just as surely as a blocked artery, swollen meninges, a bitten finger.

He touched the burnt wood, feeling how it crumbled and flaked under his fingers, leaving them black as coal.

Behind him he heard someone coming across the gravel and assumed it was Weird Nick.

The fire had taken a good bite out of the bottom of the shed before being extinguished with Weird Nick's mother's very expensive water. Patrick knelt in the weed-cushioned gravel and looked through the hole it had made. In the warm spring afternoon, his eyes took a while to adjust to the dark cavern that was the inside of the shed.

There wasn't much to see. The weeds continued from the outside to the inside, across the cracked concrete floor of the shed, as if there had never been a barrier there. Against the far wall he could see cobwebs draped like curtains.

He lay down to get a better view. Between the burnt wood and the cobwebs, Patrick could just make out a wheel of a car.

He stood up. 'There's a car in there.'

'Fuck,' said Weird Nick softly. 'Is it her?'

'I don't know,' said Patrick. His voice sounded the same, but the urgency inside him was growing with every breath he took.

He jogged to the ruined greenhouse. Among the debris were things he remembered from his childhood; things that had *always* been there, between the glass and the grass and the cement gone hard in its bags.

One of them was an old, rusted hatchet.

He grabbed it and ran back across the gravel, and didn't even slow down before driving the hatchet into the wooden door.

'Shit, Patrick!' said Weird Nick, shielding his head from the splinters, but Patrick ignored him, using the hatchet like a hammer, and when he'd made a hole that was big enough, tearing at the planks with his bare hands. The wood was old and rotten and soon he tore off the latch itself, and one door creaked crookedly open just a few inches on a rusted hinge.

'Patrick, *wait*!'

Patrick did, panting and suddenly frightened, while Weird Nick stepped gingerly forward and opened the door.

'It's OK, Patrick,' he said. 'It's not her.'

'What *is* it then?' Patrick stepped forward to look into the shed – and stared in disbelief. 'It's our old car.'

It was.

Under a thick layer of dust was the old blue Volkswagen. In an instant, Patrick remembered how deep the back seat was – so deep that he'd have to kneel if he wanted to see out of the windows, and covered with a comforting velour. A back seat for sleeping, as he loved to do. He remembered how his mother had seemed so small in the plush driver's seat, and how his father would laugh at her and pat her on the head and make her laugh too. He remembered his father opening the bonnet and showing him the plugs and the air filter and where to top up the radiator. He could do it right now; it was so fresh in his head.

But he didn't remember the damage.

The front edge of the bonnet was crumpled, the radiator grille smashed, the VW badge popped out, leaving only a black circle in its place. And in the middle of the bonnet was another dent – a shallow pan impressed in the metal, as if someone had taken a medicine ball and dropped it there.

Patrick stared at it.

For no reason at all, he thought of his mother's stinging hand on his backside when she'd caught him testing the lock on the shed door.

No means no, Patrick!

Was the car in here then?

Why would she hide it?

People hide things because they don't want anyone to know about them.

His mother's words. Telling him something as surely as the dead man had. In a slow fog, Patrick reached out and touched the distorted metal – ran his thumb along the steel creases, with their seams of rust.

'It's been in a crash,' said Weird Nick.

And that was all it took – to hear the truth spoken aloud.

With a lurch of his insides that actually made him sway, Patrick saw his father's hips crush the front edge, his legs smash the radiator grille, his head bounce off the place that looked as though it had been punched by a monster fist.

A strangled shout escaped him and he clapped his hand over his mouth in surprise.

His mother had killed his father.

But *why*?

Because Weird Nick's mother was out, they took her car, even though they weren't allowed, and even though neither of them had ever driven on the roads.

Patrick drove because Weird Nick said that it was *his* emergency and that his mother would therefore be more likely to forgive Patrick if anything happened to her car.

Patrick didn't follow the logic but assumed his neighbour must be right. He was more concerned that the word 'emergency' had made him realize he'd left Meg's phone on the kitchen table next to his tuna sandwich. He wished he had them both.

Driving Weird Nick's mother's car was nothing like Grand Theft Auto. Patrick steered and braked and pressed the clutch whenever Weird Nick said so, and Weird Nick changed gears, looked both ways at junctions, and kept an eye out for small children running into the road in the villages, and sheep thereafter.

At times they reached speeds of thirty miles an hour.

'I hope we're not too late,' said Weird Nick.

Patrick remembered, 'The kettle was still a bit warm. She can't have been gone for long.'

They lurched to a halt beside the Fiesta, which was parked opposite the Storey Arms at the base of Penyfan. It was only then that Weird Nick realized he was still wearing slippers, and was therefore ill equipped to climb the highest peak in South Wales.

'I'm such an idiot!' he wailed.

Patrick didn't answer pointless statements. Instead he just got out of the car, jogged across the road and started up the slope alone.

56

At a shade under three thousand feet, Penyfan was little more than a very steep hill, really, but it still took some climbing. It was also deceptive. It started broad and shallow, with an inviting footpath passing through gentle fields, bathed in sunshine. A family might ascend, with small children; maybe Nana in a wheelchair!

But soon there was a stile, and then a mean descent into a cheating valley, before the real rise began again from below the original starting point.

By halfway up, the slope was a proper incline that required the bowing of the head, the lifting of the knees and the sending back of children and the elderly, while the drop on either side of the stony footpath grew closer and closer, until it seemed that to stray too far from the path might be a rash thing to do.

Here the winds gusted hard, cooling any sun and

blowing one briefly raised leg across the other in an effort to trip the unwary walker.

Halfway up there was a monument to a five-year-old boy who had died of exposure on the spot, having wandered away from a local farm and tragically walked up, instead of down.

After that it got steeper.

And narrower.

Until the footpath itself had to narrow to stay atop the new moon of a ridge that fell away steeply on the left-hand side, down carved swathes of dark green, as if giants had slithered down the face, digging their fingernails in all the way down.

It *felt* like a mountain now.

Patrick had been up Penyfan on several occasions, but never in T-shirt and trainers.

The setting sun was bright, yet up here it was a cruel mirage observed through the iced window of an igloo. Its warmth was dashed away by the wind that roared in his ears and pummelled his chest, then his back, then his sides – each time waiting until he had adjusted his weight into it, before dropping suddenly to make him lurch without its support, and running round behind him to try to push him over while he was still catching his balance.

As soon as he reached the crescent with the steep drop, Patrick walked with his head up, his watering eyes slitted into the wind, to look for his mother.

If she wanted to kill herself, it would be from this sheer ridge. Now and then he walked carefully close to the edge, or dropped to his hands and knees and crawled there, and looked over the side.

He couldn't see a body, but it didn't mean it wasn't there.

The sun lost its brightness and turned orange as it sank towards the horizon. What little warmth it had lent to the wind was reduced still further, and Patrick's teeth started to chatter.

He would have to turn back. It wasn't logical to go on. It wasn't safe. Even now he'd be cutting it fine if he wanted to get back down before dark. Penyfan by day was one thing; by night it was quite another. Even colder, even steeper – and the footpath seemed to shift just that little bit closer to the drop . . .

But he kept going, kept going.

'Mum!' he shouted twice, then stopped, because it was disconcerting how quickly the sound was torn from his lips and tossed aside by the wind.

He looked behind him and stopped while he watched the red sun squeeze itself down behind the Black Mountain. It disappeared, sucking the last of the thin warmth from the air, and left a leaden warning in Patrick's belly. Night was coming. He had to go back. Not to was stupid – possibly fatally so.

Instead he went on.

In the dusk the curved drop had turned black. No longer grass-covered rock, but something dark and subterranean rising up through the Beacons. Something unnatural.

'Mum!' he shouted again, although he didn't know whether it was for her, or for himself.

He found her close to the summit, in almost complete darkness. Another ten minutes and he could have walked right past her. She was sitting hunched at the edge of the drop, her legs dangling off it like a child on a swing, her head bowed over her lap, her arms crossed, her hair and her thin cardigan whipped around her by the wind like foam on a stormy sea.

She didn't move.

'Mum?'

She turned her head and looked at him. All he could see was the pale smudge of her face.

'Patrick?'

He went towards her and she shrank away from him.

'Don't touch me!' she screamed. 'Don't touch me!'

He stopped a few feet away. 'I wasn't going to.'

'Of course you weren't,' she said.

He was close enough to hear her now, even though the wind did its best to rip up her words and scatter them across the hills like confetti.

'We have to go down,' he told her.

'Go then,' she said.

He was momentarily confused.

'*We* have to go down,' he repeated more clearly.

'I'm staying.'

'You'll die if you stay here.'

'So what? You read my letter.'

'Yes,' he said.

'I didn't have the guts to jump,' she said with a nod at the drop below her sandals. 'So I'll just stay here until it's too late to get back.'

Patrick didn't know what else he could say, so he walked the last couple of yards to the edge of the ridge and sat down close to her. Lowering his feet off the side made him feel giddy, even though he could barely see the dark hole that might swallow him if the wind caught him off-balance.

He found she was right – that the only real way to sit here was to clasp his own forearms across his ribs and hunch down to protect his head from the worst of it.

Darkness fell fast and everything melted into blackness, and sitting at the edge of a three-thousand-foot drop became much more like sitting on the pier at Penarth, dangling his legs and watching the little yachts scud by on the white-tops.

Apart from the cold.

The cold was like falling into iced water. The cold would kill them both – or render them so stupid that they would tumble off the pier and into the black ocean below.

He wondered how long Weird Nick would wait for him, before panicking and taking his mother's car home. He didn't blame him, not even for the slippers.

'I found the car,' he told his mother through chatter-ing teeth, and she nodded very slowly.

'Then why did you come after me?'

He thought about that. Why *had* he?

He worked it out while he spoke. 'Because I want to know the truth. And being dead makes that difficult.'

She said nothing and looked down at her feet, pale against the void.

'Why did you kill him?' he asked.

'I didn't mean to.'

'But you hit him with the *car*.'

She nodded slowly again and for a long time said nothing.

'I didn't really mean *any* of it to happen. I just got in the car. I know I shouldn't have – I'd had a drink. I was going to come and pick you up anyway . . . but then . . . but then I saw you crossing the road . . .'

She looked up at the darkening sky and wiped her nose on her sleeve.

'It happened so fast. You stepped backwards, and he stepped forwards . . .'

She shrugged and shook her head.

Patrick remembered the moment and thought she must be remembering it too – but from a different angle. He tried to imagine how they had looked, cross-ing the road outside the bookies: him pulling away, stepping back.

His father turning towards him, into the path of the car.

Where *he* should have been.

'You wanted to hit *me*.'

She said nothing. She stared out across the sinuous hills that stretched all the way to the dark northern horizon.

He took her silence as confirmation, and nodded.

'That makes more sense,' he said.

She looked at him, the wind thrashing her hair around her face. 'Does it?'

'Yes,' he said. 'I understand.'

'You understand why I wanted to *kill* you?'

'Yes.'

He did. And he also understood that the accident had been just that – the unlucky culmination of a million tiny moments that had fallen into place – or out of it – on that bright spring afternoon. He understood that sometimes things happened that nobody could prepare for; that what was done was done and that there was no going back. Like Weird Nick's slippers.

His mother looked away from him. Right away.

'Well, now you know the truth,' she said roughly. 'Now you can go.'

'OK,' he said. He shuffled himself backwards and got up. 'Come, then.'

'I'm *staying*! For God's sake, Patrick! Just *go* before we *both* freeze to death.'

Death.

Patrick thought suddenly of his leap over the car-park wall and into the bitter night air. Of how his heart had burst with a sudden hunger for life, even while his head knew it was almost certainly over. He had come close – he knew that. He could still feel its breath on the back of his neck.

It made him shiver with the pleasure of not being dead.

That was a good feeling. Good enough to share. He thought of the goldfish in the tank, and flexed his fingers.

'It makes no sense *not* to come,' he said carefully. 'I know everything now. Things will be better.'

'No, they won't,' said Sarah. 'And how can I live with what I've done? To your father, and to you?'

'But Dad's dead,' he said. 'And I don't care.'

Sarah turned and stared at him in surprise, and then she laughed. She actually *laughed*.

'What?' said Patrick. 'What's funny?'

But she couldn't stop, even though they were on a wind-whipped ridge where they would both probably die quite soon.

'You don't care?' she said, wiping her eyes.

He shrugged. 'Not enough to die for.'

Sarah looked up at him, then back down into the void. As she did, one of her sandals tipped off her foot and was quickly gulped down by the hungry dark.

'Shit!' she said. 'My shoe.'

She started to cry.

She couldn't stop.

'My shoe,' she sobbed. 'My shoe.'

Patrick watched her and thought of his father and of Persian Punch and of that feeling of *connection*.

'I'm so sorry,' she wept. 'I'm so sorry.'

He had heard it a million times, but this time he believed it.

'OK,' he said. 'Take my hand.'

His mother looked up in surprise.

She glanced back into the darkness one more time, then wearily pushed her hair away from her face, and put her hand in his.

They staggered and fell, and sometimes they crawled down Penyfan. Three times they lost the path, and held on to each other's clothes while they tested the grass with tentative hands and feet until they felt the safety of stones again and went on their way. Twice Sarah begged Patrick to leave her, and he had to drag her over the sharp flint until she was hurt enough to get up and go on, every step making her weep with pain and cold and exhaustion.

Halfway down, Patrick saw lights coming up to meet them. It was a mountain-rescue team, armed with blankets, soup and heat pads for their armpits.

They put Sarah on a stretcher and Patrick walked beside it on legs he could barely feel.

In the deep valley they met Weird Nick, who had

walked as far as his slippers had lasted to come to meet them.

He hadn't taken his mother's car home; he had called the police instead.

'Thank you,' said Patrick.

57

Two days after they got home from the hospital – while Sarah was still in bed – Patrick burned down the shed.

It took a little while to get going, but once it took hold it was unstoppable.

Weird Nick was woken by the sound of crackling, spitting flames on wood and rushed outside for the hosepipe, only to find that someone had stolen it.

Instead he went next door and stood beside Patrick while the shed consumed the car and the car consumed itself, helped by whatever fumes were left in its tank.

Sarah emerged in her nightdress and wellingtons and stood on the step with Ollie winding his way around her rubber legs.

'How did *that* happen?' she said.

'It's not difficult,' said Patrick. 'I'll show you if you want.'

She raised her eyebrows at him and just for a second he met her gaze, before looking away with a little smile.

'Hey,' said Weird Nick, pointing towards the old greenhouse. 'What's our hosepipe doing over *there*?'

'You're on a meter,' said Patrick.

Patrick got a job washing up in the Rorke's Drift. He loved feeding the dirty glasses and dishes into one end of the big dishwasher and retrieving them at the other end, steaming with cleanliness and too hot to touch. He instituted a system that meant they never ran out of teaspoons, which had been a long-standing headache, and he worked so hard and fast that he quickly became a favourite with the staff, who got fewer complaints and gave quicker service, and who voted to share their tips with him – an exercise unheard of in the pub's history. At the end of the first week the landlord told him he was putting his money up.

Patrick would have done it for nothing. He was allowed to have Coke in an hourglass bottle, and once a shift he got a free meal – the chef would cook him anything he wanted from the menu. *Anything*. Often Patrick chose a toasted tuna sandwich, because he'd come home from the hospital still wanting his half-sandwich, only to find the cat had licked off all the tuna and left only the soggy toast behind.

His mother gave him an advance on his wages and he bought a new bicycle – a mountain bike this time, although still blue, obviously. He no longer had to catch the bus to work, and spent his weekends cycling across the Beacons, where he was happiest. Sometimes he found a dead sheep or a fallen crow, and often slowed to stare at it, but never picked it up.

He always took Meg's phone with him, just in case, and sometimes he called her, because she seemed to like that, and he didn't mind it either – even though the sheep scattered when he started to shout.

58

Three months after the events that marked the end of Patrick's brief spell at university, he came home from a lunchtime shift at the pub to find Professor Madoc and Mick Jarvis having tea with his mother.

They all said hello, and his mother kept smiling, so he knew there was something afoot.

'What's going on?' he said.

'Nothing bad,' said Sarah.

'No,' said Professor Madoc, 'it's very, very good! We're expanding the department, Patrick, and we'd like to offer you a job.'

'What job?' he said suspiciously.

'Trainee lab technician,' said Professor Madoc. 'You'd be Mr Jarvis's assistant. He would train you to do all aspects of his work – embalming, dissecting-room preparation, hygiene, all the paperwork for the acceptance and dispersal of donated bodies, the whole shebang.'

'What's a shebang?'

'Nothing,' said Sarah. 'It just means everything. It's just a figure of speech.'

'Oh,' said Patrick. 'I've never heard it. Shebang.' He rolled it round his mouth quietly. 'Shuuuuur*bang*.'

'It's not important right now, Patrick,' said his mother.

'I'd be very happy to have you, Patrick,' said Mick. 'I know you'd do a very thorough and professional job.'

'Yes, I would,' agreed Patrick.

'Apart from all the shoe-throwing, of course.'

Mick winked, but Patrick only said, 'It didn't hit you.'

'Mr Jarvis is only joking,' said the professor hurriedly. 'That's all in the past now. We're talking about your future here. So, what do you think, Patrick?'

What *did* he think?

They were all looking at him, and Patrick had to stop himself wriggling under their combined gaze.

He thought he was much better at that these days. He thought he was much better at a lot of things. Like being touched; he didn't *enjoy* it, but he could stand still while it happened. He answered his mother sometimes, even when her statements were pointless, and that made her happy.

He thought *he* was happier, too. He understood

more, and worried less. He had friends at the pub and a friend on the phone, and a new bicycle.

Best of all, he knew what had happened to his father, and that comforted him like an alphabet plate.

He thought that knowledge was the sweeter for having been lost along the way.

Patrick realized that they were still watching him, and waiting for him to tell them what he thought about the job in the dissecting room. He understood that they were offering him a gift, and that he needed to be grateful.

'No, thank you,' he said carefully. 'I'm sick of dead things.'

ACKNOWLEDGEMENTS

Rubbernecker was written with the generous help of Lisa Mead and Swaran Yarnell in the Cardiff School of Biosciences dissecting room. Any liberties taken with cadavers in this book are a fiction, and in no way reflect the professionalism and respect they show to their temporary charges. Thank you to Dr Jamie Lewis of the MRC Centre for Neuropsychiatric Genetics and Genomics, Cardiff University, for pointing me in the right direction, to Dr Royce Abrahams and Mr Richard Rushman, FRCS for crucial help at an early stage, and to Professor Jenny Kitzinger, for kindly sharing her knowledge of family experiences of coma and vegetative states.

Many thanks also to the entire team at Transworld, who work so hard and with such enthusiasm. A special mention to Claire Ward and the art department for pushing the envelope!

OUT NOW

BELINDA
BAUER
THE FACTS OF LIFE
AND DEATH

Every killer
has to start
somewhere

READ ON FOR THE FIRST
THRILLING PAGES

1

IT HADN'T STOPPED raining all summer, and the narrow stream that divided Limeburn ran deeper than Ruby Trick had seen it in all of the ten years she'd been alive.

The ditch that marked the crease in the gorge usually held a foot of tumbling, tuneful water. Enough to wet your knees but not your knickers.

But this summer was different. This summer, the sun had only shone apologetically through short gaps in the dirty Devonshire clouds, and the stream was fast and deep and dark. And although Adam Braund could still jump from one mossy bank to the other if he had a run up, the children all gathered to watch him now because if he fell in, it was just possible that he might drown.

The lane that rose a steep, curling mile through the forest to the main road was always mirrored with wet, while the cobbles between the cottages closest to the slip-way had never lost their green winter sheen. The trees that threatened to push Limeburn's twenty-odd houses into the greedy sea below never dried out. Leaves dripped even when the sky did not; the stream spewed from the cliff face like a fire hose, and the steep dirt footpaths that escaped Limeburn through the woods were nothing but lethal slides.

Not that that stopped anyone, of course.

There were only five children in the village so they were forced to be playmates, just as they were forced to live in this dank place that smelled of kelp.

Chris Braund was the eldest at thirteen. His brother Adam was a year younger, but a year taller. The Braunds were descended from Armada sailors washed ashore, and they all looked like gypsies. Then there was Ruby with her shock of red hair. After her came seven-year-old Maggie Beer and her two-year-old sister, Em, who slowed them all down. Both were stick thin and see-through pale. Maggie had to linger for Em, the boys went on ahead, while Ruby was always left somewhere in the middle.

To the west they were allowed to climb the path through the forest to the stone stile. In a small clearing there, a bench on the cliff looked out through a leafy frame and over the black pebble beach to the Gore. The Gore was a slim, flat spit that jutted a hundred yards into the waves before turning abruptly and stopping. It was said that the Devil had tried to build a bridge across to Lundy Island, but had been thwarted when his shovel broke.

Ruby didn't like the Gore or the story.

They made her wonder where the Devil was now.

Hanging from an ancient oak beside the bench was a

loop of fraying rope where they could swing – if they wanted to burn their palms and fall in the mud. Still, they did swing more often than not, because that was all there was to do.

Sometimes Chris and Adam climbed over the stile and went on up the pathway. 'All the way to Clovelly!' Chris had boasted on several occasions, but when Ruby had asked him to bring her back a toy donkey from the visitor centre, he said they'd run out.

Ruby never went past the stile. 'That far and no further,' her mother had warned her. That was partly why. The other part was that, even on a sunny day, the woods beyond the stile were too dark and too quiet – a tunnel of green with the threat of the unseen drop on one side, and tangled undergrowth rising on the other. The pixies in the woods would lead you in circles – even right off the cliff – if they could. You'd have to turn your coat inside out to keep them away.

At the foot of the Clovelly path was a small stone beehive-shaped hut. They didn't know what the hut was supposed to be for, but they called it the Bear Den because even in the dry it smelled like bears. The children took turns to squeeze through the tiny door and sit in the dark with their knees tucked under their chins for as long as they could stand it.

Adam held the record, which was ages.

To the east, the Peppercombe path was even steeper – a switchback of mud and wooden planking in a makeshift staircase between clinging brambles.

Halfway up was the haunted house where they weren't allowed to go. They spent much of their time there, picking among the cinders in the fireplaces and knocking glass from the empty windows at low tide, to hear it tinkle on the wet pebbles a hundred feet below. Each year the worm-chewed floor jutted out further and further over the disintegrating drop. There was one place where Ruby could lie with her eye to a knothole in the floor, where there was nothing between her and the dark grey sea.

It was like flying.

Or falling.

Ruby Trick lived in a tiny two-bedroomed cottage called The Retreat. It was owned by a family in London who had bought it and named it and then found it was too distant, too dreary, too damp to retreat to – even just once a summer – and had rented it out until they could sell at a profit.

That was never going to happen. The Retreat would cost less to demolish and rebuild than it would to repair. Ruby's father, John Trick, hammered bits of scrap wood into draughty window frames, and slapped filler at the widening cracks in the walls, but each year The Retreat fought a losing battle against nature.

The forest didn't want them there – that was plain to Ruby. While Clovelly kept it at bay with size and industry – and, ultimately, brute tourism – Limeburn was just in its way. The stream and the road and the thin line of houses were never going to be enough to keep the trees on *this* side of the coombe joining the trees on *that* side. It was only a matter of time. The advance party was already established. Ferns sprouted from stone walls like little green starfish, while rhododendrons and hydrangeas crowded back doors and shrouded rear windows. And, even as the trees surrendered their branches to loppers and chainsaws, so they tunnelled sly roots under enemy lines, breaking through pipes, loosening foundations and shifting walls out of true. In Rock Cottage the living-room floor had bulged and finally splintered to reveal a root of oak as thick as a man's leg. They'd all been in to look, and to help old Mrs Vanstone rearrange the furniture around it.

John Trick always said there were some things you just couldn't stop.

Already the houses further up the hill had been swallowed by the forest, their stone hearths now washed with rain, and home only to spiders and bloated toads, while the houses that were left had nowhere to go but the sea, which gouged relentlessly at the cliff beneath them.

The long, curved slipway tempted the water up into the village, and sometimes it came. During spring tides and storms, sandbags were packed tight behind wooden slides in the doorways, and people took their heirlooms and TVs up to bed with them, just in case.

By day, it was easy to forget that the trees and the ocean were lying in wait. By day the children played in the woods and stepped gingerly across the giant pebbles on the beach to paddle in the rockpools.

But by night Ruby could feel the tides tugging at her belly, while the forest tested The Retreat, squealing against the glass and tapping on the tiles.

And she wondered what it would be like – when the outside finally broke in.

2

JOHN TRICK DROVE them up to the main road to get the bus – Ruby to Bideford, her mother only as far as the hotel, from where she brought home leftovers so good that Ruby would sometimes get up in the middle of the night to finish them off.

Their car, once white, was now frilled with rust. The car seemed to hate them as much as the forest did, and sometimes wouldn't start. When it did, it coughed and jerked all the way up the winding mile.

The hill from Limeburn to the main road was like a ride. Ruby had been to the fair once in Bideford. The rollercoaster had been small, but big enough to frighten her, and it had started like this – with a grindingly slow pull up an incline that had looked like nothing from the queue, but which had felt so steep once she was in the little cart that she'd thought she might flip over backwards.

They were always tense in the car – waiting for it to fail. Her father hunched over the wheel, her mother gripped her bag in her lap, while Ruby's fingers ached, she clutched the headrest so tight. They all leaned forward, as if it would help, as the car lurched in bad gears around hairpins, under the murky canopy of green.

Halfway up was a stable made from an old railway carriage, and a tiny paddock of mud. There was never anything in there, but Ruby always looked.

'That's where I'll keep my horse,' she said five times a week.

'What will you call it?' her father always asked.

'Depends,' Ruby idled, 'on its colour and nature.'

'What if it has a name already?' asked her mother. 'You can't change it.'

Ruby frowned. She hadn't thought of that.

'She can call it anything she likes, can't you, Rubes?' said her father in the mirror. Then he shook his head and murmured, 'Spoilsport.'

Ruby liked it when Daddy told Mummy off. Mummy was too big for her boots, with her fancy job at the hotel and her fancy chef's uniform. Showing off – that's what Daddy called it.

They passed the stone chapel where thick ivy knitted the graves together, then surfaced from the cover of trees into daylight, next to the little shop where Ruby spent her pocket money. There was a sign that promised ice cream – although the freezer was always full of fish fingers and frozen peas – and a wire cage by the door that held a local newspaper headline to the wall. It changed once a week, or whenever Mr Preece remembered to do it. Today there was a FLOOD THREAT TO 1000 HOMES.

The car juddered to a halt and they clambered out. Ruby had to wait for Mummy to get out because there were only two doors. She could see a small knot of children already at the stop. They were divided between above-the-hills, who came from the clifftop farms and hamlets, and below-the-hills, from the beaches and the forest. Aboves had wifi and ponies; belows piled sandbags in their doorways against high tides, and their hair was always matted with salt.

Before she closed the door, Mummy bent down to look back into the car. 'Could you try to see about the bathroom window, John?'

Ruby rolled her eyes. Mummy was always going *on* and *on* about the window! Why didn't she fix it herself if she was so bothered?

'If I get time,' said Daddy.

'What else do you have to do?' said Mummy, and Daddy leaned over and pulled the door shut. Then he turned the car round in a jerky circle, and sank beneath the trees.

The above-the-hill kids waited for her mother to get off the bus before they called Ruby 'fat bitch' and 'ginger minger', and stepped on her black shoes and white socks until they were good and muddy.

John Trick was twenty-nine and had not worked for three years.

He used to do welding at the shipyard, and when there was no welding he'd done scaffolding, and when there was no scaffolding he'd done labouring, and when there was no labouring, he'd started to do nothing at all.

Then he had done nothing at all for so long that he'd gradually adjusted, until nothing had become the new something.

The new something was the drive up the hill and back and breakfast in front of the TV. It was combing the beach for driftwood, and surprising limpets for bait. It was a six-pack of Strongbow cooling in a rockpool, and pissing in the sea like a castaway.

After a while, he wondered how he'd ever found time for a job.

And on days like this, that suited him just fine. The morning rain had stopped and the cloud had thinned so that it only diluted the sunshine, rather than blocking it out completely – a reminder that, somewhere up there, summer was as it should be. The sheltered cove was always warmer than the clifftops, and the moisture was already leaving the land for the sky again in steamy wisps.

Through cheap earpieces, Johnny Cash and Willie Nelson sang to him of real men and the women who'd wronged them. Sometimes – when the wind was up – he'd join in.

Short snatches of songs carried off on the spume.

He had collected half a dozen limpets and now dug one out of its shell with his penknife and put it on the hook. The outer flesh was tough, and the creature pulsed in his fingers as he threaded it over the barbs.

He cast and felt the weight touch the bottom, then he took up the tension on the line, and settled back into his old nylon camping chair.

John fished mostly at the Gut – a squareish wound blown out of the rock with gunpowder two hundred years before, so that ships could land their cargoes of lime and anthracite. The kilns where the lime had been burned were still there, built into the sea wall either side of the long, curved slipway – fortress-like stone ovens forty feet high that were now occupied by rats and by gulls, and so acrid with the shit of both that not even the children played there.

Mackerel was his most common catch, with whiting a close second. Both were good enough eating, and if he bothered to pick his slippery way to the end of the Gore, he could catch eels as long as his arm, and dogfish. Rock salmon, they were called in fancy restaurants, and sometimes Alison rang Mr Littlejohn at the hotel and he'd say yes or no. If he said yes, he gave Trick a tenner a fish. Then cut them into eight thick steaks that he sold for twenty quid a time.

John snorted around his roll-up. A hundred and sixty quid for a fish *he* caught and his *wife* cooked. He failed to see how Mr Littlejohn could sleep at night, for the thieving old bastard he was.

He could have sold the dogfish to the Red Lion in Clovelly, of course, but he never went to Clovelly, even though he could see it from here, across the shallow curve of the bay. Clovelly was the favoured brother to Limeburn's runt, and nobody in either village ever forgot it.

The fluorescent end of the fishing rod shivered, and he tensed, ready for action. But the tip pinged back into position, pointing skywards with a trembling finger.

John subsided.

Bloody crabs.

Sometimes he would reel in and check the bait and cast again somewhere else, but it seemed like a lot of work when the air was so warm and the cider so cool.

He closed his eyes and waited.

He slept.

That night the window row began again. First the window, then how much the new tyre on the car had cost, then the mess Daddy had made cleaning the fish in the sink. Ruby went into the other room before it could get to the job.

Wherever the row started, it always ended up at the job.

It got there without her.

The Facts of Life and Death
is out now